Winks at me

Rowan McKinney

Contents

Chapter 1

Toby Wentworth's life is an absolute clusterfuck. Just to throw that out there.

Why? There are many reasons, really. But for one, he has not-so-recently discovered that he is in fact very, very gay.

So. Cue the rainbow confetti, or whatever.

But one really, really wonderful, awesome, amazing fact about this revelation is, Toby doesn't know... how to be gay.

If that makes sense.

(It doesn't. He knows it doesn't.)

Obviously, there is no rulebook. No guidelines. No constitution. No magical rainbow fairy gay-mother who waves her wand and sends Toby on his merry way with every single weight lifted off his shoulders and a complimentary bar of soap.

But is it bad that Toby kind of wishes there was?

Because at least at that point, things would be simple.

Er. Simpler.

Toby Wentworth doesn't know how to "be" gay in the sense that he doesn't know how to be gay and also be a functioning human being. Seriously. It's as though his own homosexuality is a weight he's lugged around on his back for his entire life, and as a result has crippled him at the ripe old age of nineteen, inhibiting him from playing outside with the normal kids.

Well, he knows he's still a normal kid, despite his upbringing. He managed to escape before his parents brainwashed him entirely.

Toby grew up in Hopper Village, a minuscule (and, let's be honest, probably fictitious) town down in North Carolina, where the inhabitants within hit every criteria to ever exist below the term small town mindset. White, Christian, conservative. Very very very anti-gay.

Well, that doesn't matter much anymore. The important part is, Toby got out. He escaped to Pennsylvania for college about a year and a half ago, leaving behind his way-too-clingy parents, non-disappointing older siblings, and his high school girlfriend of three and a half years.

Cough—beard—cough.

(He's no longer in touch with her. It's fine. It's fine.)

Toby Wentworth's life is a clusterfuck, but you already knew that.

And, honestly, people should be impressed by homosexuality rather than against it, because this shit is fucking difficult.

Maybe homosexuality isn't as difficult as calculus, though.

Toby's been sitting in this lecture hall upwards of forty minutes, trying, trying to pay attention and absorb what the professor is droning on about, but he just. He just can't.

(Every day that goes by is another day that he regrets going into accounting. Accounting. He can barely a-count to twenty. He doesn't know how he's alive.)

Not only does Toby not understand what the fuck this mumbo-jumbo in his notebook is, but there's also a boy—a very attractive boy—sitting about three rows in front of him that keeps turning his head and catching Toby's eye.

God. He's fucking screwed.

Giving up for whatever-number-time this is now, Toby allows his whole body to go limp and doesn't even wince when his forehead meets the table with a very audible clunk. And he doesn't look up either when he hears shuffling around him, as if people are rising from their seats. Class isn't dismissed yet, he knows. Those two words are the one thing that comes out of the professor's mouth that he does understand. He would already be gone if that was the case.

But then there's something prodding him on the shoulder blade. It startles him, and his head snaps up, blinking away the haziness that overlays his vision for a hot second. He almost wishes he hadn't, afterward, because looking down at him, a half smile on his face, is the cute guy from before.

Fuck. He's even cuter up close. Toby forces himself not to stare, but he does manage to take note of the big blue eyes, bedhead of brown hair, and the freckles—freckles—sprinkled across the bridge of his nose.

Toby opens his mouth, maybe to say hey or something—he doesn't really have a plan, as all coherency seems to have flown out the window at this point—but Freckles beats him to it.

"Do you have a partner?"

Toby blinks.

Partner. Okay. Partner. This could mean various things. Maybe he's talking about a partner in terms of some kind of activity. That would make sense. They are in class after all. Only Toby hasn't heard anything about a group project, so if that's the case, that would really suck ass.

And then there's the other kind of partner. Toby doesn't get his hopes up.

"What?" he asks dumbly, multiple seconds too late.

"A partner," Freckles says. "Do you have one?"

Oh God. That doesn't really clear anything up.

When Toby doesn't respond (out of internal gay panic), the guy sighs. Now, Toby has heard many a sigh in his day, and this one in particular sounds rather scornful, if he does say so himself. And he does.

"For the project," the guy continues.

Fuck. Toby knew he was in trouble.

In that moment, he chokes on his own spit, plunging him into a fit of uncontrollable coughs. Dear God, he honestly hopes he just dies now.

"Dude, are you okay?" Freckles reaches over to maybe pat Toby on the back, but Toby is quick to swat his hand away.

"I'm—" He hacks up another cough, pounding his chest twice with his fist. "F-fine."

(Yeah. If he chokes this easily on spit, he is definitely not cut out to be gay.)

"If you're sure," the guy says, bringing his rejected hand up to rub the back of his neck instead while Toby uses his palms to press away the tears that had sprung into his eyes.

"Um," Toby manages after a few eternal seconds. He really, really hopes everything is back to normal, but knowing his luck, he could have unknowingly sprouted a horn in the center of his forehead within the moments that passed. "No. I, uh, don't have a partner."

Either way, it's the truth. He doesn't know why the fuck it took him so long.

Freckles's face lights up a bit (okay, looking good, no horn). "Cool. Wanna pair up, then?"

There are several reasons why Toby could, and most definitely should, reject this guy.

1. He doesn't know him.

2. He also doesn't know what the fuck is going on and that is way too embarrassing to admit.

3. Freckles is very handsome, and Toby does not think he will be able to work well with someone who looks like that.

4. He generally prefers to do solo projects.

"Sure," Toby answers, plastering on the most artificial smile possible as any traces of dignity left in him disintegrate immediately.

"All right, cool," Freckles says, and that is the second time he has used the word "cool" within his past three spoken sentences, Toby notices. For some reason. As if it matters at all. "I'm Leo, by the way. Here's my number. Text me later after class, and we can meet up at the library or something to get this started."

Freck—Leo shoves a crumpled piece of paper into Toby's hand, pats him twice on the shoulder as if he were a dad—no, scratch that. A stepdad bestowing his fatherly wisdom upon his angsty stepson—and returns back to his seat without another word.

Toby spends the final ten minutes of class staring at the back of Leo's head. When his ears perk up to that all too familiar "class dismissed," he doesn't need to be told twice.

He practically flies down the aisle, down the stairs, and out the door. He counts the number of backpacks and feet he trips over and trods on in the process (seven and three, respectively). And he very pointedly does not look back once he's out, because there is something so inexplicably infuriating about that class that maybe doesn't have to do so much with calculus anymore.

He's so heated, in fact, that it takes him a good ten steps or so outside to realize that something is... off. He takes in a deep breath in an attempt to clear his head, because is that so much to ask, only to be met with a stinging sensation that zips through his nose and down his throat, sparking his second coughing fit in the span of fifteen minutes.

Only then does he remember, Oh yeah, it's January, I'm in Pennsylvania, and also apparently a fucking idiot that left my coat inside.

Toby groans and spins on his heel—which is admittedly a little bit life-endangering because of the pavement, which is slick from yesterday's (now melted) snow, but that's the last thing on his mind right now—ready to trudge back into the lecture hall, only to pretty much immediately collide with another human body. A shorter, thinner, slighter body.

"Oh, fuck," Leo mutters, unsuccessfully grasping at the various items sent sprawling out of his hands, thanks to Toby's clumsiness. His phone, a couple of pens. Toby's coat.

"S-sorry," Toby sputters. "I'm sorry, I didn't—I didn't see you."

Leo waves him off, crouching to gather his belongings. "You're fine. Don't worry about it"

Toby crouches too, to try and help, but Leo's already standing back up, so now Toby is suddenly stuck in an awkward squat in the middle of the quad. He immediately rises back to his full height and definitely does not miss the subtle smirk playing on Leo's lips.

"Shut up," Toby mutters, face flaming despite the cold, jutting his hand out to take his coat.

Leo passes it over. "I didn't say anything," he says, as Toby pulls it on and gives a small sigh of sweet relief.

He decides to pretend to be oblivious to Leo's worryingly penetrative gaze he feels resting on his fingers as he fumbles with the zipper, pulling it about halfway up the length of the coat before—three guesses as to what happens—it freezes in place, resisting his desperate upward tugs.

"For fuck's sake," Toby groans, continuing to mercilessly yank on the metal. Heat floods back to his face, though this time fueled more by frustration than sheepishness, and he's really wishing Leo would mind his own fucking business right about now.

"Okay, just relax, dude." Leo tucks his phone and pens away into the pockets of his own coat and reaches his hands out tentatively, as if Toby's going to smack them away again. "Let me help."

Toby's breath hitches in his throat as nimble fingers ghost over his for a brief moment. They're long and thin, calloused in some places, and he's so starstruck (by a couple of fingers, Jesus Christ) that he lets go of the zipper and allows Leo to take over.

And now Toby finds himself wondering so many things about this guy, this random guy he literally just met. It's like he's a dog, excited and obsessing over this new human. A new scent, a new life to learn about, a new name to file, a new face to memorize. (He's got that one down already.)

"It's kinda like a seat belt," Leo continues, each word forming a small puff of air that tumbles out of his mouth and sweeps away with the bitter wind. "You just have to be patient with it."

He tugs down on the fabric to Toby's coat while simultaneously pulling upwards on the zipper. And what do you know—a few moments later, Toby's coat is closed.

"Thanks," he says, shoving his hands in his pockets.

Leo only looks at him, a strange expression flashing over his face. Toby watches his eyes as they search his own, blue and icy and endless, and for a moment that's all he can do.

"Well." Leo breaks the silence and pats Toby twice on the chest. It must throw his heart off its rhythm—the patting, strictly the patting, because it was a relatively forceful pat, you know—because it suddenly begins to thunder against his chest in that moment. Toby also notices that the tips of Leo's fingers are pink from the cold, and he wonders if Leo has a pair of gloves to slip on.

Not that he cares. At all.

"It was nice meeting you," Leo continues. "Remember to text me later, and we can figure out a time we can meet up."

"Uh. Yeah. Okay," Toby mumbles dumbly in reply, scratching the back of his head. "Thanks—uh. Th-thanks for your help."

(It's the cold. The cold is why he's stuttering.)

But then—oh, but then—Leo, Freckles, whatever you wanna call him, that—that son of a gun, looks Toby dead in the eyes and winks at him.

And then he has the nerve to just walk away, leaving Toby standing there alone, completely rid of any air in his lungs, small as the expanse of his knowledge of calculus.

Oh, Toby thinks.

Oh no.

"What's with you?" is the first thing Toby hears as he steps through the doorway to his apartment. A remark from Reggie, his roommate (and best friend by default), who is sitting at the island on his laptop.

"Huh?" Toby shucks his coat, tossing it onto the couch. Reggie has the heater cranked up to the max, which Toby is thankful for. He hates the cold. (Makes him stutter, and all.) "Nothing."

"Nah, dude, you look all..." Reggie gestures in a circular motion around his own face. "Dazed," he decides after a few seconds. "Like, your eyes look all glazed over. You okay?"

"I..." Toby blinks, not knowing how else to get rid of said glaze. "Yeah, yeah, I'm. I'm fine. Just... tired, I guess. Long day."

Reggie shrugs. "If you say so, man."

Toby swoops up a LaCroix from the fridge (lime, obviously, because it's the best flavor) and shuffles into his bedroom. He cracks open the can, takes a long, static-filled sip, and flops face down onto his mattress, not spilling a single drop. It's routine at this point.

In the darkness behind his eyelids, a very particular face pops up, as Toby has no choice but to give in to the vision. It's chiseled and sharp, with a pointed chin and a jawline that could probably slice Toby in half. There are freckles lacing his nose, concentrated in the center of his face, but flaring out to his cheeks. His eyebrows are dark, darker than the caramel-colored hair that falls in loose strands over his eyes and around his ears, not exactly laid flat, but less wavy than Toby's own hair. And finally, the eyes. Blue, pretty much the exact color of a hydrangea, Toby realizes. His mother always kept a garden during his childhood, and the hydrangeas were his favorite part, so he knows that rich blue color any-where. In fact, he'd always secretly wanted eyes like that, eyes that looked as if they were made out of crystal—but he'd inherited plain old brown ones from his parents instead.

Is it even allowed for someone to look like that?

Preposterous, Toby thinks. Absolutely and utterly outra-geous.

Toby turns on his side and blinks his eyes open to stare at the wall. The paint is a boring off-white color, sporting darker scuffs in a few places thanks to various moments of activity. He narrows his eyes a bit, trying to remember if it's within their lease to paint the walls of the apartment. Probably not. And if they are allowed, it's too much effort to even try, anyway.

Toby lifts his head a bit to take another sip of his sparkling water. No matter what he does, he can't get Leo's criminally attractive face out of his mind.

For Christ's sake, why did he have to wink at him?

Completely uncalled for. Completely unnecessary.

Because Toby's life is a clusterfuck.

And another reason why has just been added to the list.

Chapter 2

Toby isn't sure how much time he spends staring at the wall, lost in thought. He doesn't take another sip of his water until there's a knocking at his door, and it tastes a bit less tart at this point than it did before. Shame.

"Yeah?" Toby asks, shifting his position in bed. He hadn't realized how uncomfortably he'd been splayed out on the mattress, and now his abdomen aches ever so slightly.

Reggie cracks open the door and pokes his head in, a loopy smile on his face. It suits him, Toby thinks. Reggie's a cute guy, with bright orange hair and freckles galore—far more so than Leo. But he would never dare tell Reggie that.

"I'm going out tonight," Reg informs Toby, not dropping his grin.

"Okay."

"Probably won't come home tonight."

Toby raises his eyebrows. "What, you got a hot date?"

"I do indeed, as a matter of fact. After all, it is Friday night, and I have a life to tend to. Not that you would know anything about that, dear Tobias."

Toby launches a pillow at Reggie's face, but he swiftly ducks to avoid it, so it goes flying into the hallway instead. "Shut the fuck up."

(Also, Tobias is not his name. Dear God. That would be a whole different grudge to hold against his parents.)

"Aww, is little Toby-Woby jealous?"

Another pillow, another dodge.

"You're not funny," Toby says, but he can't resist the smile that slithers onto his face. That often happens when Reggie's around. It's probably contagious.

"I beg to differ, but, you know, agree to disagree."

"That sounds like something a person who knows they're not funny would say."

This time, Reggie sends one of the pillows flying right back at Toby, and it nails him square in the face. He squawks out in surprise, wrestles the pillow into the corner of his bed, and flips Reggie off, who's cackling to himself in the doorway.

"Anyway," Reg says after the laughter has died down, extending his arms over the top of his head to stretch. He does that a lot, stretching out of nowhere. Toby assumes it's probably the gymnast in him. "She's coming to meet me here before we head out, and I want to introduce you guys, so. Don't act like a dick."

Toby scoffs. "Out of the two of us, you really think I'm the one who'd act like a dick?" he demands incredulously.

"Yep, I do. Ta-ta, now, I have business to attend to."

Reggie closes the door behind him, narrowly avoiding yet another pillow Toby sends flying just half a second too late.

Toby allows a breath to pass through his nostrils before he sets his LaCroix on the bedside table and wrestles his phone out of his pocket. 3:50. He has work from six to midnight, and then he can come home and sleep to celebrate the weekend's official beginning.

He finds his fingers inching toward his other pocket, and then pulling out the crumpled Post-It note. Toby unfolds it, and reads the digits scrawled out against their hot pink background. Then he reads them again. And again. He reads those digits until they begin to float off the paper, swirl around in front of his eyes, eventually becoming a black mass of illegible scribbles. Then he blinks, and they're laid flat against the Post-It again.

Leo had said to text him later. Well, it's been about twenty minutes since class got out, so Toby doesn't exactly have much time left to text him, never mind meet him at the library, before he has to go to work. Biting the inside of his cheek, Toby inputs the seven numbers into his phone and begins constructing a message.

hey, it's toby from calc. i have work at 6 tonight, so if you wanna meet up at some point today, it'll have to be soon

He reads it over. Yes, okay. That's fine. Then, as the thought comes to mind, he adds:

unless you have a class or something right now. sorry for bothering you if you do

He pauses. Backspace, backspace, backspace.

sorry for bothering you

He clicks send and, naturally, immediately regrets doing so.

Jesus, that was such a stupid thing to say. Why would he be bothering him? Leo asked him to text him. He asked to be bothered. Toby is simply just fulfilling his task as the recently-deemed bother-er.

He really wishes he could shake this habit of psyching himself out for such minor things. Every time it happens, he digs himself deeper and deeper into a pit. And it's not an exciting hole to dig, not one that leads to China, like the myth he used to hear about when he was a kid—no, this pit goes straight to insanity instead. Fun.

A few gentle knocks on the front door pry him from his crippling thoughts of self-doubt (thank God) and he sits up on his bed, at attention. He thinks he can probably hear Reggie smile giddily from all the way in his room as footfalls make their way from the kitchen island to the entryway.

The door opens with its usual, drawn-out groan, and Toby can't help but smile to himself when Reggie says, "Hello, beautiful," his voice laced with pure adoration. As childish and ridiculous as Reg can be, he's an absolute sweetheart, and Toby doesn't know if there's anyone else out there that deserves to settle down and be happy as much as he does.

A faint chuckle carries through the walls, followed by the click of the front door shutting shortly after. Toby exhales and pushes himself off the mattress and to his feet, the bed frame creaking in response, as if pleading with Toby to stay down and relax. He wants nothing more than to do so, but he may or may not have plans tonight, and getting back into bed will probably confine him there until a quarter before six, when he will actually have to go to work.

Toby stands there for a moment, reflects on the fact that he just mentally personified his own bed, and tries very very hard not to give in to the urge to jump out his window. Maybe the one thing that keeps him from doing so is the (un)fortunate fact that they live on the first floor.

His hands are in his pockets and he walks into the living room, where Reggie and a pretty girl with umber skin and dark, curly bangs are standing by the couch. Reg, of course, is talking his mouth off, and Toby's not really paying much attention to whatever he could possibly be saying, though he does catch the words "roommate" and "sloth," and he can only imagine how those two words are connected.

Toby softly clears his throat, and the couple turns to face him. Reggie, of course, has a toothy grin of full display.

"Vicki," he says, looping an arm around her waist and walking her closer to Toby. "This is Toby, my roommate. Toby, this is Vicki, my girlfriend."

"Nice to meet you," Vicki says, holding her hand out. Toby shakes, obviously, because although he is violently antisocial, he's not cruel enough to leave her hanging.

"You too," he responds, plastering on his go-to toothless smile that he thinks probably looks more like a grimace than anything else.

Vicki smiles back, genuinely, her plum-colored lips curling upwards, the corners of her hazel eyes crinkling as a result, an expression that looks completely natural and suits her face well. And her voice is low and soft, which earns her some bonus points, because Toby is absolutely not a fan of loud people; Reg, of course, being the only exception, mostly because he's stuck with him, and has been since he moved out here.

"Reg talks about you all the time," Vicki tells him, her smile now twisting into more of a smirk. "About how you two are, like, the bestest of buddies. It's cute, honestly."

Toby doesn't know whether he wants to laugh or hide as Reggie scoffs at her.

"I do not," he insists, making prolonged eye contact with Toby, as if to communicate don't even think about believing her. "C'mon, I finally introduce you two and the first thing you've gotta do is embarrass me?"

"It's my duty, babe."

"Well, it's pretty fucked, if you ask me."

"Hey, man," Toby chimes in, folding his arms over his chest. "If it makes you feel any better, you've been embarrassing yourself plenty for years without any help."

While Reggie flips him off, a gesture Toby has no hesitation in returning, Vicki tosses her head back and laughs. It's a full, hearty laugh, not some stereotypical Barbie doll, high-pitched giggle. Toby likes that about her. He doesn't really know why; he's just always enjoyed seeing people laugh in a genuine manner. It ignites an enjoyable warm sensation in his chest.

"You're doing exactly what I told you not to do," Reggie grumbles, then waves his hand towards Toby dramatically. "Away with you, now."

Toby blows him a mocking kiss—probably the boldest thing he's done in a while, considering it makes his cheeks warm up way too easily—and disappears back into his room.

The moment the door falls shut behind him, a ding sounds out from his pocket. He mindlessly extracts his phone from his sweatpants to check the notification, only for his heart rate to immediately spike, and his self-resentment along with it.

Haha you're not bothering me :)

Fuck. Fuck.

But yea, i'm free. Can you meet me at the library in like 15 mins? We can spend an hour or so on the project before you have to go to work

Toby has to physically restrain his thumbs for several seconds before typing out his response.

yeah sure

Nailed it.

Fifteen minutes later, Toby's standing outside the front of the library, hands shoved in his pockets, tensing every one of his muscles as if doing so would form some kind of shield to protect him from the icy gale that blows against his back. He blinks frost out of his eyes as he scans his surroundings, looking out for Leo's gangly frame, but the tear-inducing wind isn't necessarily helping his vision at the moment.

He really, really hates the cold.

There seems to be a clock stowed away in his mind some-where, documenting every second with a tick—an echoing, annoying tick that becomes extremely redundant extremely quickly, until Toby's ready to pull his hair out. For a brief moment, once he's been standing for over five minutes, he experiences an internal panic at the thought of the possibility of some kind of miscommunication between Leo and him. Leo had said the library... right? So surely he meant this one. They go to a small college, and there's only one on campus as far as Toby is concerned. So unless Leo was talking about the library thirty minutes into the city, then Toby's right where he should be. Or maybe he read the text wrong. He thinks it said fifteen minutes, unless he was hallucinating. Which, who knows, could have been what happened. Before he can get himself entirely worked up about it, he pulls out his phone to double check. (More like quadruple check. Toby wonders, somewhere in the back of his mind, how much dirt he has left before he finally hits rock bottom.)

Well, he's right. (Unless he's seeing things. For the fifth time.) And it's been over twenty minutes since Leo sent that message. Approaching twenty-five. And Toby thinks he might be approaching frostbite.

He's considering just leaving, because stressing himself out like this is most definitely not worth it (as if going home would do him any favors), until a voice calls out, labored and slightly shrouded by the wind whipping around him.

Toby turns his head to the left, and there he is, jogging toward him, slowing down as he draws nearer. When he's about four or so feet away from Toby, he doubles over, hands on his knees, his shoulders rising and falling at a rapid pace with each desperate inhale and exhale. Despite the ungodly temperature, his forehead is beaded with sweat, and he's not wearing any layers; not unless you count the flannel jacket wrapped around his waist, on the cusp of slipping right off, and the black long-sleeved t-shirt with a little white rose embroidered on the chest pocket.

"Did you... run here?" Toby asks, feeling his face subconsciously twist into a dubious expression. Leo looks up at him, still gasping for breath, but smiles.

(Maybe, if it weren't so damn cold, Toby would melt. For that brief moment, he is very thankful for the weather.)

"Yeah," Leo answers, standing up straight and resting his hands on his hips.

"Wh... why?"

He shrugs. "I don't have a car."

"You could hire an Uber or something—"

"I'm broke as hell, dude, that's not happening."

"Well—I mean, I-I could have picked you up, if you called. Or texted. O-or, you know, whatever."

Leo tilts another softer smile at him, mouth closed this time. His lips are dry, Toby notices.

Not that he's looking at his lips.

"Well, I like to run," Leo says, swiping a hand through his hair, which Toby is also not looking at. "It wakes me up, and I like the satisfaction you feel after. You know what I'm talking about?"

Toby bobs his head as if he does. Never once do Leo's lips curve downward, or even falter in the slightest. Toby wonders if he's just like that. Always smiling.

"Does hypothermia just not exist for you?" Toby asks, swiveling his body toward the direction of the library, indicating that he would like shelter now.

"I don't get sick that easily," Leo tells him as they begin to walk. Thank God.

"I don't think hypothermia really cares about that," Toby scoffs.

"Sure it does. I mean, I would know. I'm from Boston. It ain't all warm and cozy up there either, you know. Never once have I gotten hypothermia, even when I slept out in the garage during a snowstorm."

Toby has to process those words before he reacts. "Wh—why would you ever do that?"

Leo doesn't answer for a second, and if Toby's not imagining things, the smile wanes ever so slightly. But then it's back within a moment, as Leo scrunches his nose and looks up at Toby.

"Just 'cause," he says, and they step into the blissful warmth of the library. They sniff simultaneously, and then Leo clears his throat. "Well, what about you? You could have come inside, you know, instead of waiting for me out there."

And even though every part of him is shivering violently, there is still a warm rush to Toby's face. He doesn't respond to that, because he feels really, really stupid right now.

God, this guy just makes things worse, to the point where it's pretty much impossible for Toby to string together a single coherent thought when he's around.

And they've known each other for less than a day.

Toby's pretty sure this partnership will only result in one thing: his death. If not first from hypothermia or pneumonia or some other godforsaken illness, then it'll be from his own embarrassment.

So that's. That's just great.

Chapter 3

Toby wonders if Leo's into guys.

It's just a thought that merely crosses his mind. Because yes, he's cute, and no, Toby wouldn't necessarily mind if something were to happen between them. And also—the wink. The damn wink. It threw him off his game, and now he can't get it out of his head. It was deliberate and it was volitional, and Toby knows that for a fact. Leo had made direct eye contact and smiled. It wasn't some trick of the wind. No smoke and mirrors. That is one thing he is confident about.

So, naturally, he has to wonder if Leo maybe... thinks he's attractive too. Because why else would he do that? To tease him? Toby went to high school. He knows that straight guys do a lot of weird things, but winking flirtatiously at other men isn't usually one of them. For some reason, that's where they draw the line rather than borderline molestation.

As they mill about the library, searching for a table to settle down at, Toby risks a few sideways glances at Leo. He holds his chin high, he realizes, consistently. And it seems like there's always a hint of a smirk on his face, whether subtle or outright. And he has a dimple on the left side of his mouth, an indent maybe the size of the pad of Toby's pinky finger. It's much easier to see in the warm, yellow lighting of the library's interior than it had been under the fluorescents in the lecture hall or the overcast sky just outside.

"Oh, over there," Leo says, stopping short and pointing across Toby's chest. Toby follows his finger with his eyes to land his gaze upon a little two-person booth, over in the corner. He barely has time to register the area before something's tugging him in its direction by the sleeve of his coat.

"Hey," he squeaks out, nearly tripping over his own feet within the first few steps he takes. But Leo doesn't acknowledge him, and continues marching forward, his dimple looking hollower from this angle than the last.

Leo releases him after a few moments, allowing him to slide into the booth on his own—though from the way he'd been clasping Toby's sleeve, he half expected him to be thrown down, as if he was a prisoner being carted away to the cellar. Toby clears his throat and makes himself comfortable (as comfortable as he can possibly be, at least) while Leo scoots in across from him.

"All right," Leo prompts, folding his hands on the table, fingers interlocked with each other as if this is a business meeting or something. Toby glances down at them, then up at his eyes, then scares himself and looks back down again after less than a second. Fucking wimp. "So."

"S-so," Toby repeats, nodding slowly, staring at the mildly reflective surface in front of him, as if doing so will allow him some insight into this whole situation, a bit of a clue as to what the premise of this project even is, as if it's a crystal ball of some sort. But no; all he sees is a beige-ish blob in replacement of his face and his erratic blond hair, disheveled every which way because of the wind. He smooths it down whilst praying to some supernatural deity of some kind that Leo will let him know all the answers without any provocation coming from him.

But Leo doesn't say anything, and instead just looks at him for a second. Toby fidgets under his gaze, because wow. There is no peace with this guy.

Toby finally decides to be brave and lift up his head, just in time to see Leo's mouth open, words seemingly queued up on his tongue—and then the table begins to vibrate below their wrists, disturbing the awkward silence that had settled over them. Toby glances down at Leo's phone, which lies face up on the table, and just barely manages to read the caller ID before Leo snatches it up and presses it against his ear: Ariel Fischer.

Leo tosses an apologetic glance towards Toby before speaking. "Hey. I'm at the library right now."

Toby scratches the back of his neck and looks around as the voice on the other end replies, and continues to speak for what Toby thinks must be at least a minute. Leo's expression does not once waver.

"Okay, I get it," he finally says, bringing his hand up to push his bangs upwards, only for them to flop right back down onto his forehead again. "I'm sorry. I—I know, I'm sorry. I'll—yes, I promise. Just trust me, okay? Okay."

Another few seconds pass as Leo listens on, now fidgeting with some lint or something that's clinging to the front of his shirt. Toby is unsure whether he wants the call to end or to continue for as long as necessary, to the point where he doesn't have to interact with Leo and can just get to work.

"Yeah. Yeah, I know. But, look, I'm—I'm with someone right now, and I should really go. We can talk about this later, okay?" A short pause. "Okay. Love you."

Toby thinks he has maybe just experienced total annihilation, as if this is a video game, and he is the weakling protagonist that nobody wants to play as. Something in him sinks to the lowest possible part of his body as Leo hangs up the phone and lets out a long sigh.

"Sorry about that," he mutters, shaking his head slightly. "Sorry."

"'S fine," Toby says, looking down and twisting at his fingers. The question is on his tongue, and he thinks he knows the answer, so there's really—there's really no point in asking, no point in bothering to wonder, "Was that—um. Was that your girlfriend?"

Well. Never fucking mind, then.

There's a pause, and Toby doesn't know what Leo's expression looks like at the moment, and he kind of doesn't want to, to be frank. Because he just knows that, whatever the answer, somewhere on his face will be the trace of a smirk, cherry-on-topped by that dimple, and he doesn't think he wants to do that to himself.

But then, Leo laughs. He laughs out loud, and it's a single, amplified cackle, one that startles Toby to the point where he can't help but break his smirk strike to witness it. Leo's mouth is stretched wide and his teeth are white and on display, and the dimple is digging into his skin, and his eyes are crinkled in the corners and bright in the irises.

God fucking help him.

"Um." Toby scratches the back of his neck, unsure of what exactly is happening here. Is Leo laughing at him, or...?

"Oh, jeez," Leo chuckles, pressing the bases of his palms against his eyelids. "Ariel, my girlfriend?"

"I-I mean, I don't know, it was just a question—"

"No, no, I get it." Leo waves a hand at him, a few loose giggles still occasionally slipping through his lips and jostling his chest with their uprising. "Sorry, it's just—God, I just can't imagine that."

Toby clears his throat. "Oh. Well, wh—who is she?"

"My roommate," Leo answers, "slash best friend. She was calling about rent. We've known each other since high school and are total opposites, but that's what makes life interesting, you know?"

"Oh. I... guess."

"But yeah." Leo crosses his arms and leans back in his seat. "Definitely not my girlfriend. In fact, I'm single."

Toby clenches his jaw to keep his head from jumping up too quickly. "Oh."

(He really hopes it doesn't come out as a question. He's not totally sure—he thinks he might be blacking out.)

"Yep." Leo pops the p, and damn it, he's smiling again, and there's an unmistakable gleam in his eye, and Toby feels himself begin to blush furiously. "Single and ready to mingle, as us white people like to say."

Oh, for fuck's sake.

Toby wonders what a heart attack feels like and whether this is one, because Leo's done it again. He's winked at him again, and now here Toby is, overreacting from one simple gesture he may or may not be reading way too much into, short-circuiting, heart slamming against his ribcage. For the second time today.

There's a silence that settles itself over the table for the umpteenth time, something way different from the rest of the library's atmosphere. Something that, for a period of no talking from either of them, seems far too loud.

"A-anyway," Toby sputters, deciding to steer this conversation in another direction. Literally any other direction. "Um."

"Oh. Right. Calc." Leo sits up a bit straighter, and Toby hopes, prays, really, that that's as straight as he gets. Because if not, Toby is in trouble. Big trouble.

As Leo rolls up his sleeves and begins to root around in his backpack, Toby mimics him, not knowing exactly what he's looking for so instead just mindlessly sweeping his hands over his various belongings—oh, look, there's his old phone charger. When Leo finally pulls out his laptop, which is littered with what has to be dozens of stickers, Toby does the same. He extracts his own MacBook, its surface smooth and silver and glossy and boring, a direct opposite of Leo's. In that moment, he's never felt more ashamed for his lack of expression.

(The only thing he can blame is his upbringing. His parents forbade him from doing anything that might tarnish something expensive, so stickers on laptops were a colossal no-no.)

"So," Leo begins, his fingers gliding over his keyboard in a very satisfying rhythm that must have been practiced thousands of times for it to sound so seamless and natural. Toby wonders what might be important enough to Leo for him to include it in his password.

But not, like, in a creepy way. He's just curious.

"Do you have any ideas?"

Toby blinks. "Huh?"

"Ideas. You have any?"

"Uh." No. Absolutely not. "Oh, n-no, not really."

"You sure?"

Toby wants to crawl into a hole. Why did he agree to this?

(Because he's an idiot that can't control his emotions. That's why.)

He feels like a bobble head as he nods meekly for the nth time that day.

Leo peers at him over his laptop screen for what must be several minutes jam-packed into a single second, and then shrugs. "All right, if you say so. We'll figure something out."

Toby wants to breathe a sigh of relief, but the problem there is he has no air in his lungs to put to use. That, and he knows he's not in the clear just yet.

"Well, I was actually thinking," Leo continues, and Toby watches how he moves his hands with every syllable, constantly having the need to do something different with them for the passage of every second. First, palms pressed flat against the tabletop on either side of his computer. Then his elbows are propped up and he's lacing his fingers together. He's brushing a few strands of hair out of his eyes, only for them to fall right back into place immediately after. He's popping his knuckles. Typing. Gesturing.

"Sounds good?" Leo asks, his left eyebrow raised and one hand frozen in a questioning thumbs up.

Meanwhile, utter dread sinks into Toby's stomach, because he was not paying attention to whatever Leo just said and it was his opportunity.

Toby is at a crossroads. He has two options:

1. Admit he has no idea what the hell he's doing here, what the basis of this project is, and that he's very sorry and maybe this wasn't such a good idea after all and all he'll do is drag Leo down and act like even more of an idiot and probably apologize for way too much for way too long, or

2. Agree and do the exact opposite of just that.

Toby isn't great at thinking about things in the long term.

"Yep," he mumbles, and dear God, he doesn't think he's ever felt such self-loathing to this extent before. "Sounds perfect."

Maybe there is a God, because Leo, whether intentionally or not, ended up recapping the project's entire premise before they officially got started. To Toby, it was like a halo of light had been cast down upon him from the heavens, illuminating his path, assuring him that everything will be all right, at least as far as his calculus grade goes. A C plus, at the very least, is obtainable after all.

Although, he wishes something like this could happen for, you know, just about everything else in his life, but. You get what you get, he supposes.

Time slips away as he and Leo converse, and even though they're not friends, even though they're only sitting here together for academic purposes, and even though he's been acting like a malfunctioning excuse for a human the entirety of the day, Toby's shocked at how quickly he manages to fall into the groove of things, how easy it is to work with Leo (who's apparently a calculus master, hello), how little effort it takes to forget his troubles for the time being and just focus on being productive.

Toby's not bad at school. He makes decent grades. He studies. He tries.

But he's never felt so engaged before.

Maybe partner work isn't all that bad.

Chapter 4

Toby's alarm makes him jump when it sounds off, mostly because he completely forgot he even had it set.

(But also a little bit because its noise is the most anxiety-inducing noise on the planet and Toby will never get used to it.)

"Oh, shit," he mumbles, fumbling to quickly shut it off before the glares of the other students attempting to study in the library turn on him. The amount of time it takes him to silence it isn't exactly long, but it's not short either—somewhere in the middle, something discomforting. When he finally manages to do so, he stuffs his phone back into his pocket and looks up at Leo.

"I have to go," he says. "Work."

"Oh. Yeah. Right." Leo shakes his head and gives a soft chuckle. "Sorry, I totally forgot we had a time limit."

"Yeah, me too." Toby closes his laptop and secures it inside his bag.

"You know, you're super easy to work with. We made some solid progress. I've got a good feeling about this grade, since we're working together."

And Toby knows it's just a statement. Just a compliment for the sake of small talk. But he can't help the fluttering feeling that stirs in his stomach.

"Yeah," he agrees quietly, sliding out of the booth and hoisting his backpack onto his shoulders as casually as possible. "I do too."

He stands there for a moment or two afterward, looking everywhere but into Leo's eyes, because he knows that his face is red and doing so will just make him feel more like a fool than he already does. He clears his throat and, fiddling with the zipper to his coat, asks, "Do you need a ride home? Or—you know. To wherever?"

Leo tilts his head, as if he hadn't heard the question right. Maybe he hadn't. Toby's not great when it comes to projecting. (Shocker.)

Please say no, he begs internally. Please say no. Why did I even ask? Please just say no.

"I'm good," Leo finally responds. "Thanks, though."

Fuck. He said no.

Toby can't help but wonder if Leo had been weighing his options. Honestly, no was probably the best choice. Being with Leo in his car, a small, confined space, is just a disaster waiting to happen for the nervous, gay wreck that is Toby Wentworth. His heart would probably bust through his chest, and then Leo would be in a car with a bloody, heartless corpse. He'd humiliate himself even in death.

"Oh, okay." Toby nods, pressing his lips into a tight, forced smile. "I'll—uh, see you later, then."

"See you," says Leo as Toby turns toward the library's exit. Similarly to how someone might forget exactly how to breathe when they think about breathing, Toby wonders if he's walking in the way a capable human being would, because he can feel Leo's gaze on his back, piercing through his coat, and he thinks it might be hindering his ability to use his legs correctly.

It's colder than it was an hour ago, Toby notices, but the wind that bites his face is no match for the warmth below his cheeks. He balls his hands into fists within his pockets as he makes his way to his parking spot, cursing his lack of capacity for human interaction. Especially when the other human is attractive.

In all honesty, Toby doesn't like himself sometimes. And he doesn't like other people most of the time. Today, he's experiencing a weird mix between the two; the absolute worst from one side, and the best from the other. He hates—loathes—how he's pretty much fallen for this near-stranger, a person who doesn't even know his last name, within the span of three hours—the weakest three hours of his entire life. It's just... annoying.

The convenience store. That's where Toby works.

Really, it's more along the lines of a mini-Walmart crammed into a drugstore-sized building. There are only two shift workers at a time, with the manager occasionally on standby in the back room should something happen, doing whatever managers do. The shelves are stocked with basic necessities and then some, and the just-off-campus location makes the store quite the popular attraction for students at pretty much all hours of the day.

But Toby likes the dusk shift the most. While the place is still busy, it's not crawling with people like it is during the daytime. Toby is able to busy himself at the register for the first half of the shift, at least, and the final three or so hours he can relax a little bit, since there are generally less customers entering the store as the clock approaches twelve a.m. He's only had to work the graveyard shift once, and it was not only boring, but he was pretty much falling asleep the entire time. And working during the morning or the afternoon is just too much for him to handle. He's also generally the busiest then.

While nighttime does allow the most opportune moment to spring a robbery onto the place, Toby's sure it'd probably never happen, since the police station is just a little ways away, but also he'd be more than willing to dump the entire register into a pillow case if he was ordered to. As if he'd risk his life for some stupid part-time job. So, that's it. Dusk it is.

"Hey, Blue," Toby greets his coworker as he steps into the back room, closing the door behind him. Blue Brown (yes, that is his actual, legal name) is already sporting his emerald green polo, the uniform for the place, and is currently fiddling with his lip ring in the mirror. He glances back at Toby without turning his head, and Toby sees the small smile in the reflection.

"Hey," Blue responds, his words hollow due to the awkward positioning of his lips at the moment.

Toby glances up at the clock mounted on the wall; he's got about five minutes or so before his shift officially begins, so he drops his bag on a chair and pulls out his own shirt to change into.

"You doin' okay?" Blue asks from his place in front of the mirror.

"Yeah." Toby tugs his shirt off over his head. "Why wouldn't I be?"

He thinks Blue shrugs, although it's a bit difficult to tell, considering the way he's hunched over. "I dunno. Something about you seems a little off today."

Toby huffs out a semi-scoff. "What, are my eyes all glazed over? Apparently they were earlier today."

"I don't know, bro. It's just the vibes you're giving off."

Toby clears his throat. "Well, I'm fine," he mumbles, fastening the buttons to his uniform and topping the whole thing off with his lanyard. "How're you?"

"Same old," Blue says, and he sounds genuinely bored. "Life is continuously boring and meaningless. But Jack and I have our two-year anniversary coming up next week, so if he doesn't lift my spirits by then, we might have some problems."

Toby raises his eyebrows, folding his t-shirt over his arms and stuffing it into his bag for the time being. "You've only been together for two years? From the things you've told me, it sounds like you've known each other for forever."

Blue chuckles, and apparently finally decides his lip ring is in a satisfactory enough position as he steps away from the mirror, and shows Toby his full face, non-reflected for the first time today. "Well, we have. We were friends in middle school because our moms worked together," he explains. "He only finally came out and confessed his feelings after his college graduation."

Toby swallows. "Really. Uh—must have been pretty nerve-wracking for him."

Blue shrugs. "I guess so. But I'd been out since the seventh grade, so I guess he didn't have to worry about me not swinging that way. That was one weight off his shoulders."

"Seventh grade? Really?"

"Yeah. I was—am—luckier than some, I guess. It wasn't very difficult for me to realize and accept that I liked guys too. Honestly, though, I blame the Cubs for my sexual awakening. I was never a big sports person or anything, but I still found myself watching every game with my dad. I mean, have you seen the way their pants just—"

"I'm gay, actually."

Blue freezes, and his eyebrows (which, for ironic purposes, have been dyed dark blue) jump up a bit. Toby's clenching his jaw and pretty much every other muscle, he assumes, as if preparing for something to come flying through the air and strike him down.

But there it is. For the first time, to anyone, ever. Out in the world, told to a person he's only known for a few months, someone he doesn't really interact with outside of work.

"Oh. Cool."

The doors fly open and two employees enter, their shoulders sagging and eyes half open. Their shifts are up.

About two hours in, after not elaborating on anything to Blue after the end of that conversation, Toby's checked out maybe fifteen people. He hasn't really been counting. Blue's taken care of a few too, and is currently the one manning both registers as Toby assumes his task of stocking shelves and tidying up, since the store is relatively empty and there's no need for the two of them to be up front.

Toby's busy in the snack aisle when the bell above the front door jingles merrily, followed by Blue's voice as he gives the routine greeting. There's no response from whoever just walked in, but that's usually the case.

Toby hears footfalls as they approach, and senses the sharp turn the person makes into the candy aisle, which is just one over, so he pushes the final box of mini Oreos onto the shelf and makes his way there.

"Can I help you with anything?" he asks, and the customer turns her head. She's a petite, dark-haired girl, more than likely also a student. Her golden-tan skin is flushed dark in the cheeks, and her very symmetrical eyebrows are drawn together. With her expression combined with the gnawing on the knuckle of her forefinger, it's easy for Toby to assume that she's either under a lot of stress or she's had a very bad day. Or maybe both. He's definitely been there.

"Uh," she says, pulling her finger away from her mouth and crossing her arms tightly across her chest instead. Her voice is a little shaky, not in a fearful way, but more like she's teetering on the verge of tears.

"Um." Toby swallows, unsure of what else to say. "Sorry. Uh, let me know if you do need something. I'll be around."

He swivels on his heel, preparing to return to his station at the snack aisle, but that shaky voice calls out for him to wait. He does his best to don a comforting, approachable expression, but he thinks he's probably trying too hard, so he drops it and tries not to think about his facial muscles in order to look as cool and neutral as possible.

"Yeah. Sorry. Sorry, I'm just..." The girl sighs and rubs the bridge of her nose. "Uh, my boyfriend and I had a fight kinda recently, and... it's really my fault, so I'm just.... You guys have ice cream here, right? I'm trying to gather my strength to go and apologize tomorrow, but..." She gives a wobbly, humorless chuckle. "That calls for an absolute cleanse of my dignity beforehand. You know?"

"Oh." Toby... hadn't really been asking for the life story, but he doesn't mind so much. There's something about this girl that he feels like he can relate to. Maybe it's the drowning-in-the-ice-cream plan she seems to be formulating in her head. He's also been there. For different reasons.

Her eyes go wide for a split second before she buries her face in her hands. "I'm so sorry. That's so awkward. You didn't—you really didn't need to know that. I'm just... anxious, I guess. Sorry."

Toby swallows and scratches the back of his neck. "It's okay," he says, deciding to attempt the smiling thing again, without backing down this time. "But, yeah, we do have ice cream. Any particular flavor?"

She brings her hands away from her face and pushes one through her thick, soft hair. "I dunno. I'm usually just a plain vanilla type person, but... it doesn't feel right tonight."

Toby exhales a laugh. "Yeah, I know what you mean." And he does. How crazy is that? "If you're willing to take suggestions, I personally think we sell the best store-bought mint chocolate chip around."

The corners of her lips quirk up. "Really? This place?"

Toby shrugs. "Don't knock it till you try it."

Oh God. Why did he say that? He sounds like his dad.

But she gives a soft, wavery series of chuckles. "Guess so," she says. "I'll give it a try, I guess. Thanks."

"Yeah, no problem. Um—good luck. With your boyfriend."

The girl opens her mouth, then closes it and gives a nod of her head. "Thanks."

Blue checks her out maybe five minutes later, sending her on her way with a carton of mint chocolate chip ice cream. The bell jingling over the front door is Toby's signal for an all clear, and he comes to join Blue at the register.

"Did I hear you giving her a pep talk?" Blue asks, raising his eyebrows. "Shy little Toby, willingly making conversation with a stranger?"

"Shut up," Toby sighs, leaning on the counter. "It wasn't a pep talk. I just recommended her an ice cream flavor. Is that so bizarre?"

"For you? Absolutely."

Toby huffs out a breath at Blue's snickering, then glances down as Blue turns up his wrist to check the time. The hands read somewhere around eight twenty.

"So," Blue prompts, standing on his toes as if conducting a scan to ensure that the store is deserted. "Did you wanna talk some more about earlier?"

Toby's mouth dries up momentarily.

"I mean, you obviously don't have to," Blue adds hastily. "It's your business. But, you know, if you think you might ever actually need a pep talk or something... I'm here."

"Oh." Toby looks away for a second, runs his fingers through his hair, then turns back. "Um. You're... actually the first person I've told."

Blue's navy eyebrows raise up a bit. "Really?"

Toby nods sheepishly.

"Oh." Blue purses his lips, nods slowly, as if he's not entirely sure how to take this information. Eventually, he must settle on a decision, when he says, "Well, thanks for trusting me enough to tell me, then."

"I mean, of course I trust you," Toby says. "You've been out to me pretty much since we met."

"That wasn't that long ago. We're not the bestest of pals, you know."

"Yeah, well..." Toby swallows. "Out of everyone I know, you're the least likely to push me away, so... it was easier."

"I get it," Blue says softly. "I know it's definitely not an easy thing to do."

"You said it was easy for you," Toby points out.

"I said I was lucky," Blue corrects him. "I was lucky to find a label I was comfortable with, I was lucky to be able to do that mid-puberty, and I was—am—lucky to have a family that accepts me. But coming out was definitely no piece of cake." Blue leans back against the counter. "I put it off for months once I managed to accept myself. I knew my folks didn't really care one way or the other about the LGBT community, but I honestly had no clue how they'd feel about me, personally. To some people, random strangers out in the world is a totally different matter than someone living under your roof. Someone you thought you knew everything about."

"So how'd you end up doing it?" Toby asks quietly.

"On accident, actually," Blue says, chuckling a bit at the memory. "Remember how I said I blamed the Cubs? Well, my parents, my sister, and I were watching a game, and Lucía—my sister—made some remark about how hot one of the players was. I agreed with her." Blue looks down at his feet. "I was so horrified, I didn't think of attempting to pass it off as a joke. They were all looking at me, and for a second, I really did think I was totally screwed. I actually started crying. That's how scared I was."

"But everything was okay?"

"Yeah. It took several minutes, since I was a nervous wreck and my parents needed a bit of enlightenment, but." Blue shrugs. "That story's got a happy ending. But it wasn't like that every single time. I've lost a few friends over the past couple of years, but it's inevitable, I guess," he sighs. "There's really no point in mourning for the people who are willing to throw away a friendship because they found out something they didn't know before. I'm still the same person I was back then. I mean, I've got blue eyebrows, but other than that..."

"I know that," Toby says. "I know not everyone's open-minded. I guess... I'm most worried about what my family's gonna say." He rubs his eyes. "They're pretty much entirely anti-me when it comes to what they believe."

Blue lets out a long sigh. "I know it's scary. And you obviously don't have to tell them any time soon, not until you're one hundred percent sure you're ready to let them know. But if you really think there's not a single chance that they'll come around and support you, then... maybe you need to make some sacrifices."

Toby gulps down something hard in his throat.

He hates the word "sacrifice." It makes him think of pain. Of agony. Of death. And he especially hates it in this case, since he has no real idea of who exactly would be the one suffering.

Chapter 5

At around 11:30, when Toby is on the cusp of freedom, his phone pings with a text from Reggie.

dude u comin or what

Toby glances up at Blue, who's doodling something un-intelligible on a trashed receipt with his elbow propped up on the counter. The store's been empty for a little over half an hour now, and Toby hopes it stays that way till the time comes for him to clock out.

uh coming to what? i'm at work, Toby responds, releasing a yawn so powerful that he has to blink a few times to regain his vision after blacking out for a split second.

this party

yeahhh, no thanks. i'm exhausted

comonnnn bro we re having fun

i thought you were hanging out with Vicki?

ya i was and then jordan invited us to his place so were here now with a couple other ppl just chillin

Toby rolls his eyes. i'll think about it. and if i do come, i'm not staying for a long time.

don't b a party pooper man

He turns his phone off and shoves it in his pockets as a new customer staggers through the door. So close.

Toby finds himself standing at the door to Jordan Mc-Connell's apartment against his better judgement. He doesn't really know exactly why he came; maybe because if he didn't, he'd never hear the end of Reggie's lecture about how he's super lame and doesn't know how to have fun. Or maybe it's because he just hasn't had a drink in a while and truthfully does not think he would mind one right about now. Probably both, honestly.

The music is audible from outside, some hip hop song he can't think of the name of right now, but it's not obnoxiously loud. Toby hopes that's a sign that there aren't too many people here. He'd enjoy himself a bit more if there weren't.

He raises his fist to knock, but decides it's pointless and instead turns the knob (unlocked, as suspected) and walks right in. The stove light is flicked on in the kitchen, which is just to the left of the entrance, and LED lights that line the tops of the walls illuminate the rest of the place, each room glowing a different color.

Toby peeks his head into the living room, which is swallowed in red. Maybe nine or ten people are sitting around, either on the couch, the floor, or the armchair. Most of them have a drink in their hand, and the rest—Toby glances down at the Ziploc bag of brownies on the table—look like they've reached peak relaxation.

"Heyyyyy," Reggie's familiar, gravelly voice sounds out from the edge of the couch farthest from where Toby stands, a smile stretched wide on his face. Vicki is perched on his lap, her legs intertwining with his, which are propped up on the coffee table, her head resting on his shoulder. "You came."

"Toby, my man," Jordan greets, standing up from his spot on the floor in front of the TV stand and, after catching his balance on wobbly knees, claps his hand with Toby's and pulls him in for a bro hug. "Been a while."

"Yeah." Toby moves towards the vacant space on the sofa, in between the conjoined Reggie and Vicki and a girl with cat eye glasses with the full intent to sit and make himself comfortable, but Jordan tugs him away with a short disclaimer that someone's already sitting there, and they're just in the bathroom. Apparently they've been "DIY-ing cocktails," as put by Jordan, and had one too many.

So instead, Toby plops down on the ground next to Jordan, who immediately fills his hands with a cold can of beer. Toby's hands are already prickly from the outside temperatures, and the drink seems to finish the job and numb them entirely. Toby, truthfully, does not care at all. He cracks the can open, mentally saying grace in a way that his parents would probably crucify him for, before downing a long, underage, unknowingly necessary swig.

If only his parents could see him now. Gay, pining after a stranger, breaking the law. The alcohol must already be getting to his brain because honestly, he thinks he might be willing to pay money to see their reactions. Would he be terrified? Absolutely. But it would be fucking hilarious.

"Damn, dude, you have a rough week or something?" Jordan asks as Toby gulps down the beer and wipes his mouth with his sleeve. Toby just grunts in response.

The feeling of the alcohol rushing to his brain paired with his immense level of exhaustion is an interesting experience. Not that he's never felt something like this before, because he absolutely has. And every one of those nights, he slept like a baby. So maybe there's always a plus side.

A few moments later, there's a faint click somewhere else in the apartment, and the person that's been in the bathroom emerges. Toby doesn't bother paying them any attention as they stumble past him to their spot on the couch, as he is far too busy with crushing up his now empty can and summoning a new one from the person—someone he doesn't think he knows—leaning against the ice chest.

Toby's not sure how many minutes, how many beers, pass. The guests are talking amongst themselves, and he's not engaging, really. He doesn't care much for gossip about roommates or news about recent hookups or slander of cruel professors. It's not much of a party for him. Just a catalyst for free alcohol. (And it's working. Which is great.)

Whatever the case, someone speaks up, raising their voice just loud enough for everyone to hear over the music (which has been dialed down a bit since Toby's arrival). It's a girl sitting on the opposite wall, with pigtails and hair Toby thinks might be dyed pink. It's difficult to tell under the room's scarlet glow.

"We should play a game," she suggests.

"Like what?" asks Vicki, perking up from her nesting spot on Reggie's shoulder.

"There's this one we used to play at parties in high school," Pigtails says. "We called it 'seven minutes in limbo.' Basically the same as seven minutes in heaven, only you're sent in with an unknown person."

"Unknown?" some other unfamiliar voice asks dubiously. Toby thinks it might be the guy stationed at the ice chest.

"Only if you consent, obviously," the girl adds quickly. "But the point of the game is just that you're not supposed to reveal yourselves until after the seven minutes are up. I mean, technically, there's nothing stopping you from doing that, but. It would just ruin the thrill of it."

"I'm down," Vicki decides, and Reggie looks up at her with his eyebrows furrowed. She sighs at him and ruffles his hair. "Relax. I'm not going to go fall in love with another person from some stupid party game." She looks up at Pigtails, her arms now draped over Reg's neck. "How do we keep ourselves hidden from each other?"

"So, everyone gets assigned a number," Pigtails explains. "There's at least one game moderator who draws the numbers out of a hat, so if there's anyone that doesn't wanna play—" Almost immediately, the girl with the cat eye glasses shoots her hand up. "Okay, good. You can do it, then. But anyway, you only know your own number. Then everyone puts on blindfolds, and two numbers are called out by the moderator. Those two go into the closet or wherever together, keeping the blindfolds on until they get there. You can take them off once the door is closed and the timer is set, but you're not allowed to—well, not supposed to—turn on the light. You don't figure out who you're with until after the seven minutes are up."

"So the object of the game is to make out with someone who may or may not be a complete stranger," Reggie says.

"Or someone who may or may not be someone you know super well. The whole point is anonymity, at least until the end of the round."

"Kinky," Reg snickers. Vicki shoves him lightly on the shoulder.

Pigtails clears her throat. "Seriously though, if any of you guys don't feel comfortable playing, you definitely don't have to. And you can opt out at any time. I know it's a pretty dubious situation."

Toby nods in understanding with everyone else.

"Okay. So, who's willing to play?"

Everyone's hand shoots up, except for the recently dubbed moderator's. Even Toby's. Because why the hell not.

Toby gets a ripped piece of paper pressed into his palm with the number nine written on it, which, coincidentally, happens to be his favorite number. So maybe this is a good sign.

After everyone has read and memorized their number, Glasses goes around to collect them all in a drained solo cup, which she then shakes around with her palm covering the top.

"Wait," the girl with the pigtails says (who Toby learns is actually named Loretta), thrusting her arm out to stop the game moderator. (Toby still doesn't know her name.) "We need blindfolds for everyone."

"On it," Jordan says, getting to his feet and dashing into his room. A minute or two later, he returns, laden with scarves, ties, and bandanas. "Will these work?"

"Sure," says Loretta as she begins helping to pass them out at random. Toby ends up with a tie. He takes in a breath and lays it over his eyes, tying it in a half-assed knot at the back of his head.

"Okay, is everyone properly blinded?" someone asks, and it's not Loretta's voice. She's got a slight accent Toby can't quite place, so he assumes it's the moderator speaking. There are murmurs of confirmation, everyone's voices suddenly a little softer. "Okay. First two numbers then, I guess."

There's a shuffling noise, and Toby sits semi-patiently in the darkness as his heartbeat seems to migrate from his chest to his throat. Strangely, though, it's not a sensation he necessarily hates at the moment. Maybe he's needed a thrill like this for a long time.

"Five and six."

There comes the hesitant creak of furniture, then carefully maneuvered footsteps. A yelp from someone a little ways away from Toby, immediately followed by a hushed apology. Toby can't decipher either of the voices, but he thinks—maybe—one of them might be Vicki. Three pairs of feet shuffle away—Five, Six, and the moderator, as she leads them from the group—the squeak of a door, which Toby thinks might be the pantry, and then a click.

Seven minutes... they really have to wait here, blinded, for seven minutes?

Apparently so, because there's no word of otherwise from Loretta. Toby sighs and leans back cautiously until his back finds the wall, and he releases that shaky breath once it does. Seven minutes.

He thinks about the people he saw when he came in. There was Reggie, Vicki, and Jordan, obviously. There's Loretta.

So he knows who four of the other eight players are. There's a fifty percent chance that he'll end up in that closet—pantry—with a person he doesn't know the name of.

He thinks about the possibilities, and his mind immediately goes to Reggie. He doesn't know whether to laugh or to cringe at the fact that, if their numbers get picked together, he could very well wind up making out with his violently straight roommate, somewhat drunkenly, in the pantry of their mutual friend's house.

Yeah. No. Toby can't do that. If it comes to that, he thinks they'll probably just hang out for seven minutes, maybe sneak a few packs of Fruit Snacks from the box. Toby will not kiss Reggie. And Reggie probably wouldn't wanna kiss him, either.

Soon enough, the timer sounds off, and there's a slight buzz of excitement that makes its way through the room, through Toby's veins. Everyone is still silent, but he knows that, just like him, they're all aching to know the who and the what of the situation.

There's a knock on the pantry door, and the moderator speaks. "You guys can come out now."

And they do, seconds after. Toby hears the breath hitch in their throats as their identities are revealed to one another, and there's a sound Toby thinks might be suppressed laughter. Curiosity digs at his stomach.

"All right, next round," the moderator announces, and the shuffling returns as her hand is plunged back into the solo cup. "Okay, we have number two, and..."

Toby waits.

"Number nine."

He's this close to making a noise. Of surprise? Nervousness? Excitement? He's got no clue.

There's a hand wrapping around his forearm to assist him to his feet, and then he's being led off, his heartbeat echoing in his ears. He wants to know who the other person is. Really bad.

"Don't have too much fun," the moderator teases, and then he's entering the confined space that is the pantry, and there's an arm brushing up against his own, and the door falls shut.

"Oh jeez," Toby whispers, completely by accident. He thinks he's shaking. How did he get here? Why did he agree to this again? Were the blissful, devil may care effects of the beers he drank fading this quickly?

"You okay?"

He stills. The other voice is low, a whisper, barely audible—but Toby can tell one thing for sure. And that is that he is in this pantry with another guy.

He doesn't know whether to be relieved or terrified.

Toby lets out a shaky exhale, and reaches up to remove the tie from around his face. He blinks his eyes open, but can't see anything anyway. It's pitch black.

"I'm okay," he responds, at a volume equal to—if not lesser than—his partner's.

"We can just hang out here. I don't think people actually play party games like this."

It's not Reggie. Reggie doesn't choose his words like this. Reggie doesn't smell like citrus, like lemons. This person does.

"I'm fine," Toby says, and the longer he's in here the more he thinks that that's probably true. He swallows, and tacks on, "We can... if you want. We can play the game."

He can't see anything, but he can feel. Smell. Hear. Adrenaline pumps through his veins to a drum-like rhythm, and his heart is beating so fast, he wonders if his partner can hear it too.

"If you're sure," the guy says. And it's not Jordan either.

Toby doesn't know how to get this started. He doesn't know anything.

But then there are fingers brushing against his bicep, soft and long and careful. And then they're travelling down his arm, and then winding around the digits on Toby's own hand. He holds his breath as his partner guides his hand through the dark, bringing it to rest somewhere that Toby assumes must be his waist. It's lower than Toby's own. This guy, whoever he is, is shorter than him.

Not knowing what else to do, and also maybe because of natural instinct, Toby draws the person in, slowly, gently, until their torsos collide. The smell of lemons is stronger, tickling the insides of Toby's nose. The guy releases Toby's hand and pats around his chest, then finds his neck, and then his lips. The person traces Toby's mouth carefully with their thumb, and Toby thinks he might hear the tiniest exhale of laughter before both hands come to rest on the back of his neck and tug him down into a searing collision of lips.

Toby has to think hard to remember when he last kissed someone. It was relatively recently, he knows. His life seems to flash below his eyelids the moment their mouths make contact, and the memory is there, for the tiniest instance of time.

It was at a party. A house party, with at least six times more guests there than there are at this one. He'd been totally wasted, drunk off his ass—why, again? Oh, right. It was the day exams ended before the holidays, and Toby wanted nothing more than to congratulate himself on persevering.

It's hazy and he can't remember faces, can't remember names, but he does recall being flirted with, occasionally being touched in places that made it easy to pass it off as an accident, an unintentional brush of skin. His shoulder, his wrist, his back. Details were lost in between their meeting and the door slamming shut behind them as they stripped down all too eagerly in some unoccupied bedroom as the music thrummed on against the floor from below, drowning out the incriminating evidence Toby knows he provided that night.

He doesn't remember how those kisses felt. Desperate, probably. Rushed. Driven by two dubious states of mind. Destined to be forgotten, as they were the morning after.

Toby doesn't think he'll forget these kisses.

They start out soft and experimental, and Toby wonders why they stay that way for so long until he realizes it's probably because he's not contributing much in return. His heart flutters as he finally pushes back against his partner's mouth, as he guides his lips open hungrily, as Toby tightens his grip around his waist, as butterflies or fireworks or both make his stomach twist. In a good way. His mind fuzzes up again as if he's just downed another beer, but Toby thinks he likes this a lot better than alcohol.

Toby can't see anything. But he can feel. Smell. Hear. Taste.

Are they moving? They're moving. He's accidentally stumbling forwards, maybe swooning, and his legs could very well be Jell-O. He feels the unfamiliar mouth turn up in a smirk against his own, and Toby kisses back harder in response.

Then there's a thud.

"Sorry," Toby breathes out, ripping his mouth away with an enormous amount of willpower. He's backed his partner all the way into the pantry door.

"It's fine." Cool hands grab his face and pull him back under again. He groans involuntarily at the feeling of those hands on his skin, refreshing against the blush stewing in his cheeks, a strong, startling, not unwelcome juxtaposition to the heat of the stranger's mouth.

Toby's thumbs shift upwards ever so slightly, beneath the fabric of his partner's t-shirt, but he halts there. He doesn't know how much time they have left, but whatever it is, it's not enough for anything further. No matter how much Toby thinks he would like to continue.

Blood is pounding in his ears and his heartbeat is echoing in his chest and his breathing—his breathing and his partner's breathing buzzes against his lips. There's so much, so much at once, and Toby wants it all, he's so willing to succumb, he almost doesn't hear the knocking on the pantry door.

"Time's up, guys."

As his partner's hands go slack in his hair and they pull apart from each other and Toby feels the stranger's heavy breathing against his skin rather than his lips, he tries not to feel disappointed.

He steps away from his partner and, as the door creaks open and the tiniest bit of light streams in from above the stove, he crouches down to feel around for the tie he'd discarded seven minutes previously. He finds it draped over a box of Rice Krispies.

Toby clears his throat and rubs his face as he emerges from the pantry. He almost doesn't want to know the other person's identity. He's being reminded again that this is just a game, a stupid party game, just for the sake of shits and giggles. He doesn't want what just happened to be passed off as a game. He'll admit it. It felt good, and it felt right. And he'd be lying if he said he didn't want something like it to happen again.

"You can look now," the girl with the glasses tells him, and he realizes he's still holding his hand over his face, as if attempting to preserve the darkness, revel in the aftermath just a little bit longer. But Toby brings his hand down, blinks a couple times, glances up, and—

Holy fucking shit.

There's absolutely no way.

The universe can't enjoy laughing at Toby this much, can it?

"Oh," says Leo.

Yeah.

Oh.

Chapter 6

Toby laughs with Leo, and it's not even fake laughter. But he thinks—knows—that they're probably laughing for two different reasons. Leo probably thinks this is a silly little coincidence, but Toby—

Toby thinks he might be going crazy.

Leo hadn't been there when Toby walked in. Right? Of course not, because he would have noticed him and walked right back out. He would be home right now if that was the case, asleep in his bed, not having an existential crisis. No, Toby is sure of it; he'd entered the house, scanned the room, taken in every face, and Leo's—Leo's very attractive, very unforgettable face—wasn't among them.

Toby thinks this has to be a joke. This has to be a joke. Or maybe he's drunker than he thinks he is, and it's a hallucination. He's about to settle on that, about to decide that yes, that's probably it, when a wormhole so massive smacks him right in the face. He actually stumbles in place when it does, clutching onto the moderator's arm to keep him stable. (She's quick to shake him off.)

The bathroom.

There had been a person in the bathroom when he walked in, who he didn't pay any mind to when they sat back down, because he didn't think he'd have to. Is this what he gets for assuming he was off the hook for one night? One fucking night?

Fuck. Fuck him. Fuck this. Fuck everything.

"Small world," Leo whispers, smirking. Fuck him too.

Toby can't summon his voice to respond, so he nods tightly instead.

The game moderator shoos them away, and Toby sits as far away from Leo as he can possibly manage. His chest feels tight, and his heart is beating just as fast—if not faster—when there doesn't feel like there's enough room in his chest for it to do so, and it hurts.

But also. Holy shit.

He just made out with Leo, last name unknown, his partner for the calculus project, the guy who'd winked at him multiple times today, who Toby found himself frustratingly drawn to, who is hot and smart and cute. And yes, this seven minutes in limbo shit, it was just a game. It didn't really mean anything. Leo tasted like fire, and the one main rule of fire is not to touch it, not to go poking around it, especially if you've already done it once and know how bad it can hurt. But this burn that Toby feels in his face, in his lips, in his chest, is... it's...

It's scary and it's mindfucking and it's addictive.

The game ends, for everyone, at some point. Toby's not sure when, not sure how many seven minute increments float by. He doesn't know if he wants to get drunk again, maybe even drink himself to sleep, or just go home.

Reggie ends up making that decision for him when he pretty much collapses into Vicki's arms later into the night, completely hammered, knocked out cold. It's around two in the morning now, and Toby feels a headache coming on as the final blissful effects of the beers he drank fade and he grows increasingly more delirious by the second, longing for sleep. So he seizes the opportunity to escape, wraps an arm around Reggie's torso and, with Vicki's help, lugs him out to his car. Damn, it's cold outside.

He feels like a parent as he buckles Reg into his seat, trying not to wake him up, but not caring all that much to maneuver himself around in utter silence. If Reg woke up before they got home, that would be great for Toby and his lack of useful muscle anyway.

It's so fucking cold outside, and all Toby wants is to climb into his car and make the measly little five minute drive to his apartment so he can collapse in his bed and sleep for twelve hours. That's all he wants.

He's so close to making that dream a reality—his hand is literally on the door handle to the driver's seat—but then there's another hand curling around the bend of his elbow and tugging him backwards a few steps, away from the light. Jordan, he assumes blindly, but when he turns around—well. Three guesses as to who it actually is.

"H-hey," Leo breathes, a cloud of white forming from between his lips and piercing the cold. His teeth are chattering. Toby hears it.

"Hey," Toby sighs, his eyes falling shut with the slow collapse of his chest. He doesn't really know what else to say.

"So. Um. I... didn't know you're friends with Jordan."

"I haven't exactly had a reason to tell you."

Leo raises his eyebrows and nods. "Touché."

There's a silence then, and it's awkward. Not the kind of silence that they experienced a million years ago, back in the library, when Toby was too nervous to speak. Not the kind of silence that can be romanticized, passed off as a cutesy little quirk in their relationship. No, this silence is as awkward as awkward can possibly be. Toby wants nothing more than to get away from it. So he tries.

"Well, see you," he murmurs, and for a split second bothers to wonder just how exhaustion can make him much more confident in being blunt. Probably because he's just done.

"Wait, Toby," Leo says quickly, and Toby does. Mostly because he realizes that that is the first time he has heard his name from Leo's lips. Not that it matters or anything. But. It's an interesting observation.

Toby swallows. "What."

Leo glances downward, and Toby notices his dark eyelashes are glistening with frost, contributing to the twinkle in his eyes that never die out, apparently, no matter how dark it is outside. "Aren't you cold?" he asks quietly.

Toby blinks. "Uh. Yeah." Because it's really fucking cold outside, so obviously. "What, are you not?"

"I am," Leo assures him, and his dimple is there. It's always there, but Toby can't stop looking at it now, for whatever reason. "But aren't you worried you'll catch—what was it? Hypothermia?"

Just how many cocktails did Leo "DIY" tonight?

"What are you talking about?" Toby asks, knitting his eyebrows together in confusion.

Then he watches as Leo's smirk stretches wide on his face, prominent as ever, as Leo holds up Toby's coat. Toby wants to kick himself.

Twice in one day? Both times, returned to him by this guy?

"You know, you're always in such a rush to leave," Leo says, unfolding the coat and holding it up with the inside facing Toby. "Why are you always so eager to move on to the next place? One of these days, you'll get sick."

Toby's about to hit him with the "Thanks, mom," but he doesn't. Because that would be hypocritical and Toby is not a hypocrite.

Unlike earlier that day when he'd simply passed over the article of clothing, Leo seems adamant on making no such gesture this time around. Toby's heart does a ker-thump as he rotates on his heels and turns his back toward Leo, allowing him to pull the coat up over his arms and shoulders for him.

Toby turns to face Leo again and croaks out a brief "Thanks," before going to fiddle with the zipper, but Leo's already beat him to it. His long, bony fingers get there before he can, and he fastens Toby's coat slowly, as if they've got all the time in the world. As if Toby doesn't have an unconscious roommate in the passenger seat of his car.

"You're always in a rush," Leo says again, and—did he get closer? Toby's mind is reeling again, and he feels more like his usual self: less confident, at a loss for words, blushing like a schoolgirl. God. Leo's shampoo really smells like lemons. "You'll probably jam the zipper again."

"I won't," Toby squeaks. He hates how quickly his carelessness, invoked by sheer fatigue, and overpowered by gay adrenaline, just dissipated into thin air.

Leo hums skeptically, but he doesn't say anything. When the zipper reaches the end of its track, finally, he hesitates there, his hands trembling. Why the hell is he even still out—

Those fingers coil around Toby's collar and tug him downward, and their noses are touching. Leo leans forward only slightly, grants the completely bewildered Toby the faintest press of mouth against mouth, as if teasing him, and then releases him. It all happens within seconds. Or less.

"Night," Leo says, raking a hand through his hair with a satisfied grin pinned on his face, strung up by that damn dimple on the left side of his mouth. He hurries back into the apartment, leaving Toby behind, wide-eyed, cold, alone, and imploding.

When Toby wakes up the next morning, it takes a second. But he does remember everything.

He remembers how, for the entirety of the ride home with the still completely zonked out Reggie, he was... not exactly in shock. It was something more along the lines of troubled, he'd say.

Because he knew—knows—that last night was a game. Just for fun. Shits and giggles.

At least, it was supposed to be. And it was, up until the point where Leo kissed him again, willingly, knowing damn well that it was Toby, Toby's lips, Toby's heart he was sending into erratic palpitations that, by the way, didn't cease until Toby fell asleep.

(Honestly, it's a wonder he even did. Even if it was only five hours of it.)

At eight in the fucking morning, Toby's brain decides all on its own that there's no need for him to rest any more, and he should stick to routine so he doesn't fuck up his sleep schedule, and it's his own fault for not going home straight after work like he should have for optimal resting time.

Shut up brain, Toby thinks. Nobody asked.

He hauls himself out of bed and staggers toward the kitchen, taking a peek into Reggie's bedroom on the way, and—yep, the guy's out like a light, his snores practically rattling the walls. Toby's tempted to walk right on over there and shake him awake, just out of pure spite, but decides to hold off on being an asshole for now.

Toby finishes the path to the kitchen and pulls open the cabinet to pluck out a coffee pod he plans on using for a monstrous cup, but—fucking figures—there are none left. Toby knows it wasn't him that used the last one because the box is still sitting there, completely barren, rather than in the recycling bin. He reconsiders stomping back into Reggie's bedroom and full-on roundhousing him in the gut.

But again, he doesn't.

Mostly because he doesn't know how to roundhouse kick.

But also because he's a damn good friend.

With a huff, he returns to his room and undresses to hop into a quick, warm shower. When he's done, he rumples a towel through his hair as he pulls on jeans, a t-shirt, a jacket, and a beanie, and is out the apartment with his keys clutched tightly in his hand.

Despite his annoyance at Reggie for inhaling all the coffee, Toby does enjoy going to the café. It's a comfortable environment; trendy, but not cliché, magnetizing but not attention-seeking. Also, their drink sizes have normal names. So. That's another plus.

It's a short drive too, which is another thing Toby appreciates about it. It's less than five minutes by car, which is really convenient considering Toby finds himself in need of an escape from his coffee-stealing roommate more often than one might think.

The parking lot isn't crowded, but it never is. He barely allows the chilly winter wind ten seconds to nip at whatever skin of his is exposed to it before he passes beneath the light yellow sign that spells out NIM'S PLACE and is embraced by the cafe's warmth, breathing in the swoon-worthy aroma of coffee and cinnamon he's come to admire so much over the past year and a half.

He approaches the counter and greets the cashier, a middle-aged woman named Pam, before ordering his usual, a French vanilla cappuccino. Large, today. He leans against the wall as he waits for his drink, an unintentional smile poking at the corners of his mouth. That's just how it is, here.

He's flooded with an overwhelming sense of contentment no matter what else may be going on in his life.

And there is definitely some shit going on.

But, happy thoughts, Toby. Happy thoughts.

His name is called and he takes the steaming cup of coffee to the booth he usually chooses to sit at, the one where he can watch the cars pass by on the road through the window. It's therapeutic, somehow. He'll often find himself wondering the tos and fros of the people who glide past, why they're rushing, why they're taking their time. Just now, he sees a gold minivan crawl by, and through the lightly tinted windows he can see the silhouettes of what seem to be several younger children, and he his immediate first thought is, soccer mom. And he knows he's probably right.

Toby doesn't know why it's so relaxing, why enjoys watching the cars so much. Perhaps because it's a distraction, and he is more than willing to succumb to as many of those as he possibly can.

Fun fact, though: one time he watched a pickup truck hydroplane into a pole across the street. The driver wasn't badly injured, luckily. But the truck was totaled. That was an interesting day.

But, happy thoughts, Toby.

Are you available today? Wanna meet up?

Toby thinks his heart leaps into his throat as he reads the text from Leo.

Meet up. Meet up to work on the project, more than likely. But there's still a part of Toby that can't help but wonder—or maybe even hope—that there might be something more to it.

He waits until he gets home (now fully caffeinated) to answer the message. He doesn't want to seem too eager.

Which is funny, because Toby never used to understand the logic in waiting to reply to someone you like. But now he does. And he isn't sure whether that's a good thing.

Pretty much the second he turns his key in the door, his thumb is on the keypad. yeah i'm free, what time?

Gray dots almost immediately appear, and they linger there for a moment, as if waiting for Toby to close the door behind him, shuck his jacket, and make himself comfortable before presenting Leo's response.

Cool. 11, library again?

sounds good

Toby's never been more thankful for technology as he is right now. He's pretty sure that he wouldn't be able to form whole sentences in his throat if this exchange was a verbal one.

Leo beats him to the library this time, and Toby finds him waiting, legs crossed, on one of the benches out front.

"I thought you were the one that told me I should have gone in last time," Toby says in greeting. Leo's head jolts up, and that signature smirk immediately crosses his face.

"I did," he says, getting to his feet. "But, like I told you, I don't get sick easily."

"I honestly can't wait for the day you do. Just so you can be proved wrong."

"Damn. Harsh. But I'm willing to bet you'd be the first of us to come down with a cold."

"What makes you say that?"

"I don't leave my coats hanging around wherever I go."

Leo flashes his teeth, swivels on his heel, and heads inside.

Chapter 7

Toby's frustrated, because Leo hasn't said a damn word.

Well, yes, he has. He's said a word. He's said multiple words. Several of them. He's done most of the talking so far, in fact. But every single thing that has come out of his mouth is strictly about calculus. Fucking calculus. Not once does he mention what happened—what he did, that motherfucker—the night before. It's borderline infuriating, and Toby is truly beginning to wonder if maybe it was all some drunken fantasy.

Leo's saying something, but Toby's not listening, because he couldn't give less of a damn about math. Instead, he's focusing his glare on Leo's mouth as he speaks. That fucking mouth. That damn mouth that sent Toby spiraling, officially, after he was already teetering the brink of insanity. He hates that mouth.

(No he doesn't.)

"...you hot?"

Toby blinks and looks up. "Wh-what?"

Leo grins. "I said, aren't you hot?"

Toby exhales and glances down at his hands. "Oh. Uh. I'm—fine?"

"You sure? It's pretty warm in here, and you're still in your jacket."

Toby clenches his jaw. "Yeah, well. You've made me paranoid that if I take it off, I'll end up leaving it here."

Leo cocks his head to the right. His hair is messier today, sticking up in some places, defying gravity, because why not? But it's not like Toby notices. Or cares. "I was just messing with you," he says. "And besides, even if you do leave it, you know you can count on me to get it back to you."

Toby bites the inside of his cheek, as if doing so will force away the blush that rushes to his face. "So make up your mind," he shoots back before he really has the chance to think about how not to make himself look like an idiot. "Do you want me to forget it again, or not?"

"Why would you assume I want you to forget it?"

"I don't know, but you seem way too happy at the idea of being my... coat... getter."

"All right, well, if this is going to become a common theme in our conversations, you're going to have to come up with a better term than 'coat getter.'"

"What's wrong with it?"

"It's too basic. Too... politically correct."

"Yeah? What would you call it, then?"

"I dunno." Leo pulls a pensive expression and reclines back in his seat a bit. Staring up at the ceiling. Toby looks up too, just for a brief moment, to check and see if anything interesting is up there. There's not. Obviously. It's a library ceiling. "How about, 'coattail-er?'"

Toby scoffs. "That's just stupid."

"It's a pun. Clearly, you have no appreciation for advanced humor."

"Yeah, yeah, sure. Whatever."

Leo brings his head back down to look at Toby—and he does, he looks at him for way too long, to the point where Toby begins to stir under his penetrating blue gaze. For some reason, he gets significantly more nervous when Leo knits his eyebrows together.

"You're different today," he says. Toby swallows hard.

"What do you mean?" he asks.

"I don't know. You just are. Usually, you're... like, nervous around me. Did something happen?"

Toby can't fucking tell if he's joking or not.

"What do you mean, 'did something happen?'" he demands, and he knows his tone is hostile. Defensive. He has a right to be upset, confused, but maybe this is a little much. Still, though, despite his doubts, he doesn't apologize.

"It's a genuine question." Leo folds his arms across his chest. "Yesterday, you barely spoke, and when you did, it was quiet. And your face turned pink a lot. Like it's doing right now."

Fuck fuck fuck fuck fuck.

"You also waited ten minutes to respond to my message this morning," Leo adds, and Toby almost chokes on his own spit. "What was that about?"

"H-how did you—" Toby sputters, and he knows his face is getting pinker and pinker.

"Your read receipts are on, dude."

Fuck.

"I..." Toby trails off, deciding it's best to just shut up instead of saying something he might regret. Because he wants to say a lot of things. And the ones that lay in the front of his mind are the most dangerous ones.

"Look," Leo says, leaning forward until his forearms touch the table. "I'm just curious. Do you have some kind of grudge against me or something?"

"Uh—no," Toby mutters. Not yet.

"Do I, like, intimidate you?"

"No." Not exactly.

"Did I piss you off or something?"

Holy shit. He's actually not joking.

"Yes," Toby growls. "You did. You are."

And Leo has the nerve to look confused. "Why?"

Toby looks away, out toward the endless rows of book-shelves surrounding them, gritting his teeth. He won't turn red. Redder. He won't.

"Last night," he finally grits out, still not making eye contact with Leo. "Why haven't you said anything? It's—driving me crazy. I'm just waiting for you to bring it up, but—jeez."

Leo makes a noise in his throat that Toby can't exactly identify, but whatever it is, it's probably not anything along the lines of an apology.

Does Toby even want an apology?

No. Not really. Just some acknowledgement of the elephant in the room. That would be nice.

"I..." Leo trails off, for once seemingly at a loss for words. An unexpected, uninvited sense of pride swells up in Toby's chest, and it's really, really, stupid. But he can't help but think, ha, who's doing the talking now—only for that feeling to fade quickly because he remembers he cannot handle confrontation and dear God, why did he even bring this up?

Right then, Leo's phone chimes with a text message, and both his and Toby's eyes flit down to the screen instinctively. Leo snatches his phone up before Toby sees the name of the person, but he can tell that, based on the way Leo's jaw sets and his eyebrows pinch together, it's not exactly someone he wants to hear from right at this moment.

"Sorry," he mumbles typing something out in response. His thumbs fly across the screen, emitting those satisfying clicking noises with every letter he punches, but Toby isn't in the mood to appreciate them, as he normally would. The clicks just keep coming, delaying their conversation, delaying the answers Toby would love to have right about now.

Leo's typing stops suddenly, cut off by some stock ringtone. His eyes fall shut and he lets a sigh pass through his nose. "Aaaand she's calling me now," he groans.

"Who, your roommate?" Toby asks.

"No."

Leo doesn't elaborate any further. Instead, he just swipes his thumb across the screen, presses the phone to his ear, and answers with a dull, "Hello."

Toby watches as Leo listens, pinching the bridge of his nose, eyes closed, as if he's a middle aged man exhausted after a long day of work. Toby's... kind of regretting agreeing to meet with Leo today. He doesn't know what he'd been expecting—maybe just working on the calc assignment and acting like nothing happened, because that would be better than this. Awkwardness hanging in the air, diluting it to something Toby has trouble breathing in. Being ignored.

Leo doesn't open his mouth for a long time. Only after he finally says something—"Today?"—does Toby willingly space out. He finds himself counting all the books of a certain color within his line of sight, or the number of students in the library wearing glasses, or the stickers on Leo's laptop.

He gets up to thirteen when Leo's call ends, with many more left uncalled for.

"Ugh." Leo presses his palms into his eyelids and leans his elbows on the table. Toby forces down the "Everything okay?" that instinctively crawls up his throat. He won't engage in Leo's personal drama. Especially not when they have something of their own to settle right now.

There are a few beats of silence, and then Leo pries his head back up and looks at Toby. His eyes dart left and right, as if he's suspicious that the books will fly off the shelves and eavesdrop on whatever he's about to say.

"Are you bored?" he asks, and it's certainly not the question Toby was expecting.

"What?"

"Are you bored? We've been here an hour and haven't gotten much done. Do you wanna come back some other time, when there aren't as many distractions?"

"Distractions," Toby echoes.

"Just..." Leo runs a hand through his hair and closes his laptop. "Let's get out of here. Follow me."

Everything in Toby is screaming at him, demanding him to say no. Who does Leo think he is to boss Toby around? He's not some puppy dog that trots happily behind him, blind to everything except for his owner.

Or, maybe, that's exactly what he is. A yellow lab, more specifically. Blond and dumb and way too attached.

"Uh. Okay."

They leave the library through a different door from which they came in, one that spits them out into trees and walls rather than sidewalks and passersby.

Toby's just about to ask where the hell they're going when the question is answered for him.

Thirty feet from the exit, Leo grabs a hold of Toby's backpack and pushes him against the brick wall of the building. Toby's far too surprised to register the small jolt of pain that travels down his spine, and far too ashamed of the thunderous pounding of his heart as Leo takes two fistfulls of his jacket to hold him in place.

"Last night," Leo says. His face is a few inches from Toby's.

"Last night," Toby repeats breathlessly. "You—"

"I kissed you," Leo finishes, nodding. "I know."

"Okay."

"Yeah."

"So why?"

"Why did I kiss you?"

No, Leo, why does the sun rise in the east? "Yes."

"Um." Leo swallows, and his grip on Toby's clothes slackens slightly. "You mean—you're talking about after, right? After that—that game."

"Yes."

A pause. "Well, I just..." He squeezes his eyes shut for a moment. When he opens them back up, they're set on some nondescript spot on Leo's jacket. "Did—did you hate it?"

Toby feels his eye twitch. "Did—what?"

"I mean—sorry. I'm sorry." Leo lets go of him, taking a step or two back, rubbing his eyes. "I'm just thinking. A lot. About some things. And I-I was a little bit tipsy last night... I know that's not an excuse, but I'm just saying. And I was—still am, I guess—interested in you, like getting to know you, I mean—that was the whole reason I wanted to pair up with you for—never mind. But, like, when we were in that clos-et—God, that's appropriate—sorry—I know I didn't hate it, and after I guess I was on this, like, high kind of thing, and one thing led to another, and—I'm really sorry. I know I—I totally overstepped boundaries, and I didn't have any right to do that. Sorry."

He's panting. It makes sense, though, because Toby's pret-ty sure Leo didn't take a breath once throughout that entire rant. In fact, he'd be more concerned if Leo wasn't breathing as heavily as he is right now. His eyes are glazed with worry, too, and his teeth are gnawing on his bottom lip, and he won't stop fiddling with the pinky finger on his left hand, and

Toby understands that these thoughts have probably been waiting to escape since it happened.

"That..." Toby begins quietly, and Leo looks up at him with a pained expression, clearly expecting the worst. For Toby to scream at him, maybe, or just walk away. But instead, the yellow lab opens his stupid mouth and says, "I think you've out-nervoused me for the first time."

Leo blinks. "I've—what?"

"You're—ha. You're so much more nervous than I am. Than I ever have been, I think. At least around you."

"What? No, I'm not."

"You're trembling."

"Yeah, well—news flash, it's fucking cold out here."

"I know it is, but I've seen you shiver less in lower temperatures."

Leo looks him up and down, his lips parted slightly, as if scanning Toby for the audacity. Toby hopes he will tell him where it is if he finds it because he would also like to know. Leo scoffs after a few seconds, meeting Toby's gaze again, and Toby can tell that unfortunately, he has come up empty. "Fuck off."

Toby snickers. Laughs. He's smiling. He thinks it might be the first time he's done that in front of Leo, for a genuine reason other than his possible downfall into insanity.

"Anyway. For your information," Toby says, "I... didn't."

Leo raises his eyebrows. "Didn't...?"

"Hate it."

He blinks at Toby, and his eyes go a tiny bit wider. "Oh. Um. Really?"

Toby blushes and glances away. "Yeah, really. I'm..." He takes in a deep breath that pinches at the insides of his lungs and rubs a hand over his face. "I'm gay, also. So. If you were, you know. Wondering."

Toby mentally says hello to Leo's dimple as it digs into his face with the slow, upwards curve of Leo's lips.

"Well, that's good to know," Leo says, and his right hand finds the back of Toby's neck, Toby's heart slamming against his chest at his touch. They exchange a quick glance, blue eyes meeting brown, and Toby leans in, just a smidge, and Leo pulls him down, down, down, the rest of the way.

It is fucking cold out here, Toby thinks. But it doesn't matter so much, not right now, because Leo tastes like fire.

Chapter 8

Toby's never had a boyfriend before, and he hates that that's the first thing he reminds himself of when he and Leo say their goodbyes some ten minutes later, noses tinged red, eyelashes laced with frost, lips... not as cracked as they had been before. Toby knows he's probably getting ahead of himself. Because, yeah, maybe this does mark the third time they've kissed (and second time they've kissed)—but that doesn't necessarily mean anything. Not yet, at least.

Toby keeps telling himself that on the way home, but the butterflies in his stomach apparently don't get the message. In fact, they seem all too excited as well, and by the time Toby reaches his apartment door, he's a full-on walking sanctuary.

"Where've you been?" the very groggy, most definitely hungover Reggie asks from his spot on the couch. Which is the entire couch. His lean, lanky body takes up every available sitting space.

"Library," Toby says as nonchalantly as possible, placing his bag against the wall and heading for the fridge.

"Was it you who brought me home last night?"

"Yeah."

"Ugh, dude, why?"

Toby tosses a scowl at him over his shoulder. "The hell do you mean, why? Because you were out cold, and I wasn't about to just leave you there. But now I'm questioning my decision."

"Why didn't you just let Vicki take me to her place?"

"How would that have been any better? For either of you?"

"It just would've. Dick."

"Yeah, totally," Toby scoffs, cracking open a LaCroix. "It would have been super easy for her to carry your heavy ass out to her car and then into her home, and she totally wouldn't be annoyed in the slightest."

"You know what you can do right now?"

"I'm dying to know."

"Shut the fuck up."

"Yeah, well, maybe you should try taking your own advice."

They exchange middle fingers as Toby slinks into his room, LaCroix in hand. When the door closes behind him, a small smile etches its way onto his face.

He spends some time working on his other home-work—more specifically, the ten-page short story he's got due for his creative writing class by Wednesday—and taking occasional, sparing sips of his sparkling water. He's not a huge fan of what he's written so far, considering nearly all of it was done in a rush and is jam-packed with be verbs, telling rather than showing, and far too many em dash-es—but there's this sudden, strange confidence coming out of nowhere that makes him feel more motivated than he has in a long time, to the point where he's actually trying to do his absolute best. And he has good ideas, he knows. It's just a matter of getting them down in a way that isn't fatally boring. Once he finishes this up, he'll definitely have to revise to make sure his writing style is consistent throughout, because it is very much not so right now.

After maybe half an hour, forty-five minutes, Toby pushes his computer away, leans back in his chair, and looks up at the popcorned ceiling. It doesn't look as ugly today. Strange.

His phone buzzes, and his head snaps up way too quickly, and he has to blink the stars out of his eyes to focus on the screen. It's a text from Jordan. He pretends he's not disappointed.

u ok man? u looked kinda rough when you left last night

Toby bites the inside of his cheek. yeah, i'm fine. i was just exhausted lol

aight i just wanted to check up on u

thanks man, it's all good

Toby's fingers linger over the screen for a moment.

Well, while he's here....

hey! He types. And immediately deletes, cringing at his own accidental enthusiasm. Why in God's name would he ever need to use an exclamation point? He's not that desperate.

get home ok? he writes instead, and sends to Leo immediately, so he doesn't give himself the opportunity to think about it too much.

The gray dots appear after a moment, and Toby subconsciously sits up straighter in his chair, unblinking.

Yeah, but i guess chivalry is dead, huh? Ngl i was kinda hoping you'd walk me home

Toby scoffs indignantly. should have asked, then

Does a princess ask the coachman to open the door for her?

probably. Toby doesn't realize he's grinning like an idiot until right now. who are you anyway? cinderella?

Please. The only cinderella here is you, and i'm your handsome prince charming that has to give you your shit back when you forget it

Toby responds with ha-ha very funny as if his heart isn't mercilessly slamming against his chest at Leo calling himself his "handsome prince charming." Just then, Reggie waltzes right on into his room, no knocking or anything.

"Yes, please, come on in," Toby sighs sarcastically, quickly placing his phone face down on the desk. "My room is your room."

"I pay half the rent."

"So do I. What's your point?"

Reggie makes a face and moves to sit down on Toby's bed, and Toby doesn't even bother saying anything this time, because it's no use. This is Reggie he's dealing with. All he listens to is his mom and the 2003 Little Shop of Horrors cast recording. (Loudly. On repeat. Completely shamelessly. And any time Toby even tries to tease him for it, he just begins to belt "Suddenly Seymour" and doesn't stop until Toby leaves the room.)

"Who were you texting, anyway?" Reg asks, peering at Toby's phone. "A girl?"

Toby's face heats up. "U-um, no."

But of course, that's not a good enough answer for Reg, even if it is the truth. His eyebrows rise up a bit, and a sly smirk crosses his face. "Wow, you totally are."

"I am not," Toby says. "Cross my heart."

"Uh-huh." Reggie waggles his eyebrows. "I mean, it's about time you got some action in your life, Toby-Woby."

Toby groans that stupid nickname (and also a bit at Reggie's blatant incorrectness), pressing his palms into his eyes. "What do you want, anyway?" he asks. "Or did you just come in to drive me crazy."

"You're already crazy," Reggie teases, and Toby shoots him what he hopes is a very intimidating glare. Reg then shifts a bit from his spot on the bed and clears his throat, and when he speaks, his tone of voice is suddenly drastically different. "Um. Well, I was actually wondering something."

Toby's interest is automatically piqued, to say the least, because Reggie's voice doesn't get very serious very often. When it does, it means something is bothering him, and when something's bothering him, it's generally not a small thing. "What's up?" Toby asks him.

"Okay." Reg lets out a sharp exhale. "So, you know that game we played last night?" He asks, rubbing the back of his neck. "The one where—I mean, you know. Duh. You were there."

"Yeah," Toby says, nodding. "What about it?"

"Well—just curious," Reg mutters, his eyes darting around the room, looking everywhere but Toby's face. "Who were you, um, partnered with?"

Toby will absolutely not answer that question, he decides. "Uh, why do you ask?"

"No reason really, I'm just—just curious."

"I..." Toby clears his throat. "I don't know who it was," he lies. "I-I mean, I don't remember. But I—I don't think I knew them."

Reggie apparently has decided to settle his gaze on his feet. He nods.

"Why? Who were you with?" Toby asks, because it's only fair. "Vicki?"

Reg hums. "Nope."

"Who, then?"

"Mm-mm. I'm not telling you if you're not telling me," he says, waving his hands.

"All right, fair enough," Toby agrees, relief heavy in his stomach, swiveling his chair around back toward his desk.

"But—just. Sorry." Toby glances back to see Reg pinching the bridge of his nose, eyes squeezed shut. "You weren't. Right? I mean—you weren't in there with Vicki, either. Right?"

"No," Toby assures him quickly. "I wasn't."

"Okay."

"And, even if I was, I would have told you, dude. And I sure as hell wouldn't have kissed her. I wouldn't do that to you."

"Yeah. Yeah, I know."

Reggie leaves the room in a slump, and a part of Toby isn't so sure that Reggie does know.

The next day, Toby initiates conversation first.

hey, should we meet today since we didn't really get anything done yesterday?

And he thinks he deserves a pat on the back.

Seconds of waiting for a response turn into minutes, which turn into hours. The day drags on, seemingly slower than any day so far this year—granted, they aren't exactly very far into the year, but still—and not once does Toby receive even the tiniest hint that Leo's still alive, much less has read his message.

Well, obviously, he is. Alive.

Probably.

When Toby does get a text, it's at four in the afternoon, and even though he's in the kitchen when it arrives, the chime sounds out as clear as a bell. He ignores the bewildered look Reggie gives him as he bounds away toward his bedroom, leaving the fridge hanging open in his wake.

Hey, Toby. Could you take my shift tonight?

It's from Blue. Toby's head falls back between his shoulder blades as he lets out a low groan.

I'm sorry, I know you were planning on enjoying a laid back weekend, but Jack apparently booked a trip to New York for our anniversary and didn't let me know till this afternoon, so I'm gonna need the night to pack and everything. Jack calls it the element of surprise, but I call it inconvenient lol. Anyways, if you can't, it's fine. I can ask someone else

Toby sighs and flexes his thumbs over the keyboard for a few seconds before typing out a response.

yeah, don't worry about it, i can cover you. have fun on your trip!

Thanks :)

Toby places his phone face down on his nightstand and flops down onto his bed. He wonders if Leo's ghosting him. If this counts as ghosting. If he should be genuinely concerned for Leo's health. If he should just calm the fuck down and let Leo be.

Toby knows that's probably the best option (and the one that is least humiliating), but how can anyone—himself in-cluded—expect that of him? He's Toby Wentworth, for God's sake. Overthinking is what he does best.

Toby doesn't know the name of his coworker for the night until he reads it on his nametag: Carl.

Carl is a sixty-something-year-old man and the only elderly person Toby's seen so close to campus, with the exception of professors, in a long time. Carl has frizzy white-gray hair outlining his otherwise bald head, with a heavy white mus-tache residing over his top lip. He reminds Toby of the Lorax. And it's weirdly comforting.

They don't really make conversation as the minutes pass, but occasionally when they accidentally make eye contact af-ter sparing wary glances over at one another, Carl will smile, and Toby is immediately flooded with kind, pure thoughts, and a warm, fuzzy feeling around his shoulders, like a hug. (So if, from here on out, Toby hears of anyone doing anything to hurt Carl in any way, he will see to it himself that they face proper consequences for their crime. Toby's not exactly a fan of the death penalty, but for Carl—for Carl, he might just reconsider.)

While Carl is away tending to the restrooms around eight thirty that evening, the bell above the front door chimes.

Toby looks over at the door, the routine greeting on his tongue, but the customer has already vanished into an aisle out of his line of sight. So Toby swallows the words down and continues to stare into space and overthink.

He takes a peek from his phone in his pocket. Still no text from Leo.

A few minutes later, through his peripherals, Toby sees someone approaching his register so he stands up a little bit straighter and manages the absolute bare minimum of a smile.

"Oh, it's you again," the customer says cheerily, and Toby has to blink a few times before he is able to process the somewhat familiar face standing before him: the girl from Friday night, the one who was so distraught about her boyfriend dilemma.

(Toby almost wishes he had one of those. Because he'd need a boyfriend, first of all.)

"Oh. Hi," he greets, and can't help but feel glad that she seems much less overwhelmed than two nights ago. "How are you doing?"

"Great, actually," she sighs, beginning to place her items on the counter. "I think your mint chocolate chip ice cream was what gave me the courage to talk to him."

Toby looks up from the bottle of Smart Water he's scanning at the moment. "Really? You guys made up?"

She nods, a warm smile crossing her face. "Yeah, last night. We worked everything out."

"That's great. I'm happy for you."

"Thanks." Toby scans the last item and begins to ring up her total, but she stops him. "Oh, sorry. He actually came with me, and said he was going to grab something really quick. Do you mind waiting for just a second?"

"Yeah, no problem."

While they wait, Toby takes yet another peek at his phone and, of course, Leo still hasn't said a damn word. He tries to hide the scowl he feels subconsciously twisting his lips as the sound of heavy footsteps approaches.

"Sorry," a distant voice says, while Toby tucks his phone back into his pocket and rubs a hand over his face, his mind reeling. "They were in the wrong section."

"It's okay," the girl replies, and Toby looks up at them, ready to scan the final product: a package of Paper-Mate pens.

Time freezes for a second.

Toby's heart ker-thunks in his chest, and not in a good way. It's as if it's been knocked out of place—forced out of place—and is just falling, falling, falling into a bottomless pit.

Leo's dimple fades with his smile as their eyes connect.

<h1 style="text-align:center">Chapter 9</h1>

"Carl, I—I need to take a short break," Toby tells him after the happy couple departs, the bell above the door jingling cheerily in their wake. "I just—need some air."

"No problem, kiddo."

Yes problem, kiddo, Toby thinks to himself among the jumble of other thoughts swirling around in his head, nearly jumping over the counter so as to get outside faster. Big fucking problem, in fact.

Toby assumes they've already gotten in the car—together, so they could go home together, eat dinner together (if they haven't already), sleep together (one way or another, but it's not Toby's business) and be a normal fucking couple together—and leans back against the rough brick wall of the store, rubbing his face with his hands, eyes wide open, unyielding to the piercing wind.

It's so dark outside, and it's not even nine yet. And it's cold as hell, probably in the teens or twenties, and Toby is only wearing a light fleece sweater over his work shirt. But neither of those things are things that Toby exactly gives a shit about in this moment.

That is, until his voice rings out in the night, ringing in his ears, and suddenly all he wants to do is go back inside and report to Carl just how cold and dark it is right now.

"Toby," Leo says, jogging up to him. "Let me—let me—"

"No."

Toby starts back toward the door, but Leo wraps a freezing hand around his wrist. "Wait, please, let me just—"

"Damn it, let go of me!" Toby growls, yanking his arm away. "I don't want to talk to you, okay?"

"Let me explain."

"Why should I?"

"Because—because you don't get it."

"I think I get it just fucking fine. I'm not as stupid as I might look, Leo."

"You're not—I didn't say—"

Toby throws his hands up, cutting Leo off. He glances around the parking lot to, a, check for passersby that might be overhearing their conversation, and b, scan for her. "Where's your girlfriend parked?" he asks. "I'm sure she's waiting on you. I wouldn't want to interrupt your plans for the rest of the night."

"I-I told her I'd catch up with her," Leo says. "I'll—I'll catch the bus home. Or, fuck, I'll run home. I just need you to listen to me."

"You lied to me."

"I didn't—"

"Yes you did, oh my God," Toby groans, raking his fingers through his hair. "You told me you were single."

"I—"

"You lied."

"No—just let me speak, for fuck's sake!" Leo says, his hands swinging wildly in unidentifiable gestures. "I told you that because I was. I mean, I at least thought I was—"

"How the hell do you think you're single?" Toby demands. "You either have a girlfriend or you don't. It just sounds like you're resorting to ridiculous excuses—"

"No, I'm not," Leo insists, but that doesn't alleviate the unbearable stench of pure bullshit wafting through Toby's nose at the moment. "Look, we'd just gotten into a fight, and I thought that was the end of our relationship. Genuinely, I thought we'd broken up. But last night, she came over to my place, and—"

"And apologized after crying and eating a pint of ice cream and gathering the courage to talk to you," Toby finishes, an intentional bite to his words. "I fucking know. I suggested she try the mint chocolate chip."

Leo lets out a small huff of breath. "What?"

"I need to get back to work."

"Wait—Toby—" He has the nerve to grab Toby's wrist again. "I promise. I never meant to lie to you. And I would never cheat on Steph. Or—or anyone."

"But you did."

"No, I didn't—not on purpose—"

"Why are you even here?" Toby demands, twisting his arm right back out of Leo's grip. "Why are you trying to apologize to me?"

"Because, I—I told you, I wanted to—I'm interested in you."

"If that were true in the way I think you mean it, why didn't you end things for good? Why didn't you actually break up with her?"

Leo says nothing.

"Yeah. That's what I thought."

"No—wait, I really do like you, okay?" Leo says, reaching up to push his bangs up off his forehead, and then flatten them back down again. "I just—I wasn't expecting her to show up, and she was clearly heartbroken, and I just couldn't... I didn't know what to say."

"What about the truth?" Toby growls. "Are you going to tell her about me? About what happened when you 'thought' you two were broken up?"

"You're making it sound like I committed a crime."

"Not necessarily, but you dragged me into this, unwillingly, and now I feel like shit because you cheated on her. With me."

"It was just a kiss!" Leo argues. "It's not like you and I are dating, or a couple, or anything. It won't ever happen again if that's what you want. I just don't get why you care so much when it doesn't affect you nearly as much—"

"I care because I am a decent human being! I have a con- science, Leo!" Toby shouts. His skin is prickling with rage, and his eyes sting, maybe with tears, maybe just because of the cold. He's rounding on Leo, and he knows it, and frankly does not give a single fuck because it feels really good to get the anger out.

After a beat of silence backed only by their heavy breathing and the whistling of the wind around them, Toby's heels make contact with the ground again, and he hadn't even realized till now how he subconsciously pushed himself up onto the balls of his feet as they argued.

"Does Steph even know?" he asks, lowering the volume of his voice to a somewhat standard level, though he feels it shaking as it leaves his throat. "About you?"

Leo sighs out a white cloud. "What are you talking about?"

"Does she know that—that you're gay, or bi, or pan, or whatever? Have you told her? Have you hinted it to her?"

Leo stares at him for a moment, blinking, as if he's struggling to process the question.

"I-I don't..." he rubs his eyes with the sleeve of his hoodie. "I don't know what I am."

Sympathy twinges in toby's chest, but he brushes it off. "Well, does she know that, then? That you're questioning, at the very least?"

Leo's gaze falls to the ground. "No."

Toby sighs, a heavy gust of white of his own forming and then dissipating in front of him. He glances into the store through the window, watching as Carl checks out a customer.

"I have to get back to work," he mumbles.

"Toby."

"You should probably go catch up with her. With Steph. I'm sure you don't want to keep your girlfriend waiting."

"Toby—"

Toby turns and walks back into the store, very deliberately not glancing behind him. He appreciates whoever it was that invented the heater however many years ago as he returns to his station behind the register, sniffling.

"Everything okay, kid?" Carl asks, his voice creaky and hesitant and gentle.

Toby barely looks at him. "Yeah," he says softly. "Uh, you know, it's really cold outside tonight."

Thankfully, Toby receives no drunk texts from Reggie by the time his shift is up, because that's the absolute last thing he needs right now. After he clocks out and pulls on his coat, bidding Carl a meek goodbye, he pulls out his phone and scrolls through as he makes his way to his car, only for a message to come through right as he tugs on the door's handle to climb in.

Of course, now he texts back.

I'm so sorry i swear i dind't see this until just now. Steph was clinging to me all day and i never really got the chace to chck my phone. Im sorry

Toby bites the inside of his cheek as he twists the key in the ignition, the engine revving to life, along with one of his Spotify playlists. His thumbs hesitate over the screen for a moment, flexing as he considers a response, until he eventually gives in and types out a reply.

don't talk about her like that, he writes. she's "clinging to you" because she likes you and you two just made up. that's what couples do.

(Not that he has reliable experience in that field.)

Immediately, the gray dots appear, darkening and lightening, darkening and lightening. At one point, they even disappear, and a small sense of satisfaction tugs at the corner of Toby's lips, because he knows that Leo's probably struggling to formulate a response right now. Serves him right.

Finally, his message comes through, a full three minutes later, when "Sweater Weather" is beginning its descent into completion.

Yeah. You're right, i'm sorry.

you've mentioned it, Toby replies.

He waits another minute or two for the next message, "Everybody Talks" starting up at some point in between. For a moment, Toby wonders why the hell he's even still sitting here, parked in the lot of the convenience store, when his everything yearns for home and sleep. He wonders why he's still conversing with someone who brought his hopes to immeasurable heights, only to crush them just as quick with one of those brutal-looking hydraulic presses that can smash a fucking bowling ball into a bunch of bowling shards.

But before he has the opportunity to dwell on those thoughts for too long, his phone finally chimes, and it's exactly—but also remarkably different from—what he'd been expecting.

We should meet up tomorrow, like you said. We don't have to talk about anything except math. If youre free, lmk. I promise i won't bring anything esle up. You don't have to forgive me, but we shouldnt let this affect our grades.

Toby reads the message, reads it again, and then just stares at it. Not processing the words, just staring at it, until his vision goes all blurry and weird and he has to blink him-self back to reality.

He puts his phone in his pocket and shifts the gear into drive, leaving Leo to wonder when he'll reply with his answer.

Sometimes, it feels really fucking good to be petty.

Reggie's sitting on the couch with the TV on when Toby gets home, clutching a throw pillow to his chest, staring mindlessly at the screen. Toby flicks on the kitchen light, and Reggie stirs a bit, rubbing his eyes.

"Sorry, were you sleeping?" Toby asks him, voice low.

"Mm. Nah."

"Good." Toby digs into the plastic bag he'd taken home from the store and hurls a pack of Nutter Butters at Reggie, who catches them with one hand. "Got you these."

"Dude," Reg marvels, tearing into the pack the moment he's unclutched his fist from around it. "You are a blessing in disguise."

"In disguise? You wound me," Toby sighs, coming to join Reg on the couch with his own package of Chips Ahoy cook-ies. Chocolate chunk, not regular. "What are we watching?"

"I dunno. I stopped paying attention a while ago."

"Oh."

They sit there in mutual silence, one only invaded—but not necessarily unwelcomingly—by the mechanical dialogue and laugh tracks emanating from the TV and the crunching and munching of their respective snacks, contributed by the both of them. A few times, Toby sneaks a sideways glance at Reggie, each time for a different purpose: first, to take in the subtle frown to his lips, then the unusually dim gleam in his eyes, and finally, the deep sighs that continuously seem to pass through his nose. Eventually, Toby's decided he's had enough. There's no reason for the both of them to be miserable.

"Are you okay?" he asks, and Reggie doesn't even blink. His eyes are fixated on whatever show this is—either Friends or Seinfeld or Community, Toby thinks. He's not a sitcom person.

"Mhm. Why do you ask?" Reggie monotones.

"I mean. You just don't seem like your usual self. You haven't, really, for all of today."

Reggie sighs yet another sigh. "I mean..." He presses two of the fingers on his left hand onto his eyelid and rubs. "It's weird."

"You're always weird."

Reg elbows him. "I'm serious," he says, and Toby quickly discards the beginnings of the teasing smirk that had started to form on his face. "So... hm. You know how I went out with Vicki Friday night?"

"Yeah."

"Well... okay. So I know this sounds lame, but I was really proud of myself for setting up that date. 'Cause, I mean, I managed to reserve a table at her favorite restaurant, which she hasn't been to in a long time and is almost always at max capacity. Anyway. On the way there, everything was normal and fine and everything, and she seemed really excited and happy, so obviously I was stoked about that. And the date itself went great too, until after we ordered dessert, and Jordan texted her and invited her over."

Toby nods slowly as Reg passes a hand over his face. "It—I just—" He lets out a long sigh. "The problem there, to me, is that she just seemed way too willing to get out of there and head to Jordan's," he mumbles. "And I'm not, like, trying to come off as this controlling asshole that doesn't let my girlfriend spend her time with other people. She can go to whatever parties and hang out with whatever people she wants to. I'm fine with that. It's her life. I guess, at the time, it didn't really bother me, at least not as much as it does now, because I hadn't seen Jordan in a while either, you know?"

"I mean." Toby shrugs. "I think that's a good reason to be upset, after the effort you—"

"It's not just that, though," Reggie interrupts. "That game we played at the party, after you got there—when that girl suggested it, whatever her name was, Vicki—I don't know if you noticed, but she, like, almost jumped off of me. She was all for it. And, like, I get that it was just a fun, stupid thing. I get that. I didn't exactly refuse to play either, but... after, I asked who she got paired with, and she wouldn't tell me. And it just—it's bothering me."

Toby raises an eyebrow. "So... what, do you think she's, like, cheating on you, or something?"

"No," Reggie answers quickly, and at a volume a bit louder than he'd been speaking so far. "No. I know Vicki wouldn't do that. I think it's more of a me problem. I feel like..." He sighs and rakes his fingers through his orange hair. "Like she's not as attracted to me anymore. I mean, it's been eight months since we started dating. I'm just, like, making myself crazy trying to figure out what I might have done for her to feel that way."

He leans his head back against the couch cushion, and the light emitting from the TV screen dances upon his freckled face. Toby bites the inside of his cheek, trying to come up with something to say.

"Reg," he finally begins, and Reggie glances over at him, eyes half-lidded with a fatigue filled from worry. "I get where you're coming from. And it's—it's definitely normal to feel insecure."

Well, Toby doesn't really get it, considering his current situation, but it's probably what Reggie wants to hear. So what's the harm in saying it?

"Honestly, um—I think the only way you're really going to feel better about this, like, fully, is if you talk to her," Toby tells him. "It's common knowledge that nothing good ever comes out of a lack of communication. I know I don't know the nitty gritty details about the two of you, but I can tell that she clearly makes you happy. And I'm sure you do the same for her. So... make sure you let her know that, and talk it out."

Reggie's silent for a moment, before he looks up at Toby with a tiny trace of a smile. "When'd you get so wise, Toby-Woby?" he asks in the most disgusting, mushy-gushy voice possible.

Toby groans at the God-awful nickname while Reg snickers to himself, because what else would Reg do but laugh at his own non-jokes?

"Seriously, though," Reggie continues, his tone noticeably lighter. "Are you, like, opening your third eye by being in a relationship?"

Toby almost chokes on his cookie, which is a bit unnerving, considering he swallowed it several seconds before. "Wh—who said I was in a relationship?"

Reggie shrugs. "Well, this past two days, you've been texting someone constantly."

"That doesn't mean—I'm not—"

"Mm-hm. I believe you, I do."

"Reggie—"

"Introduce me to her sometime soon, all right?" Reggie says, prodding Toby with his elbow and waggling his eyebrows. "Maybe we can get some double-date action happening, or something."

"Oh my God," Toby groans, slapping his hand over his eyes, mostly to conceal any traces of a blush in his face that may be illuminated by the TV screen.

Reggie continues chortling next to him, until the point where Toby has to manually put an end to it by shoving Reg's shoulder. The laughter dies down pretty much immediately, but there's a different mood in the air now, something less stuffy and heavy and more lightweight. Pleasant. Comforting.

"But anyway," Reg sighs after a few moments. "Thanks, dude. I appreciate it."

"No problem."

"And—you know, you can talk to me about shit like this too, okay? I'm here if you think you need to vent or something."

Something hard suddenly takes form in Toby's throat, and it prohibits him from replying. Instead, he just nods, tightly, and Reg flashes a quick smile at him before diverting his attention back to Friends-slash-Seinfeld-slash-Community.

Toby can talk to him. Toby should talk to him. And right now just so happens to be a great opportunity, and not to make use of it would be foolish. All it takes is two words, and another weight will be removed from his shoulders. He just put Reg in a better mood anyways, so he won't get upset. Right? Toby tries his hardest to think about any time where Reg ever mentioned anything at all regarding gay people. Trans people. Rainbows, for God's sake. Anything.

He can't. And he doesn't know if that's a good thing or not.

Toby's not sure how many seconds fly by before he forces down the painful lump in his throat and opens his mouth. "Reg," he croaks, and his voice is significantly weaker than before.

"Yeah?" Reggie replies through a mouth full of Nutter Butter, not looking at him.

Toby swallows hard and painfully. Say it. Say it. Say. It.

"Um."

I'm gay.

"I-I'm..."

Gay. G-A-Y. I like men. Surprise!

Reggie's hazel eyes shift over to meet Toby's own, and one of his orange eyebrows raises questioningly. "You good?"

Toby feels like there's something pressing down on his chest, never letting up, just constantly pushing down, until

Toby thinks he might suffocate if he doesn't say something now.

"I'm g—I-I'm going to bed, I have—I have a class tomorrow morning," he sputters, practically leaping off the couch and to his feet. "U-um. Good night."

He stalks out of the room, his arms stiff at his sides, purposely refusing to glance back at Reggie, even when his farewell is returned.

Chapter 10

Toby sometimes wonders if, within his nineteen-and-a-half years of life, he has cosmically fucked up in any way that gives reason to the universe to have some kind of weird vendetta against him, which seems to be showing now more than ever. It would explain a lot if he had. Like, for example, what the hell did he do to deserve running into a certain familiar someone on his way to his creative writing class the next morning?

"Oh, hey!" the voice calls from behind him, and Toby whips around to face it, only to regret it almost immediately. Steph is bounding toward him, her long dark hair flowing behind her in the wind.

"You're a student here, too?" she asks, smiling, making the guilt in the pit of Toby's stomach spike, until its about eight million times worse than it had already been. Why does she have to be so nice?

"Uh—uh-huh."

"That's cool. What's your major?"

Toby swallows. "A-accounting."

"Oh." She looks surprised. "Really?"

"Yeah, it's—" Toby brings his hand to the back of his head, before he remembers he's wearing a beanie, so now it just looks awkward. "My parents. Uh, they wanted me to—go into a 'rewarding career.'"

She nods slowly. "Huh. Well, I'm in architecture, so I usually stay over on the other end of campus. Guess that's why I haven't seen you around before," she tells him, and Toby nods as if everything is just peachy.

Because it is. It totally is.

Steph seems to receive the memo that Toby isn't exactly keen on communicating verbally, so she clears her throat and speaks again. "Anyway. Uh, I just saw you, and thought I should say thank you, again. For Friday."

Toby shrugs. "No problem," he croaks. "I was just... doing my job."

"Oh, you know—I was wondering. How do you and Leo know each other?"

Toby freezes up, even though he knows he should have been expecting this question. "O-oh." Fuck fuck fuck. "Well, uh, we're in the same calculus class. We're working together on some project that we—uh, that we have to do."

"Oh, okay," Steph says, still smiling. "Small world."

"Yeah."

Minuscule.

Cora cowered, the fear rattling her body just as well as the piercing cold that surrounded her. As the muted thumps of footfalls grew increasingly louder, she scurried back, the unfamiliar, rough sand scraping her naked skin, clinging to her, as if attempting to secure its hold on her and draw her back into the wasteland that was the shore. One thought ricochet throughout Cora's mind as she moved: Water. Water. Water.

The footsteps finally ceased, and for a moment, Cora's heart slowed—but then, a man emerged from behind a family of rocks. He was slim, with brown, tousled hair that held a golden tint beneath the setting sun. His eyes were a dusty blue, and when they met Cora's, his lips hinted upwards at a kind, harmless smile, one that dug a shallow dimple into the left side of his face.

Toby slams his laptop shut and covers his face with his hands, grumbling below his breath.

This is seriously getting out of hand.

How can he possibly turn in this stupid assignment if his writing looks like that? Like... like...

Okay. Fine. It's not exactly bad writing. But it's definitely not good, either.

And it's also not like Toby meant to create his character this way. It's just. The guy's supposed to be handsome, and Toby has his own personal tastes as to what handsome is. And purely, absolutely, entirely out of coincidence, they just so happen to align with the looks of a certain someone.

Toby isn't projecting. He's not.

It's around noon when Toby's phone screen brightens to life with a message. At first, he's thankful for the distraction from the catastrophe that is his writing, but when he glances down, a scowl quickly molds its way onto his face. Because speak of the fucking devil.

Look. i get that you're upset with me. You have every right to be. And i'm really trying not to pester you. But we really do need to set aside personal issues right now and do the calc work. That is the only time we even need to talk to each other. If it's not for school purposes, i wont reach out, unless for some reason you change your mind about me. But this is a pretty important grade, and neither of us should throw it away for something that i did. Please let me know if and when you're free today

Toby grinds his teeth against each other in his mouth.

Curse his inability to maintain his pettiness for a decent period of time. It hasn't even been twenty-four hours yet.

With a defeated sigh, Toby's thumbs meet the keyboard, and he types out a humiliating response.

fine. i'm starving, so let's get lunch. i know a place.

Toby secures his spot in the café fifteen minutes before Leo is due to show up, so he decides to take another crack at this short story that's absolutely driving him up a wall. As if this attempt is going to go any better than the one he made hardly twenty minutes ago.

She met his eyes for a fleeting moment, before he quickly averted his gaze from her bare body. "Are you all right?" he asked, his voice directed down at the sand, tinted with a chilling rasp that sent yet another fervent shiver down Cora's spine.

She opened her mouth, perhaps to respond, but her vocal chords simply refused to work. And yet, she still managed to scream—it was a silent scream, one that tore at the insides of her throat, shredded it raw, until the pain of it all simmered to an ache that pulsed below her skin in harmony with the beat of her thundering heart.

"Are you all right" the man repeated, crouching down as if to prove he was no threat to her. "Will you let me help you?"

Cora stared at him, eyes clouded with burning tears that she felt pool over and fall in hot rivulets down her cheeks. Ever so slowly, he began to approach, holding his hands out away from his chest as if

"What's that?"

Toby thinks he must jump out of his skin, even if for a split second, at the sudden sound of the voice in his ear. Out of instinct, he slams his laptop shut, and shoots a glare over his shoulder.

Lo and behold.

"Sorry, didn't mean to scare you," Leo says, far too cheerily for Toby's taste at the moment. A hesitant, sheepish grin is hinting at his lips as he takes the seat opposite from Toby.

"Hmph," Toby huffs, combing his fingers through his hair in an attempt to re-situate himself.

"What were you working on?" Leo asks, as if friendly banter is what they do now, extracting his own laptop from his bag. "If you don't mind me asking."

As a matter of fact, I do mind you asking, Toby thinks. "Just some writing assignment," he answers instead.

"Oh. Cool."

Toby clears his throat and swivels his body so he can push himself out of the booth. "I'm going to order," he announces, looking down in Leo's relative direction, but absolutely not making eye contact. "What do you want."

"I can come with—"

"It's fine. My treat."

(As if Toby owes him anything.)

He spares a single glance down at Leo, one that's just quick enough to catch the inquisitive arch to Leo's left eyebrow before immediately looking away out the window.

"All right. Just get me whatever," Leo finally decides. "Seems like you're familiar with this place. Pick something you think I'd like."

Toby grits his teeth. Something I think you'd like.

"Fine," he mumbles, heading toward the ordering station.

"Toby."

He freezes, heaves a sigh, and turns back around. "Yeah?"

Leo's looking at him, chin in his hands, elbows propped up on the table, an infuriating smirk playing across his lips as if he's a child scheming some mischievous master plan.

"Thanks," he says.

Toby goes red and forces himself not to run over to the counter.

He doesn't spare a single moment more than necessary to deliberate on what he should order for Leo. Though, he has to admit, for a brief series of seconds he genuinely considers just walking back with absolutely nothing for him. He'd be lying if he said there was no part of him that wouldn't be willing to see Leo's reaction.

In the end, he just orders two roast beef sandwiches and two of the cafe's signature raspberry lemonades. Possibly his favorite thing to drink, ever.

So, if Leo doesn't like it, for whatever unfathomable reason, more for him. Win win.

"You brought a friend today?" Pam asks in a slightly hushed voice as she prepares the lemonades.

Toby scoffs. "Not exactly a friend."

"I see. Testing the waters?"

"Uh, no. No. Not doing that."

She shrugs, and seals the cups with their appropriately-sized lids. "If you say so, hon."

Toby's face is burning with mortification as he brings the food back over to the table on a little plastic tray. When he gets there, Leo looks as though he's practically salivating. Jeez, does he only eat celery, or something? Toby wonders—half-jokingly—as he passes over Leo's share.

"Thanks," Leo says for the second time, but it's different from before. This one comes out rushed and rehearsed, only something he says because it's the polite thing to do before digging in. Last time, though, there was a second layer to it. Something more behind it. Toby can't quite distinguish what exactly that something is, but he has an inkling that, more than likely, it isn't in his favor at the moment. Not that he has the energy—or cares enough—to dissect it, anyway.

They eat first, exchanging very few words in the process. It definitely does not count as casual banter, because everything about it is the absolute opposite of casual. Forced, scripted, tense. Call it what you will; Toby doesn't enjoy it in the slightest, and he's thankful once Leo polishes off his sandwich and lemonade and opens up his laptop.

"Okay, so... we're about a fourth of the way done with this thing, not including the actual presentation we have to give in class. But that's nothing, really," he says. Toby keeps his eyes glued on his own screen, noticing Leo's icon pop up in their shared document. "And it's due this Friday."

"Right," Toby says, entirely monotonously.

"So we should really concentrate."

"Right."

"And focus on this, and only this. Only the assignment. That's all."

"Yeah."

Leo glances up at Toby, and they stare at each other for a highly uncomfortable amount of time. Toby's mind is reeling with so many thoughts, far too many, it's like they're fighting each other inside his head in a King of the Hill match to the death, pushing and shoving one another out of the way in their individual attempts to be the leading man, the one that ends up flying out of his mouth.

One prevails, and Toby hates that it's this one, out of all the possible contenders:

"How long have you and Steph been together?"

Leo doesn't even blink at the question, as if he'd been expecting it the entire time. Is Toby that predictable?

(Probably.)

"Almost two months," Leo answers drily, clacking away at his keyboard. His notes appear on the planning document before Toby's eyes.

"So it's nothing serious yet." God, what is he doing, baiting him?

Toby notices Leo's jaw tighten, and his typing halts for a brief moment. Toby can practically see the gears whirring behind those soft blue eyes and long, dark eyelashes as Leo formulates a non-incriminating response.

"It's serious if she wants it to be serious," he finally girts out, his eyes locked on his own computer screen, unblinking.

How gentlemanly of you, Toby thinks.

No.

Wait.

Fuck.

He said that out loud.

The air suddenly weighs a hundred pounds. A part of Toby wants to take back his remark, as well as pretty much everything he's said and/or done since last Friday. But he stands his ground, somehow. Besides, he has every right to act like this, anyway. It's nothing compared to Leo's shitty behavior.

They sit in the tense silence for way too long. To be mathematically accurate, it's probably somewhere around forty-five seconds. But that's still an excruciating forty-five seconds too long.

"Do you have the first part of the notes on limits from last week?" Leo asks, eventually, his voice dripping with indignance. "I wasn't in class on Tuesday, so I only have the second half."

"You didn't ask anyone for them?"

"I just did."

"I mean last week, when you missed. Asshole."

"I was busy."

"Doing what? Thinking you were single?"

Leo throws his hands up. "Will you just fuck off already? For Christ's sake."

"I have every right to be pissed off at you."

"I know you do. I'm not saying you don't. But we have a project due soon, and we need to focus, which is exactly what I've been suggesting this entire time. You were the one that brought the hostility to the table. This could have been a neutral, no-feelings-involved study session, but nooo—"

"It's so strange. I found it so much easier to concentrate when I didn't know you were a lying dickhead."

Leo's palms slap the table, and to Toby, it's as loud as a gunshot. For a horrifying moment, Toby thinks the entire café goes silent as a result. But luckily, his shock (or whatever it was—adrenaline, anger, et cetera) fades and the ambient banter around them continues, and Leo's expression is downright murderous.

"Are you done?" he hisses through gritted teeth, his eyes narrowed into a steely glare. "I get it. I fucked up. I'm a shitty fucking person. I'm sorry. Can we just finish this stupid thing so it can be done? After that, you and I don't have to interact ever again if that's what you want."

Toby doesn't respond for a second.

Don't apologize. Don't apologize.

"Whatever," he mutters, sitting up a little straighter and doing his best to ignore the flames burning below his cheeks.

"Thanks," Leo says, for the third time that day. And this one is Toby's least favorite one of all.

Chapter 11

"Do you think we should add another graph in there? Like, on this slide?"

"I dunno. It's up to you."

"Would it really contribute anything to the overall presentation, though?"

"I mean, if there's no rule against it, I don't see the harm in it."

"Yeah, but then one of us would have to explain it, which would mean basically just repeating some of the stuff we already said on this slide."

"Oh, true."

"So no second graph?"

"No second graph."

"Okay. Cool."

Toby wishes, genuinely, he could explain how their interaction evolved from the swamp of tension and hostility they'd been soaking in just a few hours before to this neutral little meadow of academic collaboration. And maybe throw some daisies in there, because why not. But he can't explain it. He can't.

About three and a half hours have passed since they actually started working on this, and at some point during then, it's as if they mutually agreed, without words, just to shut the fuck up and focus on getting this stupid project over with.

Which is exactly what Leo's been suggesting since last night. So really, Toby was the only one who had to agree. But technicalities are a hassle. Plus, Toby rarely gets to be stubborn. So. Leave him alone.

Standard time has the sun threatening to disappear below the horizon at 4:30, and Toby glances out the window to take a peek at the fading sky, dressed in pinks and blues and oranges. He can't wait until daylight savings starts back up again. There is no reason darkness should completely swallow the sky by six o'clock. Too early.

"What are you looking at?"

Toby blinks, and quickly looks back at Leo. "Oh," he mutters, subconsciously rolling his right fist against the table to pop his knuckles in a swift, satisfying rhythm. "Nothing. Sorry."

But Leo turns his head to look out the window anyway, and when he turns back, the sun is a halo behind his head. Toby tries not to pay attention to how the lighter parts of his hair have seemingly become spun gold, or how his eyes look a little bit brighter, or the dimple a bit more hollow. He tries.

Whether he succeeds or not isn't important.

"Shit, I didn't even realize how much time has passed," Leo says, rubbing at his face.

"Yeah, me either," Toby replies, even though it's not exactly true. As they worked, he'd been constantly glancing at the clock on his computer, making mental ticks as to how many minutes were able to pass without them bickering with one another.

"I guess that's enough for today, then," Leo decides, leaning back against the booth, putting his hands behind his head and stretching. Toby looks away far too quickly as soon as he notices the sliver of skin become exposed below Leo's crewneck. "I'm exhausted and my brain hurts."

Toby sighs, still averting his eyes. "Yeah. Me too. Math isn't my thing."

"What is your thing, then?"

"I mean, I—I don't really have one. But if I had to choose, I guess I'd say English. Writing. Things like that."

"Oh, so you were one of the kids that actually enjoyed reading To Kill A Mockingbird."

Toby raises an eyebrow. "You mean you didn't?"

There's a brief pause, and then they both giggle. Giggle. It's probably just because this assignment seems to have fried their brains. It has to be. Because they aren't friends. They don't like each other.

Toby, especially. He most definitely is not attracted—neither platonically nor anything more—to Leo.

But that doesn't necessarily mean he enjoys being a dick.

"Leo," Toby says after they pack their things and rise from the booth. "I'm, um..." He sighs and shoves his hands in his pockets. "I'm sorry. For the way I've been acting."

Leo tilts a small, forgiving smile up at Toby. "Don't worry about it. I know I deserve it."

"I mean, maybe, a little," Toby agrees as they make their way toward the door, dumping their trash into a bin in the process. "But I took the passive-aggressiveness a little too far. I mean, there was a point where... like, passive just kind of flew out the window for a while. Sorry."

"Really, you don't need to apologize." Leo shrugs. "But thanks."

It's warmer than it was earlier today, though the weather is still frigid and bitter and overall unpleasant. The wind swirls around them as they stand in front of the cafe's entryway, looking at each other, looking away, looking, looking away.

"Uh. It's... uh, pretty cold," Toby points out as if Leo's incapable of acknowledging that for himself. "Do you... need a ride?"

Leo raises his eyebrows. "You're offering?"

"I mean—" Fuck. "Do you want me to?"

Leo opens his mouth and begins to say something, but then his face drops, and he cuts himself off, bringing his hand up to push his bangs around on his forehead.

"Well, I'd say yes," he says, his voice low and wavering. "But... I'm kinda—I-I'm heading... somewhere... that would probably be too much of an, um, inconvenience for you, I think. I-I mean, I definitely appreciate the offer, and I would totally accept, but it's just—I have this thing, and—"

"You're going to Steph's place," Toby says blandly. "Aren't you?"

The tiny flush to Leo's face, a little pool of pink that his freckles seem to swim in, tells Toby yes before the slow, almost shameful nod that follows right after.

"She—she asked me to come," Leo sputters. "I don't exactly want to go, but—you know, it'll... make her happy, I guess, and I won't have to—"

"It's fine," Toby interrupts, his voice much softer and calmer than even he expected it to be. Leo seems taken aback too, judging by the fact that his eyes go a bit wider and his eyebrows jump up ever so slightly. "I can still take you there if you want."

"You—it won't make you, like, uncomfortable?"

Toby forces down the yes that instinctively forms on his vocal chords. "It's fine," he repeats instead. "I'm just dropping you off. As a classmate. It's no big deal."

The corners of Leo's lips twitch with a hint of a smile, and he nods. "All right. Sure. Thanks."

Toby attempts a smile back as he gestures toward his car.

The drive starts off silent, with Leo resting his chin in his hand and staring out the window, occasionally mumbling out directions for Toby to follow. But Toby can't really bash on him for that, because he's not exactly making any effort to spark conversation either.

Leo's the one that actually does, in fact, five minutes later.

"When'd you know that you were gay?"

The question catches Toby so off guard, he nearly runs a stop sign that seems to just materialize out of nowhere. He presses on the brakes way too suddenly, and they lurch forward in their seats as the car jerks to a stop.

"Wh-what?" he asks, even though he knows exactly what Leo just asked and doesn't really even want to hear it again.

"Sorry, I was just... wondering," mumbles Leo, a flush of pink blooming below his cheeks. "If that's too personal, you don't have to—sorry. I shouldn't have—I shouldn't have asked. Never mind."

Toby clears his throat. "It's... fine. I can—I'll tell you, if you really wanna know."

Leo's ears seem to perk up, and even Toby is shocked by those words coming out of his own mouth. *I will?* the wimpy part of him thinks.

Hell yeah, I will, the tinier, more assertive, other part of him decides. (Like, really tiny.) *He's probably confused. I could help him, maybe.*

"Well, uh... I guess I got my first real crush when I was in junior high," Toby explains, doing his best to ignore the heat creeping up the back of his neck and the penetrating gaze from the passenger seat boring into his cheek. "But I don't think I really realized it until later. There was this one friend I had, Ian, and I was so attached to him. Like, I would do things for him that he didn't ask me to do, I constantly wanted to hang out with him, be the best friend I could be, and all that. At the time, I guess I just thought I was being a really, really good friend by doing and thinking those things. Because my parents... aren't all that tolerant and accepting when it comes to anything LGBT-related.

"After eight grade, Ian moved away," Toby continues, shifting his hands along the steering wheel, unable to find a comfortable position. "And then, I... uh. I got a girlfriend."

"Girlfriend?" Leo pipes up, swiveling his head toward Toby with startling speed.

"Yeah. Her name was Lily. She told me she liked me at the freshman winter dance, and I was, like... so flattered, I guess, and surprised, so I guess I kinda just nodded and went along with it. We started officially going out a little while after that."

"How long did it go on?"

Toby sighs. "Little over three years," he mutters out of the corner of his mouth.

Leo makes a weird noise, one that Toby can't quite decipher. Whatever it's supposed to be, it really just sounds like Leo's getting strangled.

"Three years?" he repeats, as if it's the most absurd thing he's ever heard.

"I mean—okay. We broke it off after graduation because we were going to different colleges. I was too nervous to end it beforehand because I was worried people would get suspicious." Toby tightens his grip on the steering wheel. "Stupid, I know."

"How'd you manage to stay with her for so long if you weren't even attracted to her?"

Toby sighs again. His face is boiling. "Abstinence," he answers meekly.

Leo chokes.

"She had super religious parents—like, super religious—so she was completely set on waiting till marriage for sex," Toby says quickly. "So I managed to fly under the radar. All I had to do was kiss her and hold her hand and be nice. I was good at pretending to be straight, believe it or not."

"I don't, really. But please, go on."

Toby almost doesn't even notice the remark, as he was preoccupied with mortification and the desperate desire to just disappear, but he catches it at the absolute last second.

"I—wow. Okay," he scoffs. "I... don't know whether to be offended or not."

"Just forget about it," suggests Leo, waving his hand. Toby can see his smirk through his peripheral vision. "Seriously, please, continue. And turn left here."

Toby does, taking advantage of the moment to gather his thoughts and form a quick, coherent storyline that will bring them to the end of this godforsaken discussion as fast as humanly possible.

"Anyway," he says through a huff of breath, debating on rolling down the window to allow the icy wind outside to infiltrate the car and possibly cool down his face. He doesn't, though. "I guess I really knew in... junior year, maybe? I dunno, it kind of just... clicked. I worked it out on my own. I was terrified, obviously, because I had no idea how I was going to break the news to my parents. I still don't." He clears his throat. It doesn't really need clearing. "When I got to college, I guess the individuality kinda boosted my confidence and I became more interested in exploring my sexuality. So I—you know. Hooked up with a couple guys, just to... confirm it, I guess, even though I think a part of me knew it was already pretty much set in stone. Um. So. Here I am now. Very gay."

Leo's not saying anything, and it's not helping calm Toby's racing heart.

And then he does, and he says: "This is it."

Toby blinks. "What?"

"This is her place. You can turn in here."

"Oh." Toby's stupid, slow brain processes Leo's words. "Oh."

He almost misses the turn into the parking lot, but manages to make it at the last minute, sending Leo careening leftwards in his seat. Toby apologizes profusely, because holy fuck, this is embarrassing—but Leo's laughing.

"Oh my God, your face is so red," he manages through his cackles, which Toby definitely does not pay attention to at all, especially not when Leo snorts, making him laugh even harder.

"It is not," Toby insists, even though he knows damn well that that's a straight up lie.

"Uh-huh."

"You know what—" Toby pulls into a parking space and throws the gear shift into park. "Just get out of my car already."

"But we're having so much fun."

"Yeah. Fun. Because that's what this is. Try interrogation."

Leo snickers to himself and unhooks the seatbelt with a satisfying click. "You didn't have to tell me all that if you didn't want to," he says, and Toby knows he's right, but refuses to admit it out loud. So instead, he watches as Leo roots around in his backpack, which lays on the floorboard, for a couple moments. And then it gets to the point where those couple moments seem to have gone on for way too long.

"What are you looking for?" Toby asks eventually. Leo cocks his head up to look at him.

"My napkin," Leo responds casually, as if that's a totally normal answer, before ducking back down.

"Your—what?"

"I had a napkin at the café, and I brought it—or, at least I thought I brought it with m—oh, wait—aha. Found it. It's in my pocket."

"What are you—?"

"Here."

Leo presses the crumpled up napkin into Toby's hand, manually folding Toby's fingers over top of it. Leo's hands linger there for a second too long, and Toby purses his lips as his heart jumpstarts and begins thumping hard against his chest.

"Um—wh-what—"

"It's just something I did," Leo says, still not removing his hand, his blue eyes boring straight into Toby's. "You don't have to keep it. But it's for you."

"Um. Okay, but—"

"I'll see you tomorrow after class so we can finish the project. Assuming you're free?"

"I—yeah. Yeah. I can do tomorrow."

"Okay."

Leo stretches his lips into a smile, and he finally takes his hand away, leaving Toby's own oddly cold. For whatever reason. Leo grabs his bag and moves to make his way out of the car, and Toby is so close to being able to breathe freely. But Leo's not entirely gone just yet. No, because that would make things too easy for Toby.

"Hey," Leo says, the door half open, cool hair sweeping through the car's interior, through his hair, blowing the dark strands up out of his eyes for a brief moment. "Sit next to me tomorrow."

Toby blinks at him. "Um. Okay," he mumbles.

"Don't forget."

Finally, finally, Leo fully climbs out of the car and closes the door behind him. Toby watches as he climbs the stairs, watches as he knocks on the door labeled 117, as his girlfriend greets him with her hands around his neck and a kiss on his lips. He wonders what they might be saying to each other.

You're early, she's saying, probably. Maybe.

I got a ride, he's replying. Possibly.

She kisses him again.

I missed you.

Missed you too.

Maybe that's what they're saying to each other.

Her hands slide down to his arms and she pulls him inside, a dazzling smile on her face. Leo's expression is hidden from Toby. All he gets is the back of his head. Maybe it's a good thing.

Toby thinks back to Lily. The two of them together—the way they acted was similar to what Toby just saw. Or thought he saw. Maybe he's projecting and not even realizing it. A viable possibility.

He tries not to think about how similar Steph's face looked to Lily's whenever Toby would come over. He tries not to hope—no, he doesn't hope—that maybe Leo's thought process is similar to how Toby's was back then, every time he saw her.

Toby lets out a long exhale, and allows his forehead to fall forward to rest on the top of the steering wheel with a low thunk. It hurts, and a throbbing feeling sprouts below the point of impact. But Toby can't find the energy to pick himself back up.

Chapter 12

She had long, golden hair that was often twisted into a pair of neat French braids that extended down to just above her shoulder blades. When she wore her hair down, though, it was longer and shinier, wavy, falling in loose strands around her neck and shoulders and arms, bouncing when she walked, swaying with the air around her when she stood stagnant, whipping around her face when she ran or danced or jumped or twirled.

One of her eyes was cornflower blue, and the other chestnut brown. Toby doesn't remember which was which. But even though—even though he didn't like her in the way she probably hoped, he still constantly found himself staring into them—into those eyes—and unable to look away. They were probably one of the main reasons he felt so drawn to her in the first place. Because there was something different about her, something that set her apart from the rest—and she owned it. And he wanted to own it too.

Not his identity. Not then, at least. When he met her, he hadn't quite figured that part out about himself just yet. But there's something else about Toby that he knew—knows—makes him unique, a bit different from all the others even if, most of the time, nobody could see it.

The splotches down his back started out small, barely a shade paler than his normal skin, way back when he was in elementary school. He hadn't thought much of it then. He barely even knew it was there. But, then again, he didn't really feel the need to stare at his one back in the mirror as a prepubescent child.

But over time, the splotches grew in size and morphed in color, stretching across the skin on his back like ice freezing over a lake, taking on a pinkish-whitish-peachish hue. After one of the guys pointed it out in the locker room during seventh grade—"Yo, dude, what the heck is on your back?"—Toby made it a habit to go home and twist and turn and stare at himself in the mirror of his bathroom, that one comment never leaving his mind. As the days, months, and years passed, he'd just stare at himself, stare at the spots, never noticing how they continued to expand in size because he went back every day, and every day they always looked the same as they did that first time. Until he finally realized that they weren't.

Lily had different eyes, and Toby had different skin.

The way she carried herself, the way she smiled, the way she lived—it was as if everything was normal, everything was ordinary about her. As if both of her eyes were the same color. Or, as if both of her eyes had no color, and neither did anyone else's.

She made Toby feel normal. Ordinary. Colorless when it came to the skin on his back. And that's probably why he felt so drawn to her.

Toby's alarm rings out from his phone, which rests on the bathroom counter, alerting him that he has class in half an hour. He reaches over, shuts it off, and pulls his shirt on over his head with a final glance at the pinkish-whitish-peachish blotches of skin that now expand from the small of his back all the way up to his shoulders and neck.

On the napkin is a drawing. The ink is smudged in some places, and the feeble paper is slightly torn in others, but the overall image is clear nonetheless.

A mermaid.

Her face is indistinct because of scale factor, but that doesn't really even matter because everything else about her is beautiful and majestic and mesmerizing. The way her hair flairs out below the water, the meticulous cross hatched shading of the scales on her tail, the webbed fin that looks translucent even against its brown, crinkled background.

Scrawled on the back, in loopy, semi-messy handwriting, is a note:

Confession: I may or may not have been reading your paper over your shoulder for longer than you realized. But it's fine. Because it was really good. Like, really. If you're open to it, I'd love to read the finished product.

- Leo :)

P.S., the love interest sounds super hot.

"You forgot."

Toby's head snaps up from its previous position, which was hunched in a nearly painful manner over his phone, looking up at Leo with wide eyes. "What?"

"I told you to sit next to me," Leo says, plopping his bag down and sliding into the seat next to Toby. "But you forgot. And I specifically told you not to forget."

Toby goes warm. "Oh. Sorry."

But Leo seems to have already moved on to the next matter at hand. He's taking something out of his bag, whatever it is crinkling with his movement. Toby's tempted to crane his neck to see what's going on, but at the same time does not want to engage.

"Here." Suddenly something is hurtling toward his chest, and he catches it right in the nick of time. (Thank you high school basketball.) He blinks a couple of times, buffering, then looks down to see what exactly he's currently holding in his hands.

"M&Ms?" Toby looks up at Leo, who's sitting there with a satisfied grin on his face, an identical sharing size bag of his own resting on his lap as if it's a participation trophy.

Leo shrugs. "You bought me lunch yesterday, and gave me a ride," he says. "I owe you a lot. This is me making up part of my debt."

Toby can't think of a response in his head. Why the hell can't he wrap his head around the simple idea of being paid back?

"Oh, shit, you're not, like, allergic to dairy or anything, right?" Leo asks quickly. "I just assumed—sorry, if you are,

I can get you something else. But I just took a chance, 'cause I figured pretty much every normal person likes M&Ms—"

"I like them," Toby interrupts, clearing his throat and stowing the bag of candy by his feet. Leo's shoulders visibly relax. "They're my favorite, actually. So. Thanks."

Leo raises his eyebrows at that, as if it was a weird thing for Toby to say—Toby doesn't really think that it was—but then his expression softens, and that classic Leo grin returns.

"They're my favorite too," he says, eyes bright and shining, like a wondrous child. "The more you know."

The lecture hall doors burst open, and the professor storms in, looking aggravated as all hell. The students that had been out of their seats, milling about and conversing with one another just moments before, practically teleport back to their places.

"Oh, boy," Toby hears Leo huff under his breath as the professor barks out orders, followed by a snide remark about the apparently massively-failed quiz they were given the week before. Everybody pulls out their materials in a silence filled with a tension so thick, it could be cut with a knife, Toby and Leo exchanging accidental glances as they do so. And Toby isn't looking at Leo's freckles. He's definitely not counting them as class begins. He definitely doesn't get to twenty-two before Leo nudges him with his foot below the desk, and he most certainly does not go warm in the face when Leo's foot doesn't move away from his.

He doesn't. He just. Doesn't.

Toby eventually pulls his foot away.

His heart races for the entire lecture.

It's unrelated.

"The napkin," Toby says as they leave the lecture hall, making their way toward the parking lot. He doesn't say anything else after, because he's pretty sure he doesn't have to. The M&Ms rattle faintly from within their sealable bag, which has been stuffed into his backpack.

"Oh, right." Leo shoves his hands into his pockets. He's actually wearing a jacket suitable for the weather. For once. "Did you like it?"

"It—yeah, it was a good drawing."

"Thanks."

"So, are you, like, an artist?"

"Yep."

Toby blinks, and for some reason, realizes that this is coming as a shock to him. But it's also not. Like, it makes sense, but.... Weird.

"Wait," Toby begins, elongating his next few strides ever so slightly so he can regain that half a step he lost after pausing for a fraction of a second. (It isn't hard. Leo's legs are shorter than his.) "Wait. So you, like... do that? Drawing, and stuff?"

"Yes, Toby. I do that."

"I-I mean—for a living?"

He shrugs. "I do commissioning. Sometimes. If I'm motivated enough."

"So why aren't you at an art school somewhere?" Toby asks. "What are you even majoring in, if you're talking calculus?"

"Psychology," Leo says. "And I'm not at an art school because I couldn't afford it. Any more questions, Mr. Math-Isn't-My-Thing-But-Writing-Is-And-Yet-I'm-Still-Torturing-Myself- With-Fucking-Accounting?"

Toby pauses.

"Touché," he mumbles, suddenly taking a particular interest in the small white cloud that forms from the shape of his words.

"Anyways," Leo says as Toby unlocks the car, and they climb in. "Will you let me read it?"

"Read what?" Toby turns the key in the ignition, and the engine roars to life.

"Your paper. Or whatever it is. When it's finished."

"Oh. Absolutely not."

Leo looks offended. "What? Why?"

"Because it's not a storybook, it's homework. And it's a shitty excuse for either one of those, anyway."

"Are you kidding? What I read was great."

"What you read behind my back, you mean."

Leo shrugs and pops a few M&Ms from his own bag into his mouth. "Details, details," he says. "Not my fault you're not observant enough to notice when someone's behind you."

"Well, maybe—and this is just a thought—you should stop poking your nose in other people's business," Toby suggests. "That way, you won't get your hopes up."

"Maybe. But if I were the kind of person to do that, we wouldn't be friends, now would we?"

Toby doesn't answer. He also doesn't like admitting that he's wrong.

But that's unrelated.

It's just a fun fact, is all.

When they get to the library, there's a couple sitting in the booth that Toby and Leo have chosen the past two times they've been here. Toby knows they're a couple, because they're holding hands and giving each other the grossest goo-goo eyes he's ever seen.

He doesn't really think much of it and starts to walk in another direction, toward one of the free tables, but a hand is clasped around his forearm and holds him in place before he gets anywhere.

"Uh, what are you doing?" Toby asks, half heartedly attempting to retrieve his arm back from Leo's grasp.

"They took our spot," Leo pouts. Literally fucking pouts.

Toby tries his absolute best to ignore the innocently crestfallen expression on Leo's face. But he doesn't think he succeeds, considering the sudden fluttering he feels in his stomach.

"Our—? I-I mean, it's not really... our spot. We didn't, like, stake our claim or anything."

Leo huffs out a breath. "I'll do it right now then."

Toby doesn't know if he's being serious or not, but he doesn't really feel like finding out. "Um, no. Let's not do that, and just... sit over there instead."

Toby has to practically drag Leo away until they're a safe distance from the innocent couple, and when Leo twists his arm from Toby's grip and grasps his hand instead, Toby's pretty sure he blushes the color of a tomato. But he doesn't pull his hand away.

Friends hold hands. Right? When Toby was in kindergarten, he held friends with his classmate named Kuro all the time. And just like back then, this is totally normal and okay and perfectly peachy.

And, besides, they're not even technically holding hands. Toby's bringing Leo somewhere by the hand. Surely that's how everyone else sees it. There's no way anybody would look at them and then look at the couple at the table and assume they're in relatively similar situations. Obviously, nobody would do that, because they're not.

Leo has a girlfriend, anyways. Leo. Has. A. Girlfriend.

And Toby has a conscience.

He isn't an asshole.

He isn't selfish.

He isn't...

He isn't.

Toby let's go of Leo's hand as the drumming of his heart slows to a sad, somber beat and the butterflies in his stomach disintegrate into dust.

Chapter 13

They finish the project in near silence, despite Leo's multiple efforts to strike up conversation. Toby hardly speaks at all the entire hour and a half they're there, only nodding and shaking his head should he need to contribute any kind of feedback.

"We did good," Leo says as they exit the library.

"Yeah."

"So now that that's over with, do—"

"We go our separate ways."

Leo stills and looks toward Toby with a confounded expression tugging at his eyebrows. "What?"

Toby clears his throat. "Um. We—we agreed that after we finished this, we wouldn't have to talk to each other anymore."

Leo stares at him, his mouth hanging open for a brief moment before he manages to snap it shut, his teeth audibly clacking together in his mouth.

"Wait," he says, running his fingers through his hair. "Wait, okay, I thought—I thought we're friends now. I thought we were getting along."

Toby keeps his gaze set on the ground. "We were getting along," he agrees quietly. "But I think we should just go back to not knowing each other."

"But—why?"

"Because. I-I just... don't think I can be friends with you."

He spares a tiny glance up, and Leo looks as though he's just been backhanded across the face. Guilt stabs at Toby's stomach, but he forces himself to refrain from pressuring the wounds that gradually begin to seep. It's agonizing.

"Look, it's not that I... like, don't like you, or something," Toby tells him. He feels feverish. "Actually, it's—it's kinda because—"

Because I do.

"Okay. Look. I know we got off on the wrong foot," Leo says, speaking with his hands again, flapping them around in distress. "And I'm sorry for that. I really, really am. But I still want to be friends with you. I think you're—I think you're really cool, and—funny, and... stuff. I won't—I won't try anything. I promise."

Toby swallows. "I believe you," he croaks. "But this... is more about me. I guess. So just... don't bother me. Okay?"

Bother. The word tasted bad coming out of his mouth. Why did he have to use the word bother? It seems too harsh. Like Leo is a thorn in his side that he can't remove. It's not that painful. Bother makes it seem like Leo's an annoying little kid that doesn't know the definition of no after begging for a toy from the store. It's not that burdensome.

There were plenty of other choices. Why didn't Toby just use one of them?

Toby tries not to think too much about it—though, admittedly, it's already a bit late for that. He bids Leo farewell with a meek raise of his hand before slumping off toward his car.

Fuck. He could have at least driven Leo home first.

The person Toby least expects to see is standing in front of his apartment door as he approaches. The reason he's so surprised is because, really, it's not surprising at all—but things have been going the exact opposite of Toby's way, recently, so honestly, if he were to come home to a serial killing clown punching his doorbell, he would probably just sigh.

And run. Sigh and then run.

But anyway. It's not a murderous clown. It's Vicki. Reggie's girlfriend. Someone who is actually likely to be near their home.

"Oh, hey," she greets him looking up from her phone with a half smile. "Toby, right?"

"Uh, yeah," he responds, scratching the back of his head with one hand and digging for his keys with the other. "What are you doing out here?"

She sighs. "Reg asked me to come by, and said he'd take a shower while he waited, but would leave the door unlocked." She gestures to the doorknob. "But. I have been locked out for the past five minutes."

Toby shakes his head. "Sounds like Reggie."

He opens the door for them and allows her to head in first. As Vicki makes her way over to flop down on the couch, Toby tosses his things into his room and enters the kitchen.

"Do you want anything to drink?" he asks her.

"Sure."

"Water? LaCroix? Soda?"

"A LaCroix is fine."

Toby smiles and scoops up two limes from the fridge, bringing one over to her and taking the seat next to her on the sofa. "Good to see you have taste," he says. "Whenever I offer Reggie one of these, he says it tastes like expired battery acid."

Vicki snorts, cracking her can open. "Of course Reggie says that."

They sip in undisturbed silence for a minute or two, both busying themselves with their phones, and for some reason, it's hardly awkward at all. Toby knows he should probably be suspicious, considering his shitty day. But he decides that perhaps this is a mercy of sorts from the universe, and he is more than willing to accept it as such.

"Hey, you were at Jordan's place on Friday night, right?" Vicki asks suddenly.

"Oh. Yeah. Briefly." Toby tries to set up a mental dam to prevent the memories from rushing in, but that's literally impossible at this point. So he lets the damn crumble. "I stopped by after work."

"What'd you think of that game?"

Toby scoffs and leans back. "Well. To be honest, here. I—I really don't think that agreeing to play was the best decision. On my part, I mean."

Why is he telling her this?

"Shit, did something happen?" Vicki's eyes are wide. "You okay?"

"No, yeah, I'm... fine," he says. That's the easiest word he can manage right now. "It's just—it's complicated. I guess."

"You went in there with that short guy, right?"

Toby blinks. "Sh—short... guy?"

"Well, okay, he was about my height I guess. Five six, seven-ish. I think he had brown hair? You know who I'm talking about? He was super cute."

"U-um—" Toby nearly spills his drink as he sets it down on the table. So... no going back now. "Uh. Yeah. That—that was him."

"Hey, you sure you're good?" Vicki places a gentle hand on Toby's shoulder. "You went kinda red all of a sudden."

"No, I'm fine," Toby mumbles, covering his face with his hands. "Sorry. I'm okay."

"I didn't mean to touch a nerve... sorry. It wasn't even my business."

"No, it's—it's okay. Really. It's fine."

"You don't have to talk about it."

"Actually, I—I think—" Toby drags his hands down his face and sits back up, though he doesn't meet Vicki's eyes. "I feel like I do need to talk about it. It's—kind of driving me crazy."

What the fuck is he doing?

"Oh. Okay." Vicki turns her knees toward him, and places her can down on the coffee table next to his. "If you want, go ahead. Say whatever."

Toby looks up to meet her eyes for a brief moment. "Are you sure?"

"I feel like I should be the one asking you that question."

"I mean, it's just—we don't know each other that well, so I don't want you to feel like you should have to—you know—"

"You don't have to say anything to me if you don't want to. But I'm here right now if you really need to vent."

Toby sighs. "You... won't tell anyone?"

She scoffs. "'Course not. I'm not an asshole."

Jesus. Why is it so much easier to talk to strangers than to people that Toby knows and trusts?

He takes a deep breath.

"Well. Okay. For starters, I'm... kinda gay." He pauses. "No. I'm—I'm very gay. I mean, like, not overly gay, but—just—I'm gay." Fuck. He's already fucking this up. Can this count as a practice round? "And I've only told one—no, two—well, three people, now, so please don't go around telling anybody else."

Vicki doesn't even blink. "Your secret's safe with me."

"Right." Toby takes in another deep breath. "So, anyway, I kinda met him—the, uh, 'short guy'—earlier that day. I'm pretty sure he was flirting with me. I mean. He was winking, and smiling at me, and stuff, so. I dunno. And then later—well, you know. In the closet, we—you know. I mean, it was just kissing. Sorry. But—you know. Anyway. He was... pretty enthusiastic about it, and wow, that sounds super gross so I'm very sorry for wording it that way. But—you get what I mean, right? So, um. After the game was over and I was about to head home with Reggie, he kissed me again. Like, willingly. Like, not because of the rules of some game. So I... kinda got my hopes up about him, because you were so right, and he is really, really cute. But then—well, I mean, long story short, the idiot has a girlfriend," Toby groans, throwing his head back into his hands. "And I feel like shit, because the girl—she's just so freaking nice, and it's clear that she really loves him. And she has no idea. About anything that happened."

There's a short silence, but Toby's heartbeat is thundering in his ears to an intense beat only he can hear. It's out. All of it—most of it—is out to someone he barely knows, and there's absolutely no way for him to take it all back. If he could, then he... he probably...

Well. He's not so sure if he would, actually.

"Huh," Vicki finally says, and it's not cynical or sarcastic or anything; it sounds as though she's genuinely processing Toby's words, contemplating, analyzing every bit of word vomit that just spewed from Toby's mouth.

He really needs to work on his imagery.

"Pretty shitty situation, isn't it?" Toby mumbles dryly.

"Yeah."

Holy fuck. What is happening. For some reason, it's relieving that she agrees. Maybe because mutual acknowledgement of the absolute fuckery that is Toby's life makes him feel less alone. Less insane. Less worried that maybe he's just overreacting about all of it.

"So, have you talked to him recently?" Vicki asks. "After you found out about the girlfriend?"

"Yeah. I had to. We're—we're partners for this calc project. But we finished it today, and—I kind of told him that I think it's best that we don't talk to each other anymore."

"Is he going to break up with her?"

Toby's head jumps up. "What? Why would he do that?"

Vicki shrugs. "It seems like he likes you. Or, at the very least, is attracted to you. Breaking up with her would be the most decent option for everyone, especially the girl. Because right now, it seems like he's just leading her on."

"Yeah, he... is. I guess," Toby mutters. "And I feel like I'm to blame for all of this mess."

"Well, you're not. This isn't your fault. That's the most important thing for you to know."

Toby would like to respond with "I know," but considering how truthful he's been with Vicki this entire time, it feels wrong to suddenly start lying to her now. So he doesn't say anything at all.

"Do you think you like him?" she asks gently. "Is that why you feel guilty?"

Toby's face is flaming. "I-I... don't know. I don't know. Maybe. If anything, it's just some... stupid crush. A tiny, tiny crush. It's not like I'm, like, in love with the guy."

When he looks at Vicki, one of her arched eyebrows is cocked, and her head is tilted slightly to the side, as if she's waiting for him to say more. To say anything. He does.

"When we were in that closet," he begins, his voice suddenly hushed on its own accord. But then he realizes that the distant, white noise-esque sound of Reggie's shower has come to a halt at some point in between now and the last time he spoke. So he has to hurry if he wants to get everything off his chest. "It... was nice. I liked it a lot. And if it were to happen again, I don't... I'm not sure I would reject it."

Vicki bobs her head. "Okay."

"I think... that with that thought being in my subconscious ... I mean, that's probably why I've been feeling so terrible all the time. It's just a never-fading cloud of guilt that just, like, hangs over my head for all hours of the day."

"You haven't told anyone else about this? Have you told Reggie?"

"No," Toby says, his voice practically a whisper at this point. "Definitely not Reggie. I'm... I'm worried about how he'd react. He might... not want to be friends with me anymore." Toby pinches the bridge of his nose. "But he's not stupid. He can tell that something's going on, and he's been hinting at it. I'm just... too scared to say anything."

Vicki opens her mouth, but is interrupted by the clicking and creaking of Reggie's bedroom door as he finally marches out, ruffling a towel through his hair.

"Ugh, finally," Vicki groans, getting to her feet to wrap her arms around Reggie's neck. "Took you long enough. Must have been a nice shower. Also, you locked me out. Toby had to let me in and keep me company while we waited on your slow ass."

Reggie's eyes flit down to meet Toby's, and there's something... there's just something. Something that isn't quite the kind of gaze or glare that Toby is accustomed to when it comes to Reggie. He can't quite figure out what it is that's different this time, but honestly, out of all the things that are happening in Toby's life right now, he feels like this is among one of the most insignificant to worry about. Maybe he's just annoyed that Toby ruined his heroic moment of letting Vicki into the house.

Actually, knowing Reg, that's probably exactly it, Toby decides.

"Well, I'm done now," Reggie says, his gaze falling back down to his girlfriend's face. "Hello."

"Hi," Vicki replies with a smile, and she leans in for a kiss—a.k.a., Toby's cue to skedaddle.

"Well, I'll be in my room," he says, grabbing his drink off the table and rising to his feet. "You two have fun doing whatever you'll be doing. Just don't forget I'm here, and be mindful of my ears, please."

Vicki scoffs and Reggie practically growls at him as he disappears into his bedroom with a salute, one less weight off his shoulders. But when Toby hoists his bag onto his bed to pull out his computer, the M&Ms from within rattle at a decibel far louder than he thinks they should, and he feels sick to his stomach all over again.

Chapter 19

On Friday of that week—three days since Toby pretty much ran away from his problems, leaving Leo in the dust, the two of them not having communicated since—they give their presentation.

Toby scores an eighty-five. Leo gets a ninety-two.

Clearly, their professor can tell, out of the two of them, who actually understood—understands—the information they put down.

After class is dismissed, Toby hears Leo say his name once, twice, three times—and all the times, it's like a taser zaps somewhere around his head, not touching him, but just enough to make him flinch. Violently. He refuses to turn around. He made a promise to himself, and he was going to keep it, damn it.

Friday is also the day that Toby gets his grade back on his creative writing assignment. A seventy. It's like a punch to the gut, even though Toby knew that, realistically, he didn't have a chance of scoring much higher.

Imagery needs work, the professor had scribbled onto his rubric in patronizing red ink. Remember that showing is better than telling. The plot is good, but it was boring to read. Make it more immersive for the reader.

He wads up the assignment—all ten pages of it, plus his rubric—and throws it into the trash when he gets home.

Friday marks one week since the party at Jordan's. (Only one week.)

It's not like it's an important milestone, or anything. But the thought looms in Toby's mind the entire day.

Reggie's been acting a bit strange recently. Withdrawn, quiet. Very un-Reggie. Toby wonders if he and Vicki ever ended up having that conversation Toby advised him to have with her. If they did, then maybe things didn't go exactly as planned on Reggie's part. Vicki hasn't been over since Tuesday, either.

Friday, Toby has to work again. And Blue has returned from New York.

"Woah," Blue says as Toby slumps through the doors to the back room. "You look like you've seen some shit since I last saw you."

"What are you even talking about," Toby says, not fully deflecting the comment, because a part of him has no choice but to agree.

"I'm talking about the bags under your eyes, the stress zit on your forehead, the lack of pep in your step. Have you been eating, man? Staying hydrated? Are you—"

"Okay, never mind, I get it," Toby growls, pulling on his uniform. "I look like a hot mess. You don't need to paint a picture for me."

Imagery needs work.

"A hot mess," Blue agrees, nodding. "So what's up?"

Toby eyes the clock on the wall; there's about three minutes until they need to clock in, and he thinks that there is absolutely no way he'll manage to unload everything he has stored in his mind in such a fleeting amount of time.

"I'll tell you later," he mumbles, fumbling with the buttons to his shirt. "Uh, how was New York? Your anniversary?"

Toby's not even looking at him, but he can feel the atmosphere brighten with the giddy smile he just knows has crossed Blue's face. It's almost enough to make him smile, too.

"Oh my God, it was so great," Blue sighs. "I haven't been to New York in years, and going back was just—ugh. Amazing. And Jack was such a sweetheart the entire time. He was always asking what I wanted to do, what I wanted to eat, what I wanted to buy. He made it so special. Oh, he even bought tickets for Wicked ahead of time, because he knows that it's my all-time favorite show. And we also saw Hamilton, The Lion King, The Phantom of the Opera—ugh, it was all just so great. I have no idea where Jackie got the money to plan such a fantastic trip, but I mean—as long as it was legal, I'm not really gonna waste my time asking questions, you know?"

Toby snickers. "I guess."

"I don't know how I got so lucky with him. He's just—ugh," Blue gushes, and when Toby turns around, he's perched up on a bench, swinging his feet back and forth, back and forth, like a caffeinated five-year-old. "I love him more than anything, it almost makes my stomach hurt. Do you know what I mean? Have you ever felt that before?"

The deadweight gloom that seemed to have vanished for those few brief moments returns, hanging over Toby like a looming storm cloud threatening to pour down rain.

"No," Toby says quietly. "I haven't."

"Oh. Really?"

"Yeah. Love's not... it's definitely not my forte."

(Understatement of the fucking year.)

"I get it," says Blue. "But I'm sure you'll find your special guy sometime soon. I mean, who wouldn't like someone like you? You've got it all, man."

Toby gulps down something hard in his throat, but plasters on what he hopes looks more like a smile than a grimace. "All except a lip ring and blue eyebrows."

Blue drops his jaw in mock revelation. "Oh my God. You're so right. That's the key to everything."

Toby breathes out a laugh as the six o'clock alarm goes off and the workers stagger through the doors moments later, looking ready to drop dead and embrace death with open arms—but not before making their way home, first. Toby and Blue take their cues, clock in, and assume their positions.

"So, what's up with you?" Blue asks when the store is clear of all customers for the first time that night, at around nine o'clock. "You said you'd tell me later. Is it later yet?"

"Oh. Right." Toby clears his throat and turns around to lean back against the counter. "Where do I even start?"

"Wherever."

Toby combs a hand through his hair and just launches into explanation, holding back a lot less than he had been when he spoke to Vicki. But it's on purpose, because he knows that Blue is more likely to understand, more likely to relate—even though he doubts there is anything remotely relatable about this situation. For some reason, that makes Toby feel like the words he's saying, the things he's describing, are less absurd. It doesn't make sense, but it does, at the same time. Which also doesn't make sense.

"Holy shit, Toby. It's like you're living in a bad drama on the CW or something," Blue says with a snort after Toby's tank has sputtered to empty. "And all this happened in the past week?"

"Yes," Toby sighs, pinching his nose. "I feel like every other thing that happens to me is out of a fever dream."

"Damn. But at least it's over now, right?"

Toby looks up at him, knitting his eyebrows together. "What makes you say that?"

Blue shrugs. "Well, you said you cut the guy off, right? So hopefully that's the end of it for you."

"Well... yeah. I guess. Hopefully."

"Besides, it's a good thing you did," he continues ringing himself up for a pack of gum and popping a piece into his mouth. "You don't wanna be friends with someone like him. I mean, he cheated on his girlfriend, and then lied to both of you about it. You know what my mamá would call him? Un hijo de las mil putas."

Toby doesn't bother asking for a translation. He took enough Spanish in high school to be able to get the gist.

It's a relatively peaceful shift, thank God. And there are no bitchy customers or crackheads or girls in distress because they don't know how to muster up the courage to make amends with their boyfriends.

(Actually, believe it or not, Toby's never had to deal with a bitchy customer. At least, not yet.)

11:45 rolls around, and Toby is practically sleeping on top of the cash register. Blue is off in one of the aisles some-where, restocking or reorganizing or cleaning or whatever. Fifteen minutes. Only fifteen minutes until Toby can drive home, blinking sleep out of his eyes, but doing so happily because every second he's on the road is a second closer he is to curling up in his nice, warm, slightly rickety bed. Paradise.

The bell overhead the front door jingles violently as some-one quite literally runs in, and Toby bolts up, rubbing his eyes and speaking through a very powerful yawn.

"Hi, welcome to—"

"Oh, good, you are working tonight."

Suddenly, Toby is wide awake. He drops his hand from over his eyes.

"I need to talk to you," Leo says, his palms braced against the counter, panting, as if he just ran a marathon. Honestly, Toby wouldn't be surprised if he did.

"No," Toby grits out. "We're not doing this again."

"Doing what again? Look, I just—I need—"

"I'm working. If you're not going to buy anything, please leave."

"Why are you like this? One day you're all sweet and shy and giving me rides home, and then the next, you're—you're so cold, and for no reason—"

"No reason?" Toby repeats incredulously. "Are you kidding me?"

"Look, I don't want to fight about it. I just need to talk to you, Toby."

"Yeah, well, it's going to have to wait. I'm working."

"Then I'll wait right here until you're done."

"We have a no loitering policy."

"Oh, come on—"

"If you're not going to buy anyth—"

Leo blindly seizes a lighter from the container to his right and slaps it down on the counter in front of Toby.

"Ring me up," he growls.

They stare at each other, just fucking stare, for who knows how long. Toby's jaw begins to hurt from biting back on his teeth so hard, and when the pain finally begins to spark through the entire lower half of his face, he snatches up the lighter, scans it, and mutters out a cold, "One thirty-three."

Leo practically throws the five dollar bill at him, so Toby returns the change with equal courtesy.

"I don't need a bag," Leo says.

"I didn't think you would," replies Toby.

Leo takes his lighter and storms out the door. Toby leans forward until his elbows meet the counter, and then he lets out a long, tired groan.

A few seconds pass. "Everything okay?" Blue's voice calls out from somewhere in the store.

"Just fine," Toby responds, his voice muffled by the hands covering his face.

The next ten minutes fly by way too fast, because of course they do. Why wouldn't they. Toby takes as long as he possibly can without seeming weird to clock out, change back into his t-shirt, and gather his things, but even that barely spares him another three minutes.

Maybe, he thinks as he hoists his bag onto his shoulders, he's decided to just let it go.

Leo's leaning against the wall when Toby walks outside, flicking his new lighter on and off.

Wishful thinking.

"Are you actually insane?" Toby demands, not pausing to look at Leo, and instead making a beeline for his car. "It's—what, twenty degrees out here? Do you want to get sick?"

"No, I want to fucking talk to you," Leo says, his voice wavering with his hasty strides as he trails behind Toby. "This is getting ridiculous."

"No, you know what's ridiculous?" Toby whirls around and jabs a finger at Leo's chest. "You, pretending to be someone you're not, using people to keep up that fucking façade, and then acting as if it's not happening. That's what's ridiculous, Leo. Don't even try to play the victim here."

"I'm not—I'm not!"

"So what are you doing, then?" Toby snaps. "You lied to me, you lied to your girlfriend, and now we're all tangled up in this—this clusterfuck of a mess. I am allowed to not be friends with you, Leo. I don't want to be caught up in your shit, all right? I don't—"

"She told me she loves me," Leo cries, his hands balling into fists at his sides, trembling maybe from the cold, or maybe from something else. Toby can hear the lump in his throat and the brokenness of the words as they tumble out of his mouth. "Tonight. Just now—Steph said that she loves me."

Toby stares at him for a few solid moments, blinking the bitter wind out of his eyes.

"Well, congratulations," he finally grits out. "I don't know why you thought I had to know that, but there you go. There's your praise."

"I'm not looking for praise, goddammit!" Leo groans, raking his fingers through his hair.

"Then why bother telling me?"

"Because. I didn't say it back. And I—I figured you might want to know. That I didn't."

Toby is so fucking tired.

"Why?" he asks curtly.

"Why?"

"Why didn't you say it back?"

Leo scoffs. "Would you say you liked tofu if you were offered some, even if you didn't?"

"What the fuck does tofu have anything to do with—"

"I sure as hell wouldn't, because if I did, then I'd be expected to eat tofu whenever it was served to me," Leo continues, the shakiness from his hands having made its way into his voice. "And I just can't make myself come to like tofu. I've tried so many times, but I just can't."

The whistling of the wind is all that Toby hears for a few seconds.

There's a sniff from Leo's end.

Toby is so. Fucking. Tired.

"God, you exhaust me," he groans.

"Sorry," Leo mutters.

"Just—" Toby fumbles into his pocket for his keys and clicks the fob once, twice, the car beeping once, twice in response. "Get in."

Leo draws his eyebrows together. "What?"

"You're staying at my house tonight."

A pause. "What?"

"I'm not doing this because I feel bad for you," Toby assures him as they both climb in. "It's only because it is so fucking cold out here and I am way too tired to bring your ass to your place before I go to mine."

Toby turns the key in the ignition, and blessed heat begins to blast at them through the air vents.

"You're way too nice, Toby," Leo says to him, buckling his seat belt and curling his legs up into him on the seat.

"Believe me," Toby says flatly, pulling out of the parking space, "I am well aware."

Chapter 15

The entire car ride is dead silent, not that Toby cares at all. Although, maybe it's a little bit dangerous, considering the sound of the road drifting past below his tires is enough to make him nod off to sleep, which is very possible without Leo's mouth running off.

The house is silent when they arrive, thank God. The last thing Toby needs right now, on top of bringing Leo into his home, is to explain to Reggie why he's bringing Leo into his home.

"My roommate's asleep," Toby tells Leo, closing and locking the door behind the both of them. "Try not to make a lot of noise."

Leo nods, his hands fiddling awkwardly with the hem of his shirt.

Toby sighs. "My room's over here. C'mon."

Toby feels like a mother dragging her child into a doctor's appointment as he guides Leo in the right direction.

Toby throws his stuff down as Leo observes the room, his gaze floating over every wall, every piece of furniture, every nook in the desk, every bump on the popcorned ceiling. And for the first time, Toby is suddenly very aware of how bare everything is and his face flushes in shame at the bland abyss he calls home.

"Uh. Here." Toby roots around in the top drawer of his dresser for a few moments, then tosses a t-shirt and a pair of gym shorts at Leo's chest. "You can. Uh. Sleep in these."

"You don't have to—"

"It's fine. Do you want to take a shower? You can, if you want."

"Um. No, I-I'm fine. I took one this morning."

As if Toby couldn't tell. As if the pleasant lemony aroma of Leo's shampoo hadn't been harassing his nostrils earlier that morning when they gave their presentation.

"The bathroom's—uh. Right there," Toby tells him, gesturing to his right, focusing his eyes on the insides of his drawer as he scourges for clothes for himself. "You can change in there."

"Okay. Thanks."

"Mhm."

Normally, Toby wouldn't bother changing out of the t-shirt he's wearing now—it's not like he's sweaty or gross or anything. But he does, tonight. Just because. He pulls on a plain white shirt, and after it's over his head, he panics for a second when he realizes that this one might be the one with the blue stain on the front, but then there's a clicking noise as the bathroom door unlocks and prepares to swing open, so he fights his arms through the shirt as fast as he possibly can. Fuck. It might be backwards. It feels too close to his neck.

Toby doesn't look at Leo when he emerges, and instead becomes set on smoothing out the sheets and fluffing up his limp pillows. Only when the display is straighter than he could ever be does he finally decide there's not a point to it anymore, so he turns to address Leo. But he stops short.

Leo is short. Like, more so than usual, it seems. He looks so—so small in Toby's clothes. What the hell. What the fuck. The shirt is only a size medium, and yet it seems to hang off of Leo's torso like drapes off a curtain rod. What the hell. The shorts are too big, too, but Leo must have cinched them to his waist using the drawstring on the inside, considering they aren't actively sliding down his legs.

"You like Queen?" Leo asks, jolting Toby back down to Earth. Not that he'd gone anywhere else.

"Huh?" Toby forgot what he was even going to say before.

"The band, Queen?" Leo looks down, gesturing to his shirt—Toby's shirt—which displays the album cover for A Day at the Races.

"Oh." Toby clears his throat. "Oh. Yeah. I do."

Leo smiles. "Me too."

Toby looks away.

"Um. Cool." He scratches the back of his head. His eyes are aching, and only now does he finally notice. "Um, I have to—I have to take my contacts out, so I'll, uh. Be right back."

Leo's head jumps up. "Contacts?"

Damn it.

"Yeah. Sorry. Be—be right back," Toby says again, already rushing to the bathroom.

Toby hates his glasses. They make him look weird. Weirder. He only wears them at night before bed. Sometimes he doesn't even do that, though. He won't do it tonight. Definitely not.

When he returns, everything is fuzzy, but it's not anything he's not used to. Well, the fuzziness. Everything else about this moment is pretty damn unfamiliar.

"Where are your glasses?" Leo asks. He sounds expectant. Hopeful.

"I'm not wearing them," Toby responds. No shit.

"So are your eyes really brown?"

Toby draws his eyebrows together. "Pardon?"

"Sorry, it's just—" Leo chuckles. "My friend, Ariel—she wears contacts sometimes, but they're a bunch of different colors. So I was just wondering if, you know, other people with contacts do that. Guess not."

Toby is thankful that the room is dark right now. For some reason, knowing that Leo knows that his eyes are brown is—weird. Or something. Why does Leo know that?

"Soooo, I don't get to see them?" Leo asks, a smirk stretching across his lips.

"S—see what?" Toby says.

"Your glasses, dummy."

"Oh. No. Sorry."

"C'mon. I bet they're cute."

Stop. No. Stop it.

"Sorry," Toby says again, the word flying out of his mouth at incredible speed. He grabs a pillow and a throw blanket off his bed and begins marching toward the door. "Uh, anyways—you—you can have the bed. I'm sleeping on the couch." He opens the door, a very brief "Good night" on his tongue, but a hand wraps around his forearm, and he freezes in place.

"Wait. I'll take the couch," Leo offers. "You should sleep in your own bed. You're exhausted."

"I-it's fine, really." Toby pulls his arm out of Leo's grip. "If Reg gets up early, I don't want him to, like, freak out about a stranger being in the house."

"Then I'll sleep on the floor in here."

"That's ridiculous. It's fine, I promise. See you—"

"Let's share the bed."

Toby's heart seems to both sprout wings and plummet into the deepest depths of his stomach. Lovely. "Do what?" he asks meekly.

Leo rolls his eyes. Bastard. "I'm not trying to get in your pants," he says. Toby steps back from shock. Just—who does he think—? "It's called a compromise."

"Uh." Toby swallows. Aren't compromises supposed to benefit both parties? What does he get out of this? "It's okay. Really. Thanks, though."

He attempts another step toward the door, but this time, Leo's hand clasps onto his shirt. Is he pulling him back, or is Toby moving on his own?

"Toby," Leo says, and his voice must be less than a foot from Toby's burning ears. "It's not the end of the world if we sleep in the same bed. The only one making it awkward here is you, man."

Man. That's something Reggie and Toby call each other. It doesn't feel right right now.

"I..."

"Look. If you're really so against it, then by all means, sleep on the couch." Leo says, letting go of Toby's shirt. Fuck. It is the one with the blue stain. Good thing it's dark. "I'm not going to stop you. But I'm just trying to help you out."

Toby turns a bit, glances at the bed, at Leo, at the bed, and at Leo. Then at the bed. Then he looks down.

Leo's—Leo's right. This isn't a big deal. It's not. So why is Toby acting like it is? Why is he making it one? He knows it's probably just that pesky little overthinking habit of his rearing its ugly head yet again, forcing worries and thoughts and other bad things into his brain that he definitely doesn't want there.

"Fine," Toby finally agrees. His voice is quiet. Shy. He's not shy. "But I'm sleeping on the left side."

He's not shy.

Toby can't sleep. Despite the fact that, minutes ago, he was exhausted to the point where his knuckles practically dragged along the ground with every step he took, he can't sleep.

It's probably not exactly Leo that's keeping him up. Instead, it's just his presence. Toby isn't used to another body lying so close to him (especially not the one of a cute boy), or the gentle puffs of air that exit his lungs ever so often in a steady rhythm, or the occasional shuffling beneath the covers, or the sparing moments when their legs accidentally brush together and Toby nearly launches himself off the bed in shock.

A double bed can only allow so much space between them.

Toby's not sure how many minutes tick by while he just lays there, forcing himself to remain facing away from Leo, his eyelids aching to fall shut but also aching when they do, his right arm slowly falling asleep because of his stubborn idleness. Maybe ten. Maybe fifteen. Maybe it's a whole damn hour.

"Still awake?" Leo's voice, low and gravelly, asks from behind him. Toby's entire body stiffens up in surprise for a moment.

He lets out a breath. "Yeah."

Leo makes a hm noise. "Am I making you uncomfortable?"

"N-no. Not—no. You aren't."

There's a brief pause.

"Thanks for letting me stay," Leo says. "You really didn't have to do that. I could have gone home."

"It's whatever."

"Well. I mean. Considering you're super pissed off at me—which I understand—I feel like it isn't. Plus, we've literally only known each other for a week. I'm pretty much a stranger."

Toby's quiet for a minute. "You know, you're right," he decides. "You could be an axe murderer for all I know, and here I am, letting you sleep in my bed, in my clothes, less than a foot away from me."

"Damn. You caught me."

Toby thinks for a second. Then he chuckles.

"What?" Leo asks.

"Nothing. I just—I just realized something. I don't even know your full name."

"What? Really?"

"I mean, you never told me."

"I know, but it was on our presentation. First slide. Right above yours."

Toby's arm is really starting to cramp. "O-okay. Well. I was always too—preoccupied. To bother looking."

"Preoccupied."

"Shut up."

Leo scoffs. It's not a mean scoff, though. It never is.

"So what is it then?" says Toby.

"My last name?"

"Yes. Duh."

"Why are you asking as if you expect me not to know?"

"What? I'm not—I wasn't—Jesus. You're irritating."

It's Leo's turn to chuckle, quietly, and Toby can feel the mattress rippling below them. "I get that a lot."

"Yeah? From who?" Toby asks.

"Ariel. My best friend. The contacts one. There's nobody that complains about me more than she does, but there's also no one that has stuck around as long as her."

"And you said you've been friends since high school, right?"

"Yep." Leo pops the p. "We met freshman year."

"God. I'm sure she's already got gray hairs from being around you for so long."

"Hey."

They snigger to themselves. Just for a few seconds. And then the mood dies down again, and they're back to silence. Toby's entire right side is really fucking hurting right now—maybe he'll turn over, just for a bit, and then turn right back. From what it sounded like when they were talking, Leo was facing the wall, so with any luck, any luck at all, Toby should be good to go if he seizes the opportunity and just turns over right about—

"Oh. Hey."

Of course. Of course.

"S-sorry," Toby sputters. "Sorry."

"Why are you apologizing?" Leo asks, a soft smile on his face. He's so cute. It's really unfair. And infuriating.

"I'm just—sorry. This is awkward. Isn't it?"

"Not unless you make it awkward."

Toby thinks that that's already been taken care of. No problem. It's his specialty.

Well. Since they're already in this deep....

"So, um. What happened tonight?" Toby asks, even though he knows fully well that it is none of his business. Mortification creeps up the back of his neck, but he doesn't apologize this time. Maybe he should. "If you're—you know. Open to sharing."

Leo's grin fades, and he takes in a deep breath through his nose as he flips over onto his back. For a moment, Toby's terrified that he's finally done it and completely overstepped boundaries (fucking told you it's his specialty), but then Leo starts to speak.

"So, she invited me over," he begins, rubbing his palms into his eyelids. "And everything was normal. We ordered takeout, watched a movie, the whole shebang. And then her roommate went out, and she... you know. Tried initiating."

Toby does his best not to react. "Uh huh."

"And I... I just wasn't... I wasn't feeling it. So I asked her to stop. And she did, obviously, immediately." He pauses for a moment. "And she said that she would always respect my boundaries. But she... wanted to know. When I would be ready."

"Wait, you two haven't—"

"No," Leo groans. "And I feel bad about it. Because she has her own needs and desires and everything, and I feel like I'm being selfish. It's been two months since we started going out, so I understand that she wants to know."

He stops talking for a moment. His eyes look sad. Toby waits for him to keep going. Or not.

"So, basically, I told her I wasn't sure. When I'd be ready. And she was very sweet about it, because she's Steph, but I could tell she was kinda upset. Or, like—not upset. Not angry. I guess something more like aggravated. Anyway. We settled back down, and went back to watching the movie. And then she—she, like, had her head leaning on my shoulder, and was holding my hand, and that's when she said she loved me."

"And you didn't say it back," Toby says softly.

Leo shakes his head. "I couldn't."

"So why'd you come talk to me?"

Leo sighs, and turns back on his side to face Toby. "Well, I'm pretty sure she said it and was expecting me to say it too," he explains, "and she seemed even more upset—aggravated—that I didn't. And I can read the room, most of the time. So after the movie ended, I figured it was best to just leave, and let her be. Maybe not the best decision, in hindsight, but—you know, I didn't really know what else to do."

"Yeah. But why not go home? Why come to me, specifically?"

"I told you already. I just—just thought you'd wanna know." He sighs through his nose. "But I definitely wasn't expecting you to drag me to your place to spend the night."

"Yeah, well, I wasn't really, either," Toby says. "And I did not drag you."

"It's about the imagery, Toby. You're a writer. Shouldn't you know all about that?" Leo teases.

Imagery needs work.

"Theoretically," Toby says, "I guess I should."

Leo doesn't ask any questions.

They sit there in silence for a few moments, facing, looking at each other. Toby's heart skips a beat as Leo's eyes bore into his own, as if they're picking him apart, dissecting him, trying to find out all there is to know about Toby. What's Toby's story?

"All right," Leo says eventually, flipping onto his back again and draping his right arm across his eyes. "I feel a bit better now that I've talked about it. Without yelling. So I'm going to actually try getting some sleep, now."

"Oh. Okay," Toby says, about to return to his position from before, but he stops. "Wait."

"Hm?"

"You never told me."

Leo lifts his arm ever so slightly to peek at him. "Huh?"

"Your last name. We talked about it, but you never actually told me what it is."

"Oh." Leo smirks and drops his arm again. "Maybe I should just keep it a secret from you. Make you find out on your own."

"Uh, I think not," Toby says, giving him a soft shove on the shoulder. "I'd really like to know just who I'm letting sleep in my bed tonight. Before I start to worry if you actually are an axe murderer."

Leo scoffs. "Rosales."

A small huff of air escapes Toby's nose. "Leonardo Rosales," he says.

"Hey, hey, hey, we do not use my full first name around here," Leo says, returning Toby's shove. "It's just Leo."

Toby raises his eyebrows. "All right. Got it."

"You better, or else I'm gonna start calling you Tobias."

"Okay, well, that's not even my—"

"I know it isn't. Good night, Wentworth."

Toby blinks at him. He turns back over. His eyelids don't ache when they fall shut, and it's easier to breathe comfortable air. And he doesn't mind the sound of Leo's breathing, or the presence of his body less than a foot away from him. He doesn't mind when their legs accidentally brush up against each other. And his side isn't hurting, either.

As he drifts into a dreamless slumber, though, Toby can't stop thinking about what Leo'd said before, and just seemed to glaze over, never offering more reasoning or insight as to why.

I just thought you would want to know.

Toby doesn't think he wanted to know. He didn't even have to know. It's not his business.

And yet, now that Leo's told him, now that the cat's out of the bag—Toby thinks that maybe, for whatever reason, it's important that he does.

Chapter 16

When Toby wakes up the next morning, Leo is gone, and the gym shorts and t-shirt are folded in a neat stack on top of his dresser.

With a sigh, Toby rolls over to the other side of his bed, expecting cool sheets. But they're still warm. It makes Toby sit upright, face flushed, as he reaches blindly for his night-stand to grab his phone. There's a text he can't read, so he digs into the drawer for his glasses. It's from Leo, sent about five minutes ago.

Hey, thanks again for letting me stay. You looked so peaceful so i didn't wanna wake you up lol. Also i ran into your roommate on the way out. Seems like a nice guy but he looked so confused haha

Panic creeps down Toby's spine as he throws the covers off of him and staggers toward his door. When he yanks it open, he crashes into Reggie, and they both grunt in surprise. Toby flails for his glasses, which have flown off his face. He doesn't put them back on.

"H-hey," Toby says, stumbling back a bit and grasping onto the door frame for support. "Morning."

"Hi. So, uh, funny thing happened," Reg begins, raising his orange eyebrows and crossing his arms over his chest. "I was eating breakfast on the couch, minding my own business, and then I see a complete stranger walk out of your room, make eye contact with me, and throw up a peace sign before leaving."

Toby bites the inside of his lip as his stomach caves with a silent laugh. Of course Leo would just flash a peace sign and explain absolutely nothing.

"Um. Okay. So, I can explain," Toby says, rubbing his arm.

"I hoped so. Otherwise there's a whole 'nother issue on our hands."

"Um. Yeah. So, uh, basically my—my friend was dealing with some girlfriend stuff, and came to talk to me about it while I was at work last night. I mean, long story short, I invited him to sleep over. Not a big deal, right?"

"I mean, no," Reggie says, stepping back. "I've just never seen him before, so I was confused. For a second, I wondered if he was, like, some drunken late-night hookup or something 'cause of the way he acted. Good thing he's not, huh?"

Toby goes rigid, and it's suddenly much harder to breathe.

"Ah... y-yeah. Good—good thing."

reg said he thought you were a one nightstand

Lmao. Tell him you're not that lucky lol

Toby slams his phone face down onto the table—his table, at Nim's—and buries his face in his hands. Leo is not making this any better.

Good thing he's not.

Good thing he's not.

Good thing he's not.

Reggie's voice is echoing in his brain, clanging around from wall to wall, bouncing off the sides like in a pinball machine. He wants it out, wants it gone, but he can't stop replaying that moment, when it felt like the weight of the air on his shoulders became more than he could bear and the utter dread bubbled up in his stomach and all the air was sucked out of his lungs and he worried he might actually be sick, all over Reggie's socked feet.

He was hoping, hoping, that Reggie would be different. That he would have at least one person on his side that he was close to, someone he could rely on for pretty much all hours of the day, someone he could talk to, all without being hated.

But Reggie had said, Good thing he's not, huh?

And everything is ruined.

There's a gentle knock on his table. "Hey, stranger."

Toby looks up, attempting to blink away the stinging in his eyes, and tries his best to smile up at Vicki. "Hey."

"You okay?" she asks, sliding into the booth across from him. He can't see the cars as well with her there, but he hadn't been paying much attention to them, anyway. "I got your text. You seemed pretty upset."

"Yeah, I just..." Toby brings his right hand up to rub at his eye. "Stuff."

Vicki nods, as if she completely understands. "Stuff."

Toby sighs and wraps his hands around his coffee mug. It's warm, not as hot as it had been, and probably just the perfect temperature to drink. But he can't make himself do it, not with the churning going on in his stomach at the moment.

"So..." He shifts a bit in his seat. "It's about Reggie."

Vicki raises her eyebrows and takes a sip of her drink. She's drinking the raspberry lemonade. Toby would like to tell her she made a good choice, but that seems a little off topic and he just wants to be able to breathe again, as soon as possible.

Toby gives her the same brief rundown of last night's events that he'd given to Reggie before—friend, relationship, spent the night, yadda yadda yadda, the whole nine yards—and this time tacks on a summary of his and Reg's conversation as well.

"I'm freaking out, to be honest," Toby groans, raking his fingers through his hair. "I was hoping I could come out to him soon—like, I really was going to try—but now, I'm scared. He's not gonna wanna be roommates anymore, much less friends. He'll think I'm weird and gross, and—and he'll hate me. But I can't just never tell him. Keeping this secret from him for much longer than I already have will start to take its toll on me, probably sooner rather than later. I'm losing my fucking mind. I don't know what to do."

"Okay. Okay. Try to calm down," Vicki says softly, reaching across the table and taking hold of one of Toby's hands, gentle stroking her thumb across his skin. Her acrylic nails tickle a bit, but it's not necessarily a bad feeling. "Breathe."

Toby tries. His chest is very tight.

"Are you sure Reggie didn't mean something else, and maybe you're just overthinking it?" she asks, not letting go of his hand. Toby's glad. He thinks he probably needs the support, something to keep him grounded. "Maybe it wasn't exactly an anti-gay thing."

"Then what could it have been?"

"I... don't know. Maybe he doesn't like the idea of you hooking up with someone while he's home."

Toby nearly laughs. "Yeah, right. Reg thinks I'm a sad, lonely straight guy. He'd applaud me if I told him I had sex with a girl, even if he was home."

Vicki bites the inside of her cheek. "So. Why did you want to meet me here, then?"

Toby pinches the bridge of his nose with the hand that Vicki isn't grasping. "I guess I just needed someone to talk to. After I told you everything before, I kinda felt a little better, so... I don't know, I guess I figured it would work again."

She squeezes his hand. "Do you feel better?"

"A little, I-I guess. But I'm still worried."

"What should I do for you?"

Toby swallows the lump in his throat. "I don't know. Have you... has Reg ever mentioned anything around you, about—just, like, gay people in general? He hasn't said any-thing to me at all, I don't think, so I'm just. I'm in the dark, here, and it's stressing me out even more." Toby sighs. "Like, if I knew he was okay with it, then—obviously, this would be so much easier. And if I knew for sure that he wasn't, then maybe I could manage to keep from telling him, or at least have the balls to cut ties with him after I do if he ends up hating me. But I don't know anything. I don't know how I should act around him. I don't know how or when or even if to come out. I—ugh." His neck goes limp, and his forehead hits the table with a low thunk. "I feel like I'm gonna puke."

Vicki's thumb continues tracing along his knuckles. It's really, really soothing. Maybe Toby is a little—a lot—touch starved. "He hasn't said anything around me," she admits glumly. "I'm sorry, Tobes."

Toby doesn't even mind the nickname. "Me too," he responds against the table.

"If you ever want me to talk to him, I will."

"No. Don't. I'd prefer to do it myself, on my own terms. I... I've gotta prepare for every consequence. I'm honestly expecting a much worse reaction from my parents than one Reg could ever have, so... maybe doing this will be good for me. Practice, kind of."

His forehead vibrates. Toby looks up, and Vicki picks up her phone, hazel eyes scanning the screen, reading a text.

"Well, speak of the devil," she mumbles, finally letting go of Toby's hand to type out a response.

"It's Reggie?" Toby asks, wrapping a hand around his mug and finally mustering up the willpower to take a sip. It's not as good and enjoyable as it would have been if he drank it several minutes ago.

"Yeah... uh. Please don't freak out," Vicki says, and Toby sits up straighter, fully prepared to freak out. Maybe this is where the thread pops. "So, when you asked me to meet you, I guess I didn't really think a lot about it, so I didn't realize it was going to be about Reggie. So I just planned to have him meet me here for lunch after."

"What?" Toby exclaims, his palms hitting the edge of the table.

"But it's—it's okay. He just told me he doesn't feel well and can't come after all."

Toby lets out a breath. "Oh. Well. That's kinda weird. He seemed fine this morning."

"Yeah." Her eyebrows furrow as another message comes through. "Uh, weirder: he told me I should 'just get Toby to drive me home.'"

The two of them exchange a confused glance.

"Wait, does he know I'm here?" Toby asks. "I didn't even realize he knew this place existed. I don't think I've ever really mentioned anything about me coming here."

"I don't know. You didn't text him, or anything?"

"No."

There are a few beats of silence as Vicki reads the texts again, flexing her thumbs over the keypad, as if she's not sure of how to respond.

"Hey, has he been acting... like, weird around you, lately?" Toby asks. "Like, distant? Quiet? Absolutely not Reggie-like at all?"

"I mean, I guess. Weird, for sure. But not like that. He seems more attached to me than ever. It's not like I mind it that much, but it's weird. Different from normal."

Toby shakes his head. "Wonder what's up with him."

"No clue. He hasn't talked to me about it."

"Yeah." Toby takes a final sip of his drink, despite there still being over half a cup left. "Me either."

When Toby gets home, Reggie is sitting hunched over at the table, his hands tangled in his hair and his back facing the door.

"Hey, man," Toby greets cautiously, tossing his keys onto the counter. "You feeling okay?"

Reggie whirls around in his chair, and Toby actually takes a step back, because he looks pissed. His jaw is set and his eyes are filled with fire, and his eyebrows are drawn into a frown so tight, Toby worries that just the one expression will cause everlasting wrinkles.

"I can't believe you," Reggie growls, getting to his feet and stomping toward Toby. "I can't fucking believe you."

In that moment, everything in Toby plummets. His stomach, his heart, everything. Did Reggie find out? How did he—Vicki wouldn't—?

"Do you just not care? Do you not give a fuck about anyone else?" Reggie demands, and Toby can't find words. "I cannot believe you, Toby, I thought—I thought you were so much better than this. I never would have expected you to pull some bullshit like this."

"Reggie," Toby squeaks out, but that's all he can manage to say before Reg is at it again.

"Out of everyone—out of all the women you could possibly be attracted to—"

"Reggie—"

"And you've been lying to me this whole fucking time! I completely trusted you, and all you did was spit out lies!"

"Reg—"

"How long has this been going on? Huh? How long have you been sneaking off behind my back, having your own fun, and then lying to my face about it? You are disgusting."

Oh God. This is so much worse than Toby ever could have imagined.

"Reg, come on," Toby says, his voice trembling, holding his arms out toward Reggie, who is continuously rounding on him. "I know you're upset, but—let's just talk about it, please—just calm down—"

"How the fuck do you expect me to calm down?" Reggie roars. "You're acting like this is no big deal, like it doesn't matter one way or the other—what is wrong with you, Toby?"

"Look, it's—it's not exactly something I can help—"

"Not something you can help my ass. Do you think I'm stupid?"

"No—"

"What the fuck do you expect me to believe, then? That you just tripped over your own goddamn feet and accidentally landed in a bed with my girlfriend?"

Whoa.

Wait—

Wait.

Wait.

"What?"

"Yeah, pretty fucking stupid story, if you ask me," Reg sneers. "So how did it happen, then? How'd you end up—"

"No—hold—hold on. What the hell are you talking about?"

Reggie stares at him for a moment, blinking, as if he's been slapped across the face and doesn't really know how to process that.

"It's—it's a little fucking late to pull the innocence card," he growls, his hands curling into fists at his sides. "Nice try."

"Reggie, I genuinely have no idea what the fuck you're talking about—"

"I'm talking about you sleeping with my girlfriend!" Reggie shouts, and after that, everything is silent. Toby can't hear his heartbeat, or the blood pounding in his ears, or Reggie's labored breathing. His mind is too busy reeling, trying its hardest to put the puzzle when all he has is fragments of two completely different pictures.

"Wait," Toby says, rubbing his forehead. "Wait. Hold on. You think—you think that I'm sleeping with Vicki?"

"I don't—I don't think, I know. You two are clearly not as good at hiding it as you might think you are."

"Reggie, you—I don't know where you got that from, but I promise you, there is nothing going on between Vicki and me. I'm—I would never do that to you."

"Yeah, that's what I used to think," Reggie spits. "Pretty fucking stupid of me."

"Why would you even suspect something like that?"

"Oh, I don't know, the secret conversations you two like to have when I'm in the shower? The hooking up in closets at parties and then telling—promising—me that you didn't? The holding hands across the table at some hole-in-the-wall café you might think I don't know about?"

Toby cannot fucking believe this is happening right now.

"Okay. Okay." Toby squeezes his eyes shut and waves his hands around in indistinct gestures, trying to gather his thoughts. "Just—everything that you just said is either wrong, or completely taken out of context. I am not going out with Vicki. There's been a mistake. Many mistakes, actually."

"I swear, I would like nothing more than to believe that, Toby, but from what I've seen and heard—I'm just tired of you lying," Reggie sighs, rubbing a hand over his face and taking a few steps backward. "I mean, you already admitted to it, so I honestly don't know why you're still trying to—"

"What are you talking about, admitted to it?"

"Just now, when I was—when I was yelling, you said you wanted to talk about it—"

"I-I thought—I thought you were talking about something else."

Reggie pounds his fist on the countertop. "God, you two were in that goddamn closet together, and you were holding hands at that place—I only introduced you to her a week ago. Or has this shit been going on for longer?"

"We weren't—holy fuck, will you please let me explain?" Toby cries. "You've got everything, everything, mixed up, and you're only making yourself even more upset."

"I don't know how you could possibly come up with an explanation that isn't just more lies—"

"I'm not lying to you!"

Toby thinks there might be tears in Reggie's eyes. "You are, you are—"

"Why are you trying to be the victim?"

"I'm not, I'm just—I'm so fucking angry right now, and I can't think clearly, and any excuses you think might be able to convince me that you two aren't together seems like a load of—"

"I'm gay, Reggie. How's that for an excuse?"

Chapter 17

Toby and Reggie are sitting at the table, not talking and not looking at each other. Toby is ready to jump out of a window while anticipating some kind of reaction—literally anything—but all Reggie's doing is bouncing his leg and staring down at the glass surface.

Unfortunately, they still happen to live on the first floor.

"Are you okay?" Toby asks meekly, distancing himself as inconspicuously as he can just in case Reg feels like beating him to a pulp. Not that Toby thinks he would—he's never seen Reggie lay a finger on anyone—but, you know. This is a special occasion of sorts, isn't it?

"Are you really gay?" Reggie says, still not meeting Toby's eyes.

Ah, yes. Stage one. Denial.

"Yes," Toby sighs, leaning back in his chair. "I am."

"How long have you—you know."

"Been gay?" Toby almost scoffs. "Forever, dude."

"No, that's not—I meant, how long have you been waiting to tell me?"

Toby raises his eyebrows. Reggie's finally picked his head up.

"Um." Toby scratches a nonexistent itch on the back of his neck. "I dunno. I—I guess since we met. I mean, since we'd be living together, I knew it would have to happen, at some point."

"Why didn't you tell me sooner?"

"B-because, I didn't—I wasn't sure how you'd feel about it. I was worried you'd... you know. Not... wanna be friends with me anymore."

"Dude," Reggie mumbles. "I know I can be a douchebag sometimes, but I'm not a complete asshole. I don't care who you like." He pauses. "Just as long as it isn't my girlfriend."

Everything is suddenly lighter, the air is breathable, a significant weight no longer presses down on Toby's chest. It's okay. It's okay. Everything is okay.

"Oh, God," Toby sighs, rubbing his face. "You have no idea how relieved I am right now."

"I've always got your back, man." Reg cocks a half smile in Toby's direction, but it diminishes after a second or two. "I'm... sorry about all that. Before. 'S fucking embarrassing."

"No, it's—I get it. I would be pissed, too."

"Just—could you—I still kinda want some things to be cleared up," Reggie says, drumming on the table with his index and middle finger. "About what's been going on. With the two of you."

"Yeah. Sure." Toby has no secrets anymore. It feels fucking great.

Reg sighs. "So... last time Vicki was over. Tuesday, I think? I was in the shower, right?" Toby nods. "So, I got out, and I heard you two talking, and—I know I shouldn't have eavesdropped. But I was already feeling a bit paranoid, and dumb, but—anyway. I mean. I heard you say something about that party at Jordan's. And how 'we' were in that closet. And how you felt guilty, and didn't... didn't wanna tell me. Because you thought I'd get mad. Or something."

Toby's mouth falls open. "Oh. No, that wasn't—I wasn't talking about Vicki. I was... it was..." He takes a breath. "I was in there with someone—a guy—and basically found out, like, two days later, that he had—has—a girlfriend. So. I was only talking to Vicki because she... I guess 'cause she was just there, and volunteered to listen. But that was it. The only reason I didn't tell you, was... I mean. You know."

"You were worried about coming out. Okay." Reg rubs a hand over his eyes. "Yeah. That makes—that makes sense."

Toby manages a closed-mouth smile. "Anything else?"

"Yeah. Uh, what about the café? I—okay. I pulled up to meet Vicki for lunch, and saw through the window that you were—you two were holding hands. And you know, I'd been... worrying, already, so I kinda just. Flipped my shit. So, if you could—?"

"I asked to meet her there," Toby tells him. "To talk again. And she was just being nice and, like, trying to calm me down. I promise, nothing—nothing sketchy is going on."

Reggie exhales, ruffles his hair, and cracks the knuckles on both of his hands. "Okay. Okay."

"You know, I kinda noticed that you've been acting differently since earlier this week. Vicki told me she picked up on it too. Guess that was why."

"Oh. Yeah, I guess," Reggie mutters.

"I really think you should talk to her about this."

"Yeah. I will." Reggie clears his throat and pushes his chair away from the table. "I'm sorry. I'm really sorry, dude. I shouldn't have freaked out like that."

"It's okay." And Toby thinks it is okay, probably. "All good."

Reg nods and begins to head toward the door. Toby twists back around to the table, but then something pops into his head.

"Wait, Reg," Toby calls, and Reggie turns, eyebrows raised and his jacket halfway pulled on. "Uh, this morning. After—um, after my friend. Left. You remember what you said, right? You thought we—yeah." Toby clears his throat. "Uh, just out of curiosity. Why'd you say it was good? That he wasn't?"

"Oh." Reg looks down, then back up. "Oh, yeah. Well, you know. Up until a couple minutes ago, I just thought—I mean, I assumed you were straight. And I was worried that maybe you'd had, like, a rough night or something, or a few too many, and ended up bringing him home. I figured that if that was the case, you'd, like, freak out, since you weren't—since I thought you weren't—into guys. And I wanted to make sure that everything was good. That's. That's it, I guess."

Toby sighs and smiles again. "Oh. Thanks. I appreciate that."

"Always got your back, man."

Reggie gives a half wave and walks out the door. Toby thinks he could sing.

So are you still on that friendship strike, or what?

The text comes the next Tuesday in the middle of their calc lecture. Toby spares a diagonal glance over at Leo, who's sitting a few rows down and to the right from him, his laptop open and his notebook teeming with notes. As if he can sense Toby's gaze—or maybe Toby's just predictable—Leo turns his head ever so slightly and shoots a subtle grin up at him. Toby looks away as fast as he can.

haven't decided yet, Toby replies. didn't anyone ever tell you not to text during class?

Could ask you the same question. Figure you probably need to pay more attention than me since this "isn't your thing"

you know what, maybe i still am on strike

Aw come on. I gave you a giant bag of candy, dude

you told me you were paying back a debt??

Well, yea, but wasnt that such a nice gesture still? Wasn't it nice i even thought about you at all?

you are ridiculous

If i agree with u on that will you come get a bite with me? Im fuckin starving

Toby raises his eyebrows. i don't know if that's a good idea.

As friends, dude. Pinky promise. We've forgotten all that other stuff, right?

Toby gnaws on the inside of his cheek, deliberating. Eventually, Leo's merciless stare gets to be too much for him, and he finally replies.

fine. but only if you agree that you are in fact ridiculous

I'm ridiculous. I'm painfully ridiculous, of the utmost ridiculousness, so utterly ridiculous you are already regretting saying yes!!

Toby sniggers to himself, and then drops the smile as though pretending he didn't.

"If there was one thing you had the chance to do over, what would it be?"

Toby furrows his eyebrows and takes a sip of his cream soda. "Why?"

Leo shrugs, throwing a couple of fries into his mouth. "Just wondering."

"Do you ask all your friends this question?"

"I do, actually."

"Really."

"Really. Ariel told me she never would have approached me on the day we met back in ninth grade if she knew she'd be stuck with me till now, but obviously, that's not her real answer. She knows how blessed she is by my existence. Because I am amazing."

"And humble, too."

"You get it."

Toby feels like a middle school girl at a sleepover as he and Leo break into a fit of unwarranted giggles. It's probably the soda. Toby doesn't have sugar as often as he would like.

(Old habits.)

"So anyway," Leo says, coughing away the few remaining chuckles in his throat. "What's your answer?"

"Ugh, I don't know," Toby says, swirling his straw around in his glass. "Too many mistakes to count."

"C'mon. Just tell me one of them, then."

Toby sighs. "I don't know. I guess... if I had to pick just one, it would—it would probably be accepting Lily's confession, back in high school. Because when I did that, I made myself look like something I'm absolutely not. And now, it feels like the entire time we were together, I was just... leading her on. Because I pretended to like her back, I ended up giving everyone close to me false expectations that... sooner or later, I'm gonna end up having to crush, I guess."

Fuck. Maybe that was too much information. Maybe he wasn't supposed to say anything that serious. Leo isn't saying anything. He's just nodding slowly, sipping on his—what was it he ordered again?—cherry Coke.

Toby clears his throat. "Anyway," he mumbles, looking down at his lap. "What about you?"

"Nah, I don't have an answer."

"What? But you made me tell you—"

"That doesn't mean I am willing to do it also."

"You know, this is exactly the kind of thing that will make me go back on that 'friendship strike,' or whatever you called it."

"Are you just going to keep threatening me with that?"

"Threatening is a pretty technical term. But yes."

Leo sighs, and leans back in his seat. "You are ruthless."

"You brought this upon yourself."

The corners of Leo's mouth quirk upwards. "All right. Fine. You win," he concedes. "But don't expect a sob story. I'm just giving you the basic details."

"I'm listening," Toby says, putting his chin in his hands and leaning forward to prove it.

Leo scoffs and pops a fry into his mouth. He runs a hand through his hair, revealing his forehead for a fraction of a second. Not that Toby pays attention. "So. Long story short. Something... happened. When I was a kid. And it was pretty bad. Like, it fucked me and my family up for a while. And, since then, I've always thought about how if I had done just one thing differently, before the incident, then probably everything would have turned out... better. I know I'm being vague. It's just—it's a pretty personal thing to me. So. There you go."

Toby isn't as insecure about his answer anymore. "Damn."

Leo shrugs. "Life. You know?"

Toby doesn't know, not really. His life isn't exactly trauma-free, especially considering the heavily religious, conservative environment he grew up in as a closeted gay man, but the way Leo is describing his story sounds endlessly more devastating than anything he's ever experienced. But Toby doesn't say any that. So he just nods instead.

"So anyway," Leo says, clearly attempting to segue into a new conversation. "How'd that story come out? The one you said you'd just love for me to read?"

Toby has to realize it's a joke. "Oh. Ha-ha," he grumbles. "Yeah, I got a seventy on that."

"Wait, what?" Leo looks genuinely appalled.

"I told you, it wasn't good."

"I don't believe you. What I saw—"

"Without my permission."

"Details, details," Leo says, waving his hand. "But really, it looked good. You sure you didn't, like, turn in the wrong paper, or something?"

"My professor said that imagery was the biggest issue," Toby says, pinching a couple of the remaining fries out of the basket. He doesn't like to take the last pieces of anything, so he leaves the rest for Leo. "Showing, not telling, all that. According to her, it was 'boring to read.'"

Leo looks as though he was the one with the barely-passing paper. "What?"

"It's really not a big deal, it didn't affect my grade that much. I still have an A in the class, so it's all fine. I'll just make up for it with the next project we have to do."

Leo huffs out a breath. "Well, I'm on your side."

"My—? There are no sides, Leo. A grade is a grade—"

"Until you let me read the story in its entirety, I have no choice but to assume it was beautifully written all the way through and that your professor wronged you by giving you that grade," Leo declares in a way that isn't unlike a politician's inauguration speech. "Imagery-shmimagery, I say."

"Mature of you," Toby says, purposely making his tone bitter, but he can't hide the smile he knows is tugging on his lips.

Leo shrugs. "What can I say. I'm a loyal fan."

"Shut up."

The banter between them flows along naturally and undisturbed, and Toby would be lying if he said he doesn't kind of enjoy it. Leo's a funny guy, albeit very much a thorn-in-the-side at times, but somehow, Toby manages to forget all the trouble Leo has caused him throughout the past week and a half as if it's nothing, getting swept away into Leo's stories about high school and Ariel and painting and the time he got a tattoo at a really cheap and sketchy place that he refuses to show to Toby. He can't help it. He's already latched onto the hook—this is old news—and now Leo is reeling him in, and Toby finds himself less and less desperate to swim away from the shore.

That is, until said banter is interrupted, several minutes later.

The bell above the diner's door jingles, and Toby turns his head to see who it is, as is his instinct from working at the convenience store for months now. But instead of it being some faceless, nameless stranger, someone he won't bother giving a second glance, it's—

"Steph," Leo says, looking up at her with a crease in his brow. "H-hey."

"Oh, hey," she greets in return, her smile warming the air around them. "Didn't expect to see you two here. What's going on?"

"Just—grabbing some food after class. You?"

"I'm ordering to go. I've gotta be at the dance studio in an hour, so. I was craving something greasy before having to deal with the little kids."

So she's an architect and a dance teacher. Smart and like-able. Toby thinks he's probably zero for two right now.

"Oh. Right. It's Tuesday."

"We haven't talked since yesterday. I meant to text you earlier, but I guess I got caught up in some stuff. How was class?"

"Just... same old. Grumpy professor, vague notes, in-evitable failure."

And there goes the fishing rod, bending again as Toby watches this exchange unfold before his eyes. There's only a matter of time before it snaps and is broken for good, and Toby swims off with his half still attached to the line hooked in his mouth.

"How are you, Toby?"

Toby blinks away the metaphors swirling around in his head and plasters on a painful, toothless smile. "Oh. Good. I'm good. Busy, with school and work and everything, but. Good."

"That's good," Steph says, and she is so fucking nice and Toby is such a fucking asshole.

Someone behind the counter slaps their hand down onto a bell and calls out, "Pickup for Aquino?"

Steph swivels her head around and back. "Well. Gotta go." Then she leans down and presses a kiss to Leo's cheek. "See you later, babe. Nice seeing you again, Toby."

Leo doesn't look at him until Steph has her bag of food and is out the door.

"So," Toby prompts, slumping a bit in his seat and picking at the grease-stained wax paper that lines the empty basket of fries. "How are... things between you too?"

Leo sighs and lays his head down on top of his crossed arm. "We made up," he mumbles to the sleeves of his hoodie.

"Figured."

"She—she basically just said she was sorry, if I felt like she was pressuring me. Going too fast. And... I knew she really was. Sorry. So."

Toby sighs and guzzles the remainder of his soda. "That's great," he deadpans, hardly trying to hide the disappointment in his voice. "Happy for you guys."

Leo lifts his head up so that his nose and eyes are visible over his arm. "Please don't tell me you're going back on strike."

Toby considers it. Briefly.

"No," he decides, looking out the window. He can't see any cars in this restaurant. "I think my strike days are over. At least for now."

Chapter 18

The days turn into weeks and blow right past. They seem to blur together, until Toby can't remember off the top of his head which assignments are due when, when he has to work shifts, what tests and exams he should be studying for sooner rather than later, what days he and Leo plan to meet up at Nim's or the diner or the library or somewhere else just to talk after class.

So. In case anyone was wondering, he has yet to grow a pair and stop this insanity, despite the fact that with every day that passes, he feels himself falling deeper and deeper into a pit that he knows will just destroy him if—when—he attempts to climb back out of it.

But then there's the fact that Leo is really fucking good at math. And Toby is most definitely not.

All of a sudden, fucking February is drawing to a close at a pace faster than Toby can live. He's pretty sure his hand is permanently cramped from desperately scribbling down deadlines and notes-to-self and any information that might make things the slightest bit easier to handle. Never mind the actual assignments.

Soon enough, it's the twenty-fourth, and Toby is on his way into the English hall for his creative writing class when someone calls out his name from afar. He hasn't heard the voice as many times as he's heard others, but he certainly knows it well enough to be able to place a name to it before he even gets the chance to turn around and come face to face with none other than the lovely Steph Aquino.

"Hey," he greets as cheerfully as he can muster. As far as Toby is aware, Leo hasn't said a word to Steph about... anything. So that sinking, guilty feeling he gets whenever she comes around and approaches him with that kind, genuine smile on her face is getting worse and worse every time it happens. He doubts there is anyone else in the world right now that deserves what has happened behind her back less than she does.

"Hey. Do you have a second to talk?"

Several profane words pop into Toby's head at that, and his stomach twists around itself as if it's a wet rag forever trying to rid itself of water. She probably hasn't found out. But what if she has? What if she's finally giving Toby what he deserves?

"Um. Yeah, sure. I've got a few minutes," he says, and he hopes the wavering in his voice is only a trick of his mind.

"Okay. So." She claps her hands together, but they make more of a muffled thump than a clap sound because of her gloves. She then points at him with finger guns. "I need your help."

Relief washes over Toby, but he tries not to let it show. "Me?"

Steph nods and rocks on her heels. "So, this Sunday is Leo's birthday. The twenty-eighth. And I want to throw a surprise party for him."

"Oh. That's... that sounds fun."

"Yeah. So, you know, I was wondering if there was any chance I could recruit you to help me set it up?"

Toby raises his eyebrows. "You want me to help?"

"Yeah. If you can."

"Why?"

Steph scoffs, as if it's a silly question. "I mean, you guys are like, BFFs," she says, beaming at him. "Honestly, I think he might hang out with you more often than he hangs out with me."

Toby can feel his face go beet red.

"Oh, we—we're really not that close," he mumbles, looking away. "And I'm not... uh... I mean, if this is a surprise party, I'm not—I'm really not all that great at keeping secrets."

That's a damn lie. Toby's entire life is a secret.

Steph's smile wavers and her shoulders sink a bit. "Oh," she says, crestfallen. "Are you sure you wouldn't be willing to help out a bit? I—I know you might have your doubts, but I think Leo would really, really appreciate it."

Toby sighs and pushes his hand through his hair. His eyes land on the entrance to the building, on a few random passersby as they stroll down the sidewalk, and finally back on Steph's face. He should really get to class soon. He's only got so long.

"All right," he finally agrees. "I can help."

Steph's face lights right back up again. "Really?"

"Yeah. Why not."

(There are a lot of reasons why not.)

"Thank you so much," Steph says, fumbling around in her pocket for her phone. "Here, can I get your number so I can text you? I'm hoping the party can be this Saturday night, so we'll have to get everything prepared before then."

"Oh. S-sure," Toby says, entering the digits into her phone. "Um. Have you asked anyone else? Or am I the only one?"

He hands her phone back, and she takes it. "Well, I tried," she tells him, reaching up to play with the dark braid that cascades over her left shoulder. "I talked to Ariel—his roommate—but she said she was too busy. She's in, like, pre-med, or something. Anyway. As of right now, it's just... you and me."

Maybe Toby looks worried, because Steph quickly reaches over and gives him a reassuring squeeze on the arm.

"Don't worry, it's not going to be anything major. I'm thinking we'll invite ten, fifteen-ish people max. Nothing too crazy. We got this, okay?"

Toby nods tightly. "Okay."

"Okay. Thank you, again. I'll let you get to class now."

Another thing to add to Toby's agenda. Lovely.

~ ~ ~

When Toby walks into the convenience store Saturday afternoon, practically arm in arm with Steph, of course there's none other working there than Blue Brown. And some other person that Toby thinks is named Lynn.

"Do you need help finding anything?" Blue asks, raising his eyebrows and shifting his gaze between Toby and Steph.

"We're fine," Toby mumbles, and he has to try his absolute hardest not to manually steer Steph away. "Thanks."

"Well, let me know."'

Toby has to say, Blue certainly does an impeccable job at following the script. Because Toby definitely knows where everything is in the store.

"You work with that guy, right?" Steph asks as they swing into a random aisle. "He seems nice. I like his eyebrows."

Again, it's the genuine, kind, pure remarks like that that make guilt bubble up in Toby's stomach.

"Yeah, he's cool," he mumbles in response.

"Okay. So. Supplies," Steph says, pulling out her phone and opening a typed list. "First, cheap ass alcohol."

"Oh, I'm not—I'm nineteen," Toby tells her as he guides her to the proper section of the store. "So if you were counting on me to buy, I—"

"I'm of age," she assures him. "Don't worry. I wouldn't just dump all my responsibilities on you like that. At least, not without a warning first."

Toby gives a hesitant chuckle. Jesus, why can't he act normal?

"Okay, so I know that Leo's a big fan of fruity things," Steph says, tapping her phone against her chin as she scans over the various alcoholic selections. "What do you think? Sangria, maybe? Or—is that too much of a brunch-y drink? Ooh, we could do vodka-cranberries, or some kind of punch. Or, like, some fruit-flavored rosé or something."

As Steph deliberates on the viable options, Toby racks his brain, trying to remember what drink Leo had in his hand—if any—at Jordan's house, weeks ago. He's pretty sure everyone there was drinking beer, though, and if there was anyone that wasn't, Toby can't remember. So many things happened that night. Although, the thought still itches in his brain, irritates his hippocampus. If he could just—

"Cocktails," Toby says. It's as though a bell or something has been struck, and the memory just slips out with the vibrations. Steph turns to look at him. He coughs.

"Just a suggestion," he mutters. "Um, how old is Leo turning? Twenty-one?"

"Twenty," Steph responds, as she loads a bottle of vodka, a bottle of champagne, and a case of beer into the mini shopping cart that they picked up on the way in. "Don't tell the cops."

"Oh, yeah, I won't." Toby scratches his head. Weird how Leo and him have been hanging out more and more often since mid-January, and yet he still only just now discovered that Leo's only five months older than him. Almost exactly. (Toby will be twenty on July twenty-ninth.)

"Okay. Alcohol, check. We should grab some soda and stuff, too."

"Hey, why don't we divide and conquer?" suggests Toby with his hands in his pockets. "You can grab the sodas—they're right around the corner, by the way—and I'll get some other stuff and meet you."

"Oh. Good idea." Steph looks down at her list, and then back up at Toby. "Okay. If you could grab... let's see. Four frozen pizzas—Leo likes cheese, but if there isn't enough or something, then just get pepperoni, I guess. Neapolitan ice cream, cranberry juice, bottled waters, and, like, stuff to assemble a platter of cheese and crackers? If they're—you're?—out of any of that, then don't worry about it—"

"Got it," Toby says, formulating his mental list and figuring out the best route to take to get all of the items in the most efficient manner. "And I'll come find you after?"

Steph gives him a thumbs off and he heads in the opposite direction, toward the freezers. Incidentally—or maybe not—a certain someone with blue eyebrows is restocking the frozen waffles.

"So who's the lady?" Blue asks, not even glancing over his shoulder to look at Toby.

Toby rolls his eyes. "A friend."

"No shit, rainbow boy. What kind of friend, I mean?"

"Would you lower your voice?" Toby hisses. "She's... more like a friend of a friend. It's his birthday tomorrow, so we're—"

"Oooh, who's he?" Blue asks, turning his head as if just to show off his waggling eyebrows.

"Her boyfriend." Toby looks straight ahead as he opens the door to the frozen pizzas.

"Ah." Toby places four pizzas into his basket before Blue gasps as if he's just heard the latest drama about whatever problematic TV show he's currently obsessed with. (Pretty Little Liars, Toby is pretty sure. So. Yeah, problematic.) "Wait a minute."

"What."

"That's not her, is it?"

"What are you talking about?"

"The girlfriend of the guy you were telling me about," Blue says, his brown eyes the size of saucers. "The one who kissed y—"

"Sh-sh-sh-sh-sh-sh-sh!" Toby nearly drops the basket as he moves to clamp his hands over Blue's mouth, leaving the freezer door hanging open in his wake. "Jesus fuck, Blue!"

"Oh my God, you two are friends?" Blue's voice is muffled, but he doesn't seem to care. "And she doesn't know?"

"Shut up."

"Dude, you need to turn your life into a fucking TV show. Seriously. Y'all are working together to throw him a birthday party, and she's got no idea what actually happened between you two. It would make millions, man."

"You," Toby growls underneath his breath, "need to learn how to keep your goddamn mouth shut. This is a small store. She could hear you."

Blue stares at him for a long second, and then shrugs.

"Then at least someone would be telling the truth around here," he says, prying Toby's hands away from his face, closing the door to the waffles, and walking away.

"There you are," Steph greets as Toby lumbers into the candy aisle, weighed down by the basket hooked within his right forearm. "Got everything?"

"Yep," he says, voice straining slightly as he hauls the basket into the cart. His arm is buzzing. (He hasn't been working out much lately.) "You?"

"Leo's got a major sweet tooth, so I'm trying to pick out some candy we can set out too," she says, scanning the selection before her. She scoffs. "Only I always end up forgetting to ask what kind of candy Leo likes the most, so—"

"M&Ms," Toby says mindlessly, plucking a giant bag off of the shelf and tossing it into the cart.

Steph looks up at him, one of her dark eyebrows cocked. "Really?"

Toby has to process what just happened before his eyes go wide and he immediately turns away from her.

"Um, I mean—pretty much every normal person likes M&Ms, right?" he sputters.

Steph hums to herself. "Yeah, I guess. But since Leo likes fruit flavored things, what about, like, Skittles or Jolly Ranchers, or something like that? I think that's a safe bet."

"Oh, sure." Toby clears his throat. "But—um. I think we should still get the M&Ms. If not for Leo, then... for the other guests."

Steph shrugs, and plucks a few other bags of candy off the shelf. "Sure, why not?" she says. "But I think that's everything, now."

Toby follows her to the checkout with his eyes set on his feet, and tries his best to ignore the judgmental gaze he feels coming from Blue at the other vacant register. Of course, Toby can't blame him. He knows what an asshole he is. Blue knows, Leo knows, Vicki knows. Everyone knows except for Steph, and he doesn't think he'll ever be brave enough to tell her.

Chapter 19

The party is at Steph's place, because she said that throwing someone a party in their own home and then leaving them to clean up the mess afterward is "something that someone like Tucker Carlson would do." And, not that Toby didn't agree before, but the analogy just makes so much sense that he has no choice to agree this time.

Decoration-wise, they don't go too all out. According to Steph, Leo's favorite color is red (which, admittedly, Toby feels like he already knew, because he's seen Leo save the red M&Ms for last, despite the fact that they all taste the same), so they spruce up the place with a few red balloons and streamers, as well as set out red paper plates and napkins. And of course, the solo cups already work out in their favor.

HAPPY BIRTHDAY LEO is spelled out on a banner (not in red, because Steph thinks that would be a bit overboard—it's in a light blue instead) that hangs on the wall of the apartment opposite the entrance, just above the couch.

"So what's the plan?" Toby asks as they finish up tidying and decorating. It's the first time he's instigated conversation since they got back from the store.

"Leo's at the art gallery right now, but he'll be off at five. I'm going to pick him up and bring him here, so you'll be here with the guests as they arrive."

Something in Toby's stomach stirs at that. Maybe because of the fact that Leo never mentioned working at the art gallery, not even once, and that really bothers him for some reason.

"How many people are coming again?" Toby asks, stepping down from the stepladder he used to hang the banner.

"About fifteen, including you, me, and Leo," Steph answers, stacking and unstacking and restacking cups at the edge of the kitchen island until she's apparently satisfied enough with their arrangement and stepping away. "As long as nobody decided to go and blab to their friends about this, I mean. Because if they did, who knows how many people might try and show up."

"Right." Toby is (over)thinking about having to welcome twelve complete strangers into someone else's home, his mind reeling and the social anxiety brewing in his gut, when suddenly a rumble of thunder off in the distance rolls its way to Toby's eardrums.

"Oh, shit," Steph groans. "I was really hoping the rain wouldn't come until later. I won't be able to pick him up if it starts soon. My car's in the shop, so I'd been planning on just walking to the gallery since it's not too far—"

"I can do it," Toby offers, a bit too enthusiastically. "I-I'll pick him up for you. If you want me to."

Steph's eyes light up. "Really?"

"Yeah. It's no problem."

"Thank you," Steph says, putting one hand on her hip and the other curled up below her chin. "Okay. I'll text him that something came up, and that someone else will meet him and take him here." She pauses, and then sighs. "No, that's way too sketchy. He'll know I'm planning something."

Toby shrugs. "I mean, I can just go there. Pretend it's a coincidence or something, and then offer him a ride."

"Toby, you are a lifesaver." Steph checks the time on her phone. "Okay, so it's almost four. You can leave now if you want, maybe stop at home and change if you feel like it. Just please don't forget to text me when you've got him and get back to the building, so I can get everyone ready."

"Got it," Toby says, already grabbing and pulling on his jacket and heading for the door. "See you."

When Toby gets home, he throws on a pair of light wash jeans and a scarlet red t-shirt. Not for any particular reason. He just hasn't worn that specific shirt in a while.

Toby's been to the art gallery once or twice, and it's a pretty cool place, so he can't help but wonder why Leo has never once mentioned working there in all the conversations—or, rather, attempted conversations—the two of them have had about his art career.

But Toby can't really complain. After all, he hasn't been all that willing to share his writing with Leo, either.

He enters the building around 4:50, and is immediately noticed and warned by the (apparently British) middle aged woman at the front desk that they will be closing in ten minutes. He responds with a quick thank you, and proceeds to make a rushed lap around the first floor of the gallery to pass the time, as well as remind himself of what the place actually looks like. Last time he went was probably around a year ago, and even then he didn't get the full experience. He'll have to come again sometime in the near future.

When he returns to the foyer at two minutes to five, he approaches the woman at the front desk and clears his throat.

"What can I do for you, love?"

"I'm, uh, waiting for Leo. Rosales," Toby says. "I'm his ride home. Will he be done soon?"

"Oh, yes. He's finishing up for the night and should be out any moment now," and then gestures over to one of the benches against a front window. "You're welcome to take a seat while you wait."

"Thank you," Toby says, striding over toward the bench, but he doesn't sit down. His nerves are suddenly eating him up on the inside, which is absolutely outrageous because at this point, Leo's wormed his way into becoming one of the top five people Toby most frequently texts, so he literally has no reason to be nervous at all. He decides that really, he's just worried about flapping his loose lips a little too much and completely ruining the surprise. Which is a fair possibility.

There's the sound of a door shutting from somewhere out of Toby's line of sight, and then the familiar voice rings out, bouncing off the walls of the spacious foyer.

"I'll see you next week, Sophie. Tell Charlie and Cedric I said hi."

"Sure, darling."

Toby wipes his sweaty palms on his jeans (ew? When did this become a thing?) as Leo rounds the corner. Almost immediately, he catches sight of Toby and skids to a halt .

"Uh, what are you doing here?" he asks, several expressions appearing and disappearing on his face like a slot machine, until he remains with a confused, lopsided smirk.

"Oh." Toby rocks on his heels like a sheepish teenage girl. He stops rocking on his heels. "You know. Just going for a leisurely visit to the art gallery."

"Uh-huh."

"And, you know, funny thing; a little birdy also told me that you happened to work here, so it's not like I could just leave without seeing you in uniform."

"Shame you had to come so late," Leo says, nodding his head toward the exit, signifying their departure. "You could have caught my 4:30 tour."

"You're a tour guide?" Toby asks, eyebrows raised.

"Yep. Saturdays at 9:30, 2:30, 3:30, and 4:30."

"You boys have a lovely rest of your weekend," the woman—Sophie—calls out from the desk.

"You too," Leo and Toby respond simultaneously, pushing the doors open to embrace the falling rain.

"C'mon," Toby says, grabbing Leo's hand—not wrist, not arm, but hand—and dragging him out into the icy abyss, Leo's sputters of surprise lost to the wind rushing in Toby's ears and the giggling coming from his own throat. Giggling.

If he's like this now, all giddy and shit, he doesn't even want to think about what he might do after he's had a few drinks.

"Toby," Leo gasps once they reach his car, both of them scrambling inside as quickly as possible. "What the hell."

"I'm your ride," Toby says, buckling up and placing both hands on the steering wheel as if to prove his authority.

"Well—I mean, thank you, but—maybe a warning next time would be great."

"Sorry." Only he's not really sorry at all. It's not like he'd parked an absurd distance from the entrance, so they aren't, like, soaked to the bone. But there are raindrops sparkling in Leo's hair, shining as they cascade in rivulets down the sides of Leo's smiling face, and Toby wonders why the hell this image is something he should ever even fathom apologizing for.

(God. He's in so much fucking trouble.)

"Well?" Leo's voice wakes him from whatever weird trance he was in, and he blinks himself back to attention, hoping the burning in his face is more of a mental thing than physical. "If you're the driver, then drive. Or were you just trying to get me wet?"

There's a fragile silence that hangs in the air for a second or two as the unintentionally suggestive remark seems to resonate in their ears, until it's shattered by both of their hysterical laughter.

Toby's heart is beating so fast.

He feels really happy right now. Probably happier than he has in weeks.

When Leo catches his breath and begins to blink rain out of his eyes, Toby shifts the gear into reverse and backs out of his parking space. His face hurts from the muscles being put to work for such a noticeable period of time. When was the last time he smiled this wide? When was the last time happiness hurt like this?

The first thing that comes to mind is the last time they kissed. Outside of the library. Forever ago.

He starts talking before his stomach gets a chance to ruin the moment.

"So," Toby prompts, biting the inside of his cheek to minimize the stupid grin he knows more than likely makes him look like an absolute idiot. "Who are Charlie and Cedric?"

"It's pronounced Cee-dric, first of all," Leo corrects him, leaning back against the seat and allowing his shoulders to slump low. "But they're Sophie's sons. Twins. I met them on my first day at work. It's a funny story, actually; they were messing around on their own and, long story short, ended up crashing the very first tour I gave, which I was so unbelievably nervous for for days on end."

"And you tell Sophie to say hello to them for you?" Toby asks.

"I mean, we're cool now. Don't get me wrong, it was terrifying in the moment, but looking back, I laugh every time I think about it. They remind me of..." He stops short. "Just. Someone I used to know."

Toby raises his eyebrows. "So are you gonna tell me the full story, or not?"

Leo chuckles and pats Toby on the shoulder. "Maybe one day."

"What? Why not now?"

"It's not in the stars, young grasshopper. Wait patiently."

Toby scoffs and shoves Leo's hand off of him, and Leo cackles to himself. Toby just won't stop smiling.

"Okay, fine," he says. "Next question, then."

"Oh, I don't think I was aware this was an interrogation. My bad."

"Why didn't you tell me you worked at the gallery?" Toby asks, toning down the silliness because he does genuinely want to know the answer to this question. "I mean, it seems like a pretty cool job. And, like you said, I would have tried to catch one of your tours beforehand—"

"It's not a permanent thing," Leo says, his voice also adopting the sudden soberness. "I mean, not as permanent as part time jobs go. I won't be working there for much longer. And I only started in—November, I think? Or December. I'm not totally sure."

"Why?"

"Because. I..." He sighs. "Just think of it as, like, the gallery and me doing favors for each other. That's... all you need to know right now."

Toby doesn't prod for further details, and a full minute of rain pattering the windshield and the road drifting beneath them and the faint melody of "Iris" through the speakers eventually dismisses the topic. Until Toby clears his throat.

"Will you tell me some other time, then?" he asks quietly. "Maybe when the stars are aligned?"

He spares a brief glance to his right and sees the corners of Leo's mouth hint upward.

"Maybe so."

"SURPRISE!"

The voices all sound out in unison, Toby's included, though admittedly much quieter and less confident than the others. Leo blinks a few times, and then a smile begins to slither across his face, and then Steph pretty much throws herself onto him, clasping her arms around his waist and smiling up at him with her chin on his chest.

"Happy birthday!" she squeals, constricting her hold around him. "I hope you're not too tired."

"What—wait, so—this is all for me?" Leo turns toward Toby. "You were in on this?"

"Toby helped me put it together," Steph answers, moving off of Leo and linking her arm with Toby's. "Couldn't have pulled it off without him."

"That's probably not true, but. I appreciate the compliment," Toby says, laughing awkwardly, glancing around nervously at the abyss of people he has never met once in his life. "You definitely had this under control."

"Not really, if I'm being honest here—"

"Never mind, forget I asked," Leo says, waving his hand. "You two are both way too modest to be playing this game. We'll be standing here forever if I let this continue."

"Fair enough," Steph says, laughing. She laces her fingers with Leo's and tugs him away into the swarm of guests, all of whom seem to pounce on him as soon as possible, greeting him with too-tight embraces, hair ruffles, or awkward side hugs. Leo's eyes are bright, glowing, and the entire room seems to be, too.

After he catches up with everyone and thanks them all profusely for coming, Leo shuffles back over to Toby, who has purposely detached himself from the crowd and is cracking open a bottle of water in the corner of the kitchen.

"You are a sneaky son of a bitch," Leo mutters, nudging him on the shoulder with his own. "You know that?"

Toby smiles against the lip of the bottle. "I'm gonna take that as a compliment."

"I was wondering why you looked so spiffy when I saw you at the gallery," Leo tells him. "I mean, jeans? I think I've only ever seen you in sweatpants. And is this shirt from Urban Outfitters? Didn't think a college student would have that kind of money."

"I-I didn't—I don't know, I wasn't—" Toby has to take a breath as he looks everywhere but into Leo's eyes. "I-it's just a shirt. I wasn't going for spiffy."

(He was totally going for spiffy.)

Leo seems to believe him as much as Toby believes himself. "Uh-huh." His nimble fingers brush against the fabric of Toby's sleeve, and then tug downward ever so slightly. "Well, the color suits you," he says into Toby's ear, his voice near a whisper, sending violent chills down Toby's spine.

Toby thinks he probably turns as red as his shirt as Leo's eyebrows rise and fall in a swift, teasing motion before he re-engages himself with his guests.

Chapter 20

Toby unwillingly meets every single one of the guests at the party. And by unwillingly, he means he is literally dragged by the sleeve across Steph's apartment by Leo, introduced to each person as "Toby, my unofficial chauffeur" by Leo, and quite literally clung to by Leo whenever a conversation between the two of them and at least one other person would go on for more than a minute.

Toby hates it and doesn't, all at once.

Once everyone has been acquainted with one another and the rainfall has become drowned out by the music Steph has queued up to boom through the stereo, that knot that had formed in Toby's stomach beforehand seems to slowly become looser. He's still not exactly in a favorable environment, but now at least these people aren't total strangers, and now he knows who he thinks he will probably be straying away from as much as he can (i.e., Leo's friend named Edward, who Toby was worried would genuinely bark at him as they shook hands).

They sit, stand, dance, eat, drink, laugh, talk. It's a tame gathering, not some kind of uncontrollable frat party—Toby doesn't have to be incredibly close with her to know that something along those lines is drastically different from Steph's style—despite the copious amounts of alcohol that sit on the kitchen counters, some of it bought by Toby and Steph earlier that day, and some of it brought voluntarily by the other partygoers. People are still drinking it, of course—to not would be a tragic waste—but they're doing so with... reasonable etiquette. After all, they have yet for someone to barf all over Steph's Abaca rug.

But ten p.m. is when people seem to simply not care anymore. Least of all, in fact, Leo. Perhaps he's had one too many Vodka Cranberries, because his freckles swim in a stream of pink that flushes across the front of his face, and he starts talking more, laughing more, dancing more.

Toby learns that Leo cannot dance.

Some older rock song fades out, its essence still lingering in the air after a few brief moments, until the silence is replaced by yet another song, something more recent. And apparently something that Leo likes a lot.

"Oh, shit!" he shouts as he slams his empty solo cup down on the island and raises his arms, pointing both fingers at the ceiling, revealing a little sliver of his lower stomach that Toby doesn't look at. "I fucking love this song!"

Toby snickers at him, his own mind a bit fuzzy from the two or three beers he's had so far tonight. But the snickering stops quite abruptly when Leo's arms come swinging back down and he grabs a hold of Toby's wrists, yanking him in the direction of the stereo.

"What are you doing?" Toby demands, squirming in a desperate attempt to withdraw from Leo's surprisingly firm grasp.

"You're being lame," Leo tells him bluntly. "You haven't been enjoying yourself."

"That's—not true—"

"Dance with me."

"No."

"Dance with meeeee."

"No."

"Please?"

Toby looks at Leo, at those blue eyes shining like glass beneath their dreamy, watery glaze. He looks down at where Leo's hand is clasped around his wrist, and nearly jumps a mile when Leo's thumb makes the tiniest gesture and strokes up and down his skin. Out of instinct, he withdraws, stumbling back a bit, and pushes his hand through his hair. Leo draws his eyebrows together and opens his mouth to say something else, whatever drunken series of words queued up on his tongue, but copper arms snake around his torso from behind and Steph rests her chin on his shoulder, smiling dreamily up at him. Toby whirls around and returns to the kitchen island.

There's only one person there, one person who's been even less engaged with the other guests than Toby. Her arms are crossed over her chest, and she looks rather bored. For some reason, Toby thinks she looks familiar, but he can't put his finger on where he may have seen her before. She definitely wasn't here earlier, when Leo dragged him around the apartment.

"Not a fan of dancing?" she asks him. He can barely hear her over the music.

Toby shrugs. "Um. No, it's—it's not really my thing."

"Yeah, me either. Not a fan of any of this, really."

"Then why bother showing up?"

"Because I have to. I know Leo wasn't expecting this, but if he found out I consciously decided not to show up at all, I'd just never hear the end of it."

Toby scoffs. "Are you two close?"

"Yeah, guess you could say that." The girl holds out her hand. "Ariel."

Toby feels his eyes go wide and his jaw slacken ever so slightly. It takes him a few moments to gain control of the muscles in his arm to return her handshake. "Toby," he says. For some reason he thinks he sounds stupid saying his own name. "I'm—yeah. I'm Toby."

Ariel raises an eyebrow, and the opposite side of her mouth twitches upward. "I'm sure Leo's told you all about me by now."

"Well—I mean, not all, but—he talks about you a lot, and I've just. I've never seen you till now. I was honestly starting to wonder if you were even real."

Ariel cocks her head to the side. "You've seen me before."

"I have?"

"Yeah. Last month."

Last month? Last month? God, Toby could have been doing anything back then. He pinches the bridge of his nose,
attempting to focus his hazy mind, counting back the days,
rewinding and trying to place her face. But apparently he
takes too long.

"Jordan McConnell's house," Ariel tells him, and there's a
strange, sudden sharpness to her words that makes him
think she could probably slit his throat open with words
alone at the most unprecedented time. "I was there."

She was there. She was there. Toby wracks his brain, trying
to summon the faces of the strangers he saw that night, only
none of them quite fit the face he's looking at right now,
there's something that's—something throwing him off.

And then it hits him, and he's glad it does before Ariel can
manage to. Because she looks like she absolutely can and
will.

"Glasses!" he blurts, pointing a finger at her. "I mean—you
were the girl with—you had those cat eye glasses on, right?"

Ariel places her hand on top of Toby's and pushes his finger
down. He quickly lets it fall limp at his side. "You got it," she
says. "I was also the 'game moderator,' or whatever."

"Yeah. Yeah." Toby brushes a hand through his hair. "I-I
remember that."

Ariel stares him down. Her eyes are icy blue, lighter and
much more intimidating than Leo's, and they stand out
against her tan skin. Her hair is a similar shade to Leo's,
maybe a bit darker—Toby thinks they could probably pass
as siblings. But he doesn't know why he's thinking about that

right now when Ariel looks downright murderous, ready to rip his throat out with her teeth.

"He has a girlfriend," she grits out. "But you clearly know that, right?"

"I-I'm sorry?"

"I know what happened between you two." Toby's heart drops into his stomach. "I mean, I watched you guys walk into the pantry together, and I saw that little stunt you two pulled outside that night."

Toby looks over his shoulder, relieved to find everyone caught up in their business, far out of earshot. He looks back to Ariel, his throat full of sand, his tongue weighing a hundred pounds. "Look, what happened—we were both drunk, so—"

"I don't care if Leo's gay," Ariel continues. Toby keeps waiting for her to blink, but she doesn't. "I don't care if he's straight, or bisexual, or anything. But he's dating someone right now. If you fuck that up, you'll fuck him up, and you'll fuck Steph up."

"What—"

"You're confusing him, and I know you might not be doing it on purpose, so long as you're not trying to make any kind of advances on him or anything. But you don't seem like the kind of guy that would do that. But until he figures himself out, until he decides whether or not he wants to stay with Steph, it's probably best you distance yourself from him so he doesn't make any more mistakes. Honestly, it might be better for both of you if you do that."

Toby can't find words for a long time. A new song starts up during what he thinks must be a temporary state of paralysis, because he wants to move, he wants to speak, but he can't find the strength to do so until the first wave of shock finally wears off.

"I didn't know about Steph until later," says Toby finally, his voice weak and quivering. "I promise, I didn't. I never would have—I'm not trying to break them apart. In fact, I've been—I've been trying to do what you said, distancing myself, just to make sure I don't accidentally interfere again, so I don't know what—"

"That's bullshit," Ariel huffs. "You two have only been getting closer these past few weeks. I'm Leo's best friend, so trust me, I've noticed. It was you he stayed with that night he didn't come home, right? He slept over at your place?"

"Well—yeah, but—"

"If you've been 'staying away from him,' what are you doing here?"

"Steph asked me to help, because she said you—"

"And you said yes? In good conscience?"

"Do you think I don't feel bad about this situation?" Toby hisses, jabbing his finger into his own chest. "Because I fucking do. Okay? I feel like shit every time Steph looks at me. The last thing I want is to become some kind of landmine in their relationship."

"Then act like it."

Toby opens his mouth, curse words laid out flat, prepared for takeoff, but then an arm is slung over his shoulders and he feels himself be yanked downward a couple inches, and everything he wants to say to Ariel gets swallowed down in the process.

"Whatcha doing over here?" Leo asks him, alcohol heavy on his breath.

Toby looks down at his feet. "U-um. We were just—we were just talking—"

Leo makes a hm? noise, and through Toby's peripherals, he sees Leo's head turn to face Ariel and can practically hear the smile of delight twist onto his face.

"Hey!" he exclaims, immediately withdrawing his arm from Toby's shoulders and neck, and wrapping Ariel up in a bear hug. "I thought Steph said you couldn't come!"

"Well, I decided I could spare to leave work a little early," she tells Leo, patting him on the back. "But only for you. Happy birthday, idiot."

The conversation that starts up between the two of them after that seems to fade into the background, becoming another noise mingled in with the thrumming of the stereo and the rain falling outside. Now taking center stage, flooding Toby's ears, is the sudden pounding of his head and the sound of his own heart, thundering in his chest from a mix of rage and self-hatred and guilt and fear and everything everything everything that's been hiding away and building up since the very first moment, it's all flooding in all at once and Toby can't—he can't deal with it, he can't.

He doesn't know or hear the words that leave his mouth when he dismisses himself from the conversation. Maybe he says nothing at all and just leaves, glancing around desperately for an out, swiping up a half-empty bottle of vodka as he makes his way toward a room he's never been in, a room in an apartment that doesn't belong to him, a room he has no business barging into. But it's quieter and it's darker and there's no one here and it's an escape, so he sits on the floor against a bed and cries burning, shameful, cathartic tears that sting like glass.

Chapter 21

Toby's phone is in his pocket. He could easily pull it out and look at the time, see how long he's been sitting here, how many minutes or hours or years have passed since he entered the room. But he can't find the strength to do that right now, because no matter what digits end up showing up, the screen will still be bright as fuck and Toby's head is already pounding and he can't handle that right now, whatever now is. So as far as he's concerned, time just isn't, and time will continue not to be until he sobers up and reading a digital clock in the middle of a room drowned in darkness won't be so intensive.

He's not crying anymore, if that means anything at all. He thinks about it and it doesn't. In fact, he wishes he was still crying. Crying gave him something to do, a reason as to why he shut himself in here in the first place, should anyone ask. He hopes no one does, though. But crying kept him focused on the tears as they fell, counting them as if they were sheep, until the numbers got too high to where he couldn't count anymore. That's when he stopped crying. Maybe he should start from scratch. Maybe that would be good. Maybe starting from scratch would take him into morning time and he would be sober and he could go home. And he wouldn't need an excuse to be shut in his room because it would be Sunday and who wants to come out of their room on a Sunday? Not Toby, and definitely not Reggie either. So Toby could cry in his room in private on a Sunday and nobody would know nobody would find out and he wouldn't have to explain anything anything at all to anyone because it's Sunday.

The bottle of vodka isn't drained yet, but if Toby stays here an hour or two longer then maybe it will be. And then Toby would probably be dead, if he's not already dying. Maybe he should stop drinking. He's only nineteen.

And Leo, Leo's only twenty. Or, is he twenty yet? Is it midnight? It is Sunday? Toby doesn't know because as far as he's concerned, time just isn't.

Does Toby forget that he's nineteen every time he drinks, or does he remember and acknowledge and then forget, choose to forget? He doesn't know. He'll have to see next time, after he sobers up from tonight, he'll see next time he drinks, next time he drinks when he's nineteen.

The vodka makes noise in its bottle as Toby swishes it around and around. Swish swish swish. Toby counts the swishes instead of the tears because the tears still aren't coming. One swish, two swishes, three swishes, four—six, six and a half—Toby stops because the swishing is making him dizzy and his head is already hurting and maybe he can cry again if he just tries really really hard this time.

Cry, cry, cry. There is a lot to cry about, so cry. Cry to feel better about shit that makes you feel worse. Cry, cry, cry.

Cry about Ariel and the things she said and cry because she was right and because you know she was right. You can cry about that.

Or about Steph, what if you were Steph? What if you were Steph and you knew what Steph doesn't know right now, what if you were Steph and you found out what would you do? You would cry because how could you? How can you? Toby can cry about that.

Reggie said he didn't care when Toby thought he did and thank God he didn't, thank God Toby was wrong. Toby was and is so happy to be wrong he could cry. Or cry about being right, what if he had been right? What would have happened what would have happened? It would have been bad, terrible, something for you to cry about for a long time after. Cry about being right. What if you were right? What if he hated you, what if he hated you and thought you were disgusting and weird and bad? That would have been so bad, so bad you could cry, so cry, just cry, fucking cry about it already.

Why is it so hard now? Everything is so hard now, and crying is hardest. Crying isn't, and neither is time, because Toby just can't.

Time is again when the door opens and Leo says, "There you are. I haven't seen you around for, like, an hour."

"Time's it?" Toby asks. He hasn't touched the vodka in a while, so he feels a little bit better even though he still hasn't managed to cry again, not even after before when he really really wanted to.

"'Bout ten to midnight," Leo answers, closing the door with a gentle click, and plopping down on the floor right next to Toby. "Scale of one to ten, how wasted are you?"

Toby gives him a thumbs up because it seems like the right answer and Leo chuckles, and Toby smiles because he likes when Leo chuckles but wait wait wait wait wait wait wait.

"Wait," Toby drawls, pinching the bridge of his nose. "Wait. You shouldn't—be in here with me."

"Why not?"

"'Cause. It's just best if you're not."

"Does this have something to do with whatever you and Ariel were talking about earlier?" Leo asks.

Toby squeezes his eyes shut. "Did you hear us?"

"No, but I could tell it was pretty heated. You gonna tell me what happened?"

Toby sighs and shakes his head. "Shouldn't be in here."

"But I want to be."

"Why aren't you having fun? 'S your party that your girl-friend threw just for you. Why are you even in here?"

"It's peaceful," Leo says, and Toby hears and feels as he shifts his position, his right arm brushing up against Toby's left for just a brief moment. "And I wanted to make sure that you were okay and not, like, choking on your own vomit."

"'M fine."

"I think the nearly-empty bottle of vodka says otherwise."

"I didn't drink all of that," Toby mumbles. "It was halfway empty when I picked it up."

"Not half full?"

Toby thinks for a moment, genuinely trying to come up with an answer in his big stupid head, until he catches the teasing grin on Leo's face and scoffs. "Empty," he says. "Definitely half empty."

Leo sighs and everything in Toby has wings but everything in him is also named Icarus.

"Do you want to talk about it?" Leo asks gently. "If she offended you or said something rude I can go talk to her, if you want."

"Doesn't matter what she said. She was right," Toby groans, pulling his knees to his chest and resting his chin atop his kneecaps. "I'm only making things worse for you and Steph."

"What?"

"I know how much I'm confusing you."

"Who—did Ariel tell you that?"

"Yeah, but it's not like it's news," says Toby. "I mean, what happened between you and me is bad enough, and I should have—I should have stopped hanging around you, like I wanted to in the first place. It's just... better if I'm out of the picture while you figure things out, work things out with Steph."

Leo's quiet for a few moments, and when he does speak, his voice is quieter, timid, hesitant. "What about after that?"

Toby shrugs. "Guess it depends on what you choose."

"And what if I do choose to stay with Steph? What would you do?"

Toby looks up at him. Leo's face is stone, his jaw tight, as he waits for Toby's response. Toby allows the muted music in the other room to be all that surrounds either of them for a few beats. He thinks it might be something by Queen. That's nice. It would be fun to break out into song, as if life was some Disney, fairy tale-esque musical, but everything is just... too heavy to do that. So he clears his throat and places his chin back on his kneecaps.

"I'd... do my best to stay away from you," he replies quietly. "I feel guilty enough already."

There's yet another silence that follows, and the odd sense of comfort that Leo brought into the room is dispersing quickly. Toby can feel it going, leaving him, and he really wants to reach out and grasp it tight and ask it to stop, to stay, just for the night, and then after that it can leave and go and be gone forever. But he's not strong enough to do that. And when he thinks about how he isn't strong enough to do that, it's almost enough to make him cry.

"Thank you for the party," Leo says out of the blue, startling Toby. He glances over at him, meets Leo's eyes, which are soft again, soft and blue, and no longer set in a cold, hard stone as they were before.

"It was all Steph," Toby tells him, his voice hushed like her name is taboo. "I'm definitely not the one to thank."

"She said you helped her plan."

"I mean, yeah. A bit. But it was her idea in the first place, and it was like she had everything outlined in her head before she even asked me, and she knew everything about what would make you the most happy."

There's a sudden soft rattling noise as Leo pulls something out of the pocket of his denim jacket, and then shakes it in front of Toby's face. Toby squints his eyes, trying to focus on whatever it is being held up in front of him, and eventually reaches out to take it. It's a miniature plastic bag, twisted to a close. Toby opens it and reaches inside to see what this is all about.

"M&Ms," Leo says as Toby plucks a few out and holds them in the palm of his hand.

"Yeah." Toby feels warmth rise in his cheeks.

"Thanks."

"I-it was—I was just—"

"Making me happy?"

Leo's gaze is piercing, and there's a smirk sculpted onto his face, because of course there is. And that gets Toby thinking. If he were a sculptor and Leo was a statue made of clay, Toby thinks the only proper way he would manage to perfect that signature expression would be by using his pinky—not a tool, his pinky—to create that little divot in the left side of Leo's face. That would be it. He would master it that way. Probably, at least. Toby realizes he has yet to figure out if his pinky actually fits the size of Leo's dimple. What a funny thing to ask someone to clarify. He'll have to estimate, for now.

"Whatever," Toby says, his voice nearly a whisper. God, he's too drunk for this.

Leo chuckles a bit, snatches up a few of the candies in Toby's hand, and pops them into his mouth. Toby can't move for a second.

"Oh," Leo says, pulling his phone out and illuminating the screen. Just as Toby thought, he's too drunk for this, and the screen is far too bright. He squints his eyes and turns his head in the opposite direction while Leo says, "Five minutes."

"Till what?" Toby asks.

"My birthday."

"So go celebrate. Go have fun at your party."

"I'm not gonna have fun while you're sitting in here, looking absolutely miserable." The screen of Leo's phone dims again and Toby looks back in his direction, only for the bottle of vodka to be swiped away from beside him.

"Hey," he whines, but Leo's already downing a sip. Multiple.

"Oh, God," Leo groans afterward, his eyes all squinty, as he wipes his mouth with his sleeve. "That burned a bit, not gonna lie."

"Why—"

"Why not?"

Toby scoffs and shakes his head. "You're ridiculous."

"Heyyy, there's the Toby I know. Welcome back, man." Leo smacks Toby on the back and for a second it sobers Toby up entirely as the disturbance that's been stewing in his stomach threatens to come back up, but it doesn't, thank God. Toby would have no choice but never to see Steph or Leo again if he threw up right here and now. Talk about humiliating.

"Hey, why didn't you tell me that your birthday was coming up?" Toby asks once he's absolutely certain that nothing is going to regurgitate from his throat but words.

Leo raises his eyebrows, and then looks straight ahead with a shrug. "I didn't want you to think you had to do anything for me." He smirks. "But clearly, that backfired."

"Well, I—I actually do have a present for you," Toby blurts, patting at his pockets. "Hold on, let me—"

"Toby, you didn't have to—"

"No, no, it—it's not a big deal, I just—I wanted to get you something, you know, so—"

"Then why don't you wait for three more minutes?" Leo suggests softly, placing a hand on Toby's as he prepares to withdraw the gift from his pocket, all folded and crumpled and lame. "Wait until it's my actual birthday to give it to me."

Toby looks down at their hands, and then back up at Leo, who's smiling, smiling, smiling and it should be illegal to smile like that because it's probably going to kill Toby one day or another, it'll kill him if he looks at it for a second longer.

"Fun fact," Leo begins to say, and thank God because it probably would have killed Toby if he didn't begin to say. "According to my mom, I was an easy birth. At least compared to my sisters."

"You have sisters?" Toby asks and he does want to know, he does, but he also wants to know how these words will look on Leo's tongue as they leave his mouth, how he will say them, so Toby keeps looking at his lips because he wants to know, that's all.

"Yeah... I mean, I have a sister. She's only six. My mom was pretty young when she had me. My age, actually. She was twenty. God, that's crazy to think about. You said you have siblings, right?"

"I have an older sister and an older brother," Toby says. "Only, not in that order. My sister is younger than my brother, but she's older than me. Olivia and Seb. Sebastian."

"So you're the baby of the family, huh?"

"Guess so."

"I always wanted to know what that's like. After Bobbie was born, I was always having to watch over her while my mom worked. I learned how to cook and bake, how to do laundry, how to change a diaper—not a good time, let me tell you. But I didn't mind it much, because I was helping my mom out by doing it all. But I had to grow up kinda fast because of it. Like, I never got the chance to learn to drive—not that we could really afford a second car if I did—and the amount of time I spent hanging out with my friends when there wasn't a baby-slash-toddler on the floor in front of us was pretty limited."

Leo's lips are slick with vodka that never made it all the way into his mouth and he talks with his hands, except not the hand that's resting on top of Toby's and Toby wonders if he even realizes this, if he even knows what he's doing to Toby.

"Heh. One time, I went to go pick Bobbie up from daycare after school—I think she was three or four then, so I must have been sixteen or seventeen—anyway, when I got there, her teacher told me she wasn't there, and hadn't been all day."

It's an interesting story, a really interesting story.

"So obviously, I freaked out. When I woke up that morning, she was totally fine. Like, not sick or anything. So I literally ran home, not thinking to call my mom because I was totally panicking, and when I opened the door, Bobbie was sitting on the floor of the living room, covered in my mom's make-up. Turned out my mother had a super late shift the night before and just did not wake up that morning to take Bobbie to—"

Toby wonders why Leo stopped talking, because he's interested in the story, and he wants to know more about him, about his past, so why isn't he saying anything? Why did he stop? Why did he stop?

Toby doesn't know until Leo's hand comes off of his and cups his face, and then it's like Toby snaps awake from a deep sleep, and he's kissing him, he's kissing him. Toby is kissing Leo, and Leo is kissing Toby back.

He must be so drunk, because what the fuck is he doing? After what Ariel told him, after the promise he made to himself—Steph is right outside, what is he—?

Toby puts his hands on Leo's shoulders and pushes him back, panting and drunk and out of his fucking mind.

"Sorry," Toby breathes.

Leo shakes his head and leans forward again, his nose bumping Toby's, his breath smelling of alcohol, his eyes half-lidded and his lips parted, parting, speaking words that Toby can't hear and he can't take it anymore and Toby's hand slides into Leo's hair and his legs are maneuvering themselves all on their own until he's—fuck, until he's straddling

Leo and what is he doing what is he doing, what is he doing, this is bad but it's so good.

Leo's skin is cool, it's always cool, but his mouth is hot. He must be twenty now, is one of the million thoughts that bounce off the walls of Toby's brain. It must be Sunday by now, Sunday, the twenty-eighth, his birthday. His mouth is hot, and his mouth is bitter like vodka, and Toby is already so so so drunk so he doesn't mind so much.

Leo's hair is soft and longer than Toby thought, and it feels nice in between Toby's fingers, it feels nice. It must feel nice for Leo too, when Toby tugs on the strands of his hair, because he sighs right into Toby's mouth, and Toby tastes the cranberry as if he had taken a sip of his own. This is good, this is so good, but it's so bad and he can't be doing this because it's so bad. Toby is horrified and pleased all at once when Leo's hands slip beneath his red t-shirt and his thumbs dip below his jeans and rub circles into his hips, stupid jeans, he should have worn sweatpants. No, fuck. And why is Leo doing this? Why is he letting this happen? He should be pushing Toby away, scrambling away from him, screaming in his face, because that's what Toby deserves. Why is Leo pretending to not know that, why is Leo pretending as though this is fine and good and right, how can he be pretending when Toby is doing this to him? Toby wonders if he's feeling faint for a moment, but no, they're moving, moving down, and then the back of his head hits the floor, and Leo is on top of him, and they're still kissing, until Leo moves his mouth away from Toby's and relocates to his jaw and his neck. What is Toby doing to him? What has Toby done?

"No. Stop," Toby pants, and it takes so much effort, and he tightens his grip in Leo's hair and tugs his head away from his neck so quickly that Toby's worried he might have hurt him, more than he already has.

"What's wrong?" Leo's voice is low and calm and smooth and whisper-y and it's not right, he should be screaming in Toby's face.

"I'm so sorry," Toby whimpers, covering his mouth with a quivering hand and bolting upright, narrowly avoiding bumping his forehead against Leo's. Why is he the one scooting away when he's the one that started it? Leo should be screaming in his face.

"It's okay. I liked it. It's okay."

No no no no no no no those are not the right words.

"I-I should—I should go." Toby jumps to his feet way too fast and he might fall, he's seeing stars. Are stars out at midnight? They must be because he's seeing them and they're everywhere.

"You're so drunk, wait," Leo says, and there's a bit of a laugh to his voice. Why. "Let me help—"

"I should go. I'm sorry. I'm sorry."

"Toby—"

Toby throws open the door and Steph is standing there, it's Steph, and she's smiling, and peeking her head into the room, saying Leo's name, happy birthday Leo, happy birthday.

Toby pushes past her I'm so sorry and runs to the door, tripping over his own feet, but nobody's looking because they're all looking for Leo I'm so sorry because it's Sunday, it's his birthday now. Except Ariel, she's glaring at him from somewhere, he's not quite sure where exactly, but he can feel it and he knows she probably knows everything that just happened I'm so so so sorry.

Toby can't drive, he knows he can't, so he just runs. He runs like Leo does. The cold is biting his face, tearing into his skin, and he wonders if it's blood that's dripping down his face, but he thinks that blood is warmer than that, it can't be blood, no matter how sharp the wind is. So he's running and running and running and everything is crashing down, going to shit around him, crumbling where he treads, but at least he's crying again.

Chapter 22

The next day, Toby wakes up sick with a stuffy nose, a splitting headache, and absolutely no memory of whatever happened the night before, post-ten o'clock. Including how the hell he managed to get home.

"Are you okay?" Reggie asks when Toby shuffles out of bed at noon, dragging his blanket along with him as if it were a cloak and he an elderly queen. Reg's tone is just questionable enough to the point where a tiny bit of panic spikes in Toby's chest.

"I am absolutely not," Toby answers, his nose completely backed up so he sounds like a gay Donald Duck. He opens the cabinet door to their over-the-counter stash, blindly feeling around for the painkillers as he rests his head on a neighboring cupboard.

"Yeah. I'm not sure why I asked. You look like shit."

"Thanks."

"Any time."

Toby's hand encases the all-too-familiar bottle of pills, only when he shakes it, there is no satisfying rattle. It's completely empty. He wants to slam his head against the cabinet but, for obvious reasons, he holds himself back. It's tempting, though.

"Why," he whispers. "Why. Would you. Put. An empty. Bottle. Back. Into. The cabinet."

"What do you mean, me?" Reggie asks from the couch, the mock surprise in his voice only incriminating him further. "Coulda been you."

"Reggie. Reginald. I know I can be lazy sometimes, but fuck, is it really that difficult to toss a bottle into the garbage?" Toby cries, which certainly does not help the jackhammering in his skull. "Literally—literally all you had to do is turn around and take three steps! Three goddamn steps to the trash can!"

"Okay, okay! Chill! I'm sorry!" Reg says, not sounding sorry at all. "I'll gladly go grab you some more, if you want."

"It's fine," Toby sighs, slinking back toward his room. "I'll take care of it myself."

"Uh, are you sure?"

"Mhm."

"Okay, but—are you sure sure? You really don't look so great—"

"Yeah, I get it Reg. It's fine. I could use some fresh air, anyway."

"Okay." There's a blissful moment of silence before Reggie speaks again, as Toby downs a large glass of much-needed water that he can barely taste. "So, I know you told me you were going to a party, so I knew that you'd be drinking," Reg says, "but I'll admit it, I did not think you had it in you to get as shit-faced as you were last night."

Toby nearly chokes on his water, and whirls around toward Reggie with wide eyes. "Wh-what did I do?"

Reg scoffs and shakes his head. "I mean, you were just a mess, dude. You were crying, and covered in sweat, but also, like, shivering. And you kept mumbling things I couldn't understand. It was super weird seeing you like that."

"Sorry," Toby groans, pressing his palm against his pounding forehead. "I shouldn't have had so much to drink. I didn't say anything embarrassing, right?"

"Nah. I couldn't understand anything that came out of your mouth, anyway."

Toby nods and takes a few steps back toward his bedroom, peeling off his rumpled shirt and jeans—jeez, he never wears jeans—and replacing them with a significantly more comfortable pair of joggers and a freshly laundered t-shirt. He steps into the bathroom to look at himself in the mirror—against his better judgement—and Reggie's right. He looks like the living embodiment of an on-fire garbage can. His face is pale and gaunt and dead-looking, his eyes sunken into his skin as a result of the purple abyss swimming below them, attributable to his horrendous sleep schedule. His hair—God, his hair creates a whole new definition for the word calamity. The longer he stares at his reflection, the higher the desperation to rip his gaze away from it grows. And yet, Toby can't find the strength to look elsewhere.

What does eventually draw him out of his trance is Reggie shouting the f-bomb rather loudly from somewhere else in the house. Toby rakes his fingers through his bed head twice, flicks off the light, and returns to the living room.

"What the hell?" he asks, rubbing his eyes. "What'd you do?"

"Fuckin' stubbed my toe," Reg groans from the couch, sitting with one foot propped up on his knee, examining said toe. "Hurt like a bitch."

"Are you bleeding?"

"Agh... no, I don't think so."

"Good, because the last thing we need is your blood staining the rug. I'm leaving."

"Pick up some band-aids, too, please. Just remembered we need some."

Toby steps out the apartment and is immediately hit with a cool breeze that, honestly, doesn't feel too terrible. Since it's nearing spring, the weather's warming up ever so slightly—though that is to say, the temperature is still probably somewhere around forty degrees. But it's fresh air, and that's all that matters to Toby at the moment.

He staggers over to his usual parking space, only to find... nothing. His car isn't there. But of course it wouldn't be, because Toby can hardly remember anything from last night, so obviously he was far too drunk to drive. Well, good for him for being responsible even when wasted. Bad for him that the convenience store is a good fifteen minute walk away, and even though Toby just decided he doesn't mind the weather all that much, it doesn't necessarily mean he'd be willing to walk through it for a lengthy period of time. Plus, his nose is already running, and this is only making it worse.

With a sigh, Toby bunches his jacket a little bit tighter and, with his arms folded over his chest and his hands squished in between his biceps and torso, makes his way over to the sidewalk.

There are other people walking, naturally, because he lives just off campus and many college students have no other choice. But they all seem used to the harsh wind and numb fingertips and red-tinted noses, which makes Toby feel even more alone and helpless. Even though he has no reason to. He's lucky he's got his car. Talk about privilege.

Toby blinks away the stinging tears that come to his eyes as a result of the wind blasting his face head on, and when his vision is no longer bleary, he can focus on what's right in front of him—which, incidentally, happens to be a... person in a hood jogging toward him, with seemingly no intent to dodge Toby, even as he draws nearer.

Toby quickly steps to the side, closer to the street, waiting for the person to barrel past him, yet again blinking tears away, but seconds later when his eyes are shut for less than a second, a hand wraps around his forearm.

"H-hey," Toby exclaims, yanking his arm away and stumbling back ever so slightly, his fight or flight activated.

(Flight is his default. He's never thrown a punch in his life, and he doesn't really wanna start now.)

"Sorry, I didn't mean to scare you." The person pulls the hood off their head, and—well, what do you know. The birthday boy himself.

"What are you doing here?" Toby asks, rubbing his arm where Leo had gripped it way too tight. "And why are you sprinting down the sidewalk?"

Leo blinks at him, as if confused by something Toby said, but then appears to shrug it off as he clears his throat and holds out the plastic bag he's holding. "I-I... um. Thought you might need this."

Toby furrows his eyebrows, but takes the bag and peeks inside.

Painkillers.

"Oh, thank God," Toby sighs, immediately popping the bottle open and tossing two into his mouth. "My head is pounding like crazy. How'd you know?"

"You were... so drunk last night. Don't you remember?"

Toby scoffs. "Dude, anything past ten o'clock is. Just. Like it never happened."

"...Really."

"Yeah... what, did I do something embarrassing?" Toby asks, his eyebrows rising up his forehead. "What did I do?"

Leo looks down at his feet, and Toby does too. He's shifting his weight from one foot to the other, as if debating on telling Toby some information that seems very fucking important.

"Um." Leo scratches the back of his neck and looks out toward the street. "I mean, you know... you were super out of it."

Toby might lose his mind. "What did I do?"

He's picturing the worst. Giving himself a stick and poke. Jumping off the balcony and into the pool, clothes on. Or off. Blowing up Steph's oven. Dancing in front of people.

Leo clears his throat again, but doesn't say anything. All Toby can do is watch in agony as he opens his mouth, waits for an excruciatingly long moment before saying the words that send Toby spiraling. "You kissed me."

Toby stands in shock as the memories, now shaken loose, begin to rush back in. It's not everything. He doesn't have the full picture when it comes to his train of thought or lack thereof or really much else besides the horrible truth. But the horrible truth in question is, probably, a million times worse than any of the other drunken mistakes he could have made.

"Oh, shit," Toby breathes, subconsciously clapping his hand over his mouth. "I—fuck. Fuck."

"Don't freak out," Leo pleads, reaching out toward him, but Toby is staggering back, his hand now on his forehead as if in an attempt to calm the thoughts racing within his brain. (It doesn't work.) "It's not a big deal, really—"

"It is a big deal!" Toby whisper-shouts so as to not grab the attention of any passersby. "Fuck, Leo—it's a big fucking deal!"

"Look, you were drunk—you can't blame yours—"

"You—you kissed me back!" Toby hisses jabbing an accusatory finger at Leo's chest. "I remember that, you—you know you cheated on her, Leo, with me. For real this time. Fuck!"

"It was a mistake, okay?" Leo groans, entangling his fingers in his hair. "Just—don't disappear on me again. Please. We should talk about this."

"Fuck." Toby's knees buckle, and he sinks downward until he's left sitting on his haunches with his face hidden in his hands. "God, what is wrong with me."

"Toby—c'mon, just get up. We'll—we'll go somewhere to talk. The cafe, or the library, or wherever you want—"

"Does she know?"

"She—what?"

"Does Steph know? Did she see?"

"Uh... I don't think so."

Somehow, that just makes Toby feel infinitely worse. Maybe because if she had, if she had seen, the crushing pressure to own up and apologize wouldn't be another weight on Toby's shoulders. Fuck.

"Shit." Toby pushes his hair back, returning to his upright position on wobbly legs. "Fuck."

"Come on. Let's get out of the cold, and—and go somewhere. It's not the end of the world, despite what you might think. And it's not like she ever has to find out, either."

"I don't want to be a fucking—homewrecker, Leo," Toby says, pinching the bridge of his nose. "I'm not emotionally stable enough to cope with the fact that I might be the reason you two separate."

"What if you are the reason?" Leo snaps. Toby's eye twitches. "What if you are?"

"What are you talking about?"

"I'm going to—I'm gonna break up with her."

Toby can't help the scoff that escapes his throat. "Yeah, okay. You've had several opportunities to do that, and you wimped out for every single one of them."

"Well, I'm going to do it this time," Leo growls. "Tomorrow. I'm gonna break up with her."

"And you're saying it's because of me? Fantastic."

"Not—not because of you, but—you are the reason."

Toby furrows his eyebrows. "I'm not following."

"You—ugh." Leo rakes his fingers through his hair and spins on his heel to where his back is facing Toby, and after a few moments, completes the full rotation. "Just don't go back on strike."

Toby shakes his head. "I'm not promising anything."

"Toby—"

"Ariel was right when she said I should stay away from you until you've sorted things out. I'm only causing you more harm than good."

"That's not true."

"It is true, Leo. Did you hear yourself? You just said you were going to break up with your perfectly happy girlfriend because of what I did. You weren't saying stuff like that yesterday, or the day before, or the day before that."

"Well, that's because I'm a loser," Leo sighs, "and too much of a baby to take care of things before they get more chaotic."

"And you're saying I somehow changed that."

"Yes."

Toby squeezes his eyes shut and presses his palms against his forehead. "I can't do this right now," he says.

"If you don't believe me, then come with me," says Leo. "I'll break up with her in front of you, if that's what you fucking want."

"Jesus, I'm not doing that—what do you think I am, a sadist?"

"I'm not going to bring you into it. I won't even mention your name. She won't have any idea what's happened."

"So you're just gonna keep it all a secret? You're never gonna tell her?"

"I—no, I wasn't really planning on it. It's not like I want to break her heart."

Toby shakes his head. "You already have, Leo, even if you don't realize it. I have to go. I'm too hungover for this."

"Don't just leave. Can we please talk about this somewhere else?"

"I have to go," Toby repeats, turning around and heading back to the apartment.

"Your car's still at Steph's," Leo calls out from behind him.

"I'll get it later."

"Toby—"

"Please just leave me alone."

With that, Toby breaks into a jog in order to get away from there as fast as he possibly can, even though it makes his eyes burn even more. Only when he gets to the door and looks back out at the empty sidewalk does he remember he has yet to tell Leo happy birthday.

Chapter 23

Toby, shamefully, begins to think that maybe he didn't really mean it when he asked Leo to leave him alone. Because days pass, and then weeks. Weeks. And the most he's come into contact with Leo is seeing the back of his head every Tuesday and Friday during their calculus class.

All of a sudden, it's the end of March. Goddamn March. April begins next week. Spring has arrived, the weather has gotten a bit sunnier and a bit warmer, and finals are beginning to rear their ugly heads as they loom just around the corner. Good news, spring break is the week after next. Bad news, Toby has, like, four exams before then. One of which is calculus. And without Leo, he is beyond unprepared. He's beyond screwed.

Leo. Leo hasn't spoken a word to Toby since his birthday. He hasn't sent a single message. He hasn't even mailed a single letter via pigeon to Toby's window. Absurd.

Of course, though, Toby had asked for this, and Leo is only respecting his wishes. He has to keep reminding himself of that. Really, he should be happy. Because that's one less issue he has to deal with for the time being. Life can go back to being only mildly chaotic, as it was months ago.

But, still, not even one pigeon?

Toby's not staring at Leo, who is slumped in his seat and fiddling with a Rubik's Cube, and he's not focusing in on his hands and fingers, long and slender and nimble, as the professor ends the class early and the students around him rise from their seats all at once. He also doesn't notice Leo's shoulders rise and fall, or his neck crane back against his chair to reveal a bored, possibly even disappointed expression painted on his face, and he most certainly does not make eye contact with him for what must be a whole of a nanosecond before Leo instantly snaps his head back up.

"Jesus, just go ahead and ask him out, already," a voice snickers into Toby's ear, and he just about jumps out of his skin.

"Excuse me?" he says, whirling around to see a girl with faded pink hair, vicious eyeliner, and black lipstick smirking up at him (not unlike how Leo used to do), her laptop closed and propped up on her hip.

"You stare at him literally every day we have class," she says, gesturing back to Leo with her eyes, who is now literally running out the door. "I definitely love a good unrequited love story, but this? Excessive pining? Eh, it's going a little too far for my taste. It's kinda getting painful to watch."

"Uh." Toby is so taken aback, it takes him far too long to think of a single cohesive thing to say. "S-sorry, do I know you?"

"Loretta," the girl tells him. "Pretty sure we've met once."

"Oh. Oh, right, at the—yeah. The thing at Jordan's. Right?"

"Yeah, that's it."

There's an awkward, lingering silence that lasts for way too long.

"Um. Anyway." Toby clears his throat and pushes his chair back. "I don't—I think you've got the wrong idea. I have to go now."

"Wait. Sorry." Her hand clutches onto Toby's sleeve as he stands and takes a step, and when he raises his eyebrows at her, she releases him and drops her hand, which slaps her thigh as it falls slack. "Sorry. I didn't mean to, like, offend you. I shouldn't have butted into your business. That was rude of me."

Uh, yeah. "It's fine. But I actually have to go. I have work."

He doesn't, not until six. But it's still technically not a lie, so he's rolling with it.

"Right. Sorry."

She steps aside so he can pass her, but before he can get even four steps in, he sighs and turns back around to face her. He sucks in a breath and asks, "Wh-what makes you think I'm pining after him?" Because he's not. "Because I'm not."

The corners of her lips hint upwards, and she shrugs. "Well, you pay more attention to him than you do the professor. You constantly glance at your phone and, like, hover your thumbs over the keyboard while you stare at his head. Underneath one of the jots you wrote today, you typed—and I quote—'I don't know what any of this means, but Leo probably would, so maybe quit being a baby and talk to him.'"

Toby wants to die. "I-I did not write that," he sputters, averting her eyes.

He did, in fact, write that. Verbatim.

"Uh-huh," Loretta says, biting her tongue as an even wider and more wicked smirk slithers onto her face. "Whatever you say."

"Look, I'm not—this isn't some romcom, cliché, unrequited love story, or whatever you called it earlier," Toby mutters, looking down just in case there are any traces of red on his face. "He and I are friends. Sort of. We're—we're kinda not talking right now, though. So that's it. That's all there is to it."

"Okay. Sure. But I'll just say this: I definitely don't look at my friends like that."

"Well, everybody's different. Also, don't you—you sit behind me. How would you even know how I look at him?"

"Call it my sixth sense," she says. "I've got a nose for sniffing out heartache."

"It's not—"

"Right. Not heartache." She raises a hand, palm facing out, fingers spread apart. "My bad."

Toby sighs, and pinches the bridge of his nose. "All right, I'm really leaving now."

"'Kay. See you around."

"Yeah."

Toby descends the stairs, eager to get away from this girl (who allowed her to be so nosy?), but just as he approaches the front of the hall (maybe he's just salty because she was right), he notices something colorful out of the corner of his eye, right about where Leo sits.

He glances up at Loretta, who appears to be focused on something on her phone, and takes a few tentative steps toward the spot. There, on the floor, is Leo's unsolved Rubik's Cube.

Toby might laugh. Maybe he does a little bit. Because this is just too unbelievable—something actually coming full circle? Toby actually being given two loose ends he can actually tie up, all neat and pretty like a bow? There's just no way.

He reaches out and picks up the Rubik's Cube. Holy fuck, this isn't a delusion.

"What's up?" Loretta asks from where she still stands, a few levels up. "You okay?"

"Great," Toby croaks, and shit, he might actually be telling the truth. "Uh. Bye."

Toby shoves the Cube into his pocket and tries his best not to sprint out the door.

So, Toby's plan to reunite Leo with his Rubik's Cube and use it as an excuse to talk to him, maybe would be a teensy bit easier to actually execute if he knew where Leo was at the moment. Because he doesn't.

It's Friday, so as far as Toby knows, Leo doesn't have a class right now. Which doesn't exactly narrow down his options. In fact, he's probably at home, minding his own business, which is great and all—except Toby has no idea where Leo's home is, so he can't exactly go there to scout him out. Also, it's a bit creepy. And Toby is not that desperate.

Not that he's desperate in the first place. But there is still a line, whether he is or not.

So Toby decides on the next best thing: To ask someone. And the first and pretty much only person that comes to mind is Steph.

He tries not to think about it too much as he makes his way toward her apartment. He also tries not to get his hopes up when the possibility that maybe she's not home forms as a thought in his brain. He knows he has no right to go and ask her; in fact, he hates that he's stooping this low. This seems like an asshole-y thing to do. And he's not an asshole. At least, not anymore.

Maybe... he could use this opportunity to apologize. Because the guilt is still weighing on him every day, constantly there as a storm cloud above his head, popping into his mind when he has nothing else to think about. It would be nice to finally get rid of it and have his peaceful, boring life back. But of course, he'll have to make the apology vague. Because if he says too much, then that could lead to disaster between Steph and Leo, and Toby definitely doesn't want or need another thing to feel guilty about. He's not sure how exactly to go about that, so. If it does end up happening today, it'll be on a whim. He's still not entirely sure whether or not luck is on his side at the moment. He's learned never to assume.

Toby fiddles with the Rubik's Cube in his pocket as he climbs the stairs to Steph's place, his throat suddenly dry and his hands very clammy. No, he definitely is an asshole. What the hell does he think he's—

"What are you doing here?"

Toby's head snaps up, and Steph is standing there in the doorway, her arms folded across her chest, her jaw set in a very un-Steph-like expression.

"H-hey," Toby mumbles, his Rubik-less hand coming up to rub the back of his neck. "Uh, good to see you again."

Toby waits for a smile. A greeting. Anything. Anything? But she doesn't budge, and instead repeats, "What are you doing here?"

Toby clears his throat. "So, um, I was wondering—uh, do you know where Leo is right now? I—I need to return something to him."

She stares at him, her amber eyes widening ever so slightly. "You're asking me?"

Fuck. What the hell is wrong with him? "Uh. Sorry. I just—I didn't know, and figured you probably would—he and I aren't really talking right now, so—uh. Sorry. I didn't—sorry. I'm sorry for bothering you."

Toby squeezes his eyes shut as if that will cleanse his body of the mortification that seems to be pumping through his veins at the moment. He makes to turn and, if he can manage to without making even more of a fool of himself, just run away. But before he gets that chance, Steph's hand grasps his arm, and she utters a cool "Wait."

Toby faces her again, though his eyes decide to focus on the door hinge rather than her face. "Do you not know?" she asks.

Toby blinks. "Not know... what?"

"What happened."

God, there is so much she could possibly be talking about. "Uh... I don't think so."

He spares a glance up at her, and she's biting the inside of her cheek, shifting her weight as if debating on actually enlightening him. Then, her voice soft and weak, she says, "Leo and I broke up."

Holy fucking shit sweet mother of Jesus God save the fucking Queen.

"Really?" Toby squeaks, and fuck, he sounds way too excited. He's not. But he sounds that way. "Wait—actually?"

"Yes."

"Wh-when?"

"Night of his birthday. He told me he couldn't 'do it' anymore."

Holy shit.

He actually did it.

"Oh," Toby says, doing his best to tame the utter shock he feels invading his every word. "Uh. Sorry."

Steph stares at him for a moment, and then shakes her head. "He told me everything, Toby."

Holy shit.

Toby's eyes go wide as Steph's expression remains stoic and bleak. "Everything?" he asks in an accidental whisper.

She nods. "Everything."

Toby doesn't know whether he wants to jump over the balcony or pump his fist. He decides not to do either because both would probably lead to more issues for Steph and God knows he's definitely caused enough of those.

"Oh," he says instead. "I-I see."

Steph sighs, and leans against the door frame. "I don't know whether I want to laugh at you or hit you right now."

"Either is fine," Toby blurts without thinking.

Steph scoffs, shaking her head. She opens her mouth as if she's going to say something, but apparently can't find the words, so she just swallows instead.

"Look, it's—it's really mostly my fault," Toby mumbles sheepishly, shoving both of his hands into his pockets and rocking back and forth on his heels. "I—I kissed him at the party without his permission, so if you blame him for that—"

"It's not just that," Steph says, her voice wobbly, sending Toby's heart plunging into the pit of his stomach. "He told me about before then, too. That stupid game you guys played or whatever, when he—" She gives a watery, incredulous scoff. "When that idiot thought we were broken up after that one stupid fight."

"Oh. Yeah." Toby curls his hands into fists, uncurls them, curls them, uncurls them. "When all that happened—yeah. I thought he was single."

Steph looks up at him, her eyes glistening with tears. Fuck, Toby is such an asshole.

"You know," she says, clearing her throat and immediately looking away, "I think I knew I wasn't making him happy."

Toby bites the inside of his lip. He doesn't know how to respond to that.

"I mean, Leo's a good guy. He's kind and supportive and—and way too much of a wimp to speak his mind," she continues. "I wish he'd told me he was confused beforehand. I would have done my best to help him through it."

Of course she would have. Because she's Steph, and she's too good for either of them. They are both assholes.

"I don't appreciate what he did behind my back, and I-I can't forgive it just yet. But I do know that when he's around you, he's more himself than he is with me. You fit him way better than I ever did."

Toby almost chokes on his spit. "I—do?"

"And Leo knows it too. He's had a difficult time coming to terms with it, but... he definitely knows. I think you can help him get through this identity struggle he's going through. Honestly. You're... probably the best man for the job."

Toby doesn't know what to say. He's half considering that maybe he's not even hearing her right. Because she should be—she should be screaming at him. There should be a red hand print painted on his cheek. That's what he deserves, not these gentle words that are coming out of her mouth.

"Steph," he says. "I'm—I don't—"

"He's at the art gallery right now," she tells him, pushing off of the door frame and allowing her arms to fall to her sides. "You two should probably have a little chat."

Toby buffers for a moment, unsure as to how he should process this information.

"W-wait," he stutters. "Wait, I thought he only worked there on Saturdays."

"It's... a special occasion. You may want to stop at home and change into something a bit nicer. Try to be there for five."

"Wh—"

"And just so you know, I don't hate you, Toby," she says, her hand resting on the edge of the door, preparing to push it closed. "I don't even really blame you for anything. This probably would have happened eventually, whether you were in the picture or not. I just need time to think."

"Oh—yeah. Of course." He clears his throat. "Um. Thanks. For not hating me."

She smiles sadly at him and closes the door.

Chapter 24

So, after deep consideration, Toby has decided that maybe he is living in a real-life romcom, because at the moment, he is partaking in one of the most infamous clichés that goes like something along the lines of "chasing after your dream man because you just realized how you truly feel about him, so quick, go, before it's too late."

Not that Leo is Toby's, quote unquote, "dream man."

But, like, not that he's not.

So basically, fuck his life.

But... not just yet. In case things go well.

Another thing about the end of March is that daylight savings time is back in business again (thank goodness), so it's not remotely dark when Toby arrives at the gallery around 5:15. A little bit later than what Steph suggested, but it wasn't his fault that Reggie chose tonight to have a meltdown about his upcoming gymnastics competition, and basically clung to Toby for upwards of twenty minutes before Toby finally managed to peel him off and get his ass out the door. So. He just hopes it doesn't affect much.

He doesn't even know what's going on here. What's the "special occasion?"

Toby has no idea, but when he climbs out of the car and sees a man in a steamed suit with a lace-adorned woman on his arm, he understands why Steph advised dressing nicely. Although, he wasn't aware she meant this nice. So all he did was throw on a white button down and a pair of black slacks, shirt untucked, and call it a day. He didn't think this would be a tie kind of deal.

Whatever. He rarely wears anything other than sweat-pants. Nobody should expect much more from him, anyway.

Toby enters the gallery after the gussied up couple and sees the same woman—Sophie, if he's remembering cor-rectly—that had been there the night before Leo's birthday, which seems like an eternity and a half ago. She glances up at him from whatever she's jotting down onto a sticky note and smiles through her red lips.

"Hello again," she greets kindly. "It's been quite a while."

Toby honestly didn't even think she'd remember him. "Uh, yeah," he mumbles, restraining himself from shoving his hands into his pockets. "I was just wondering—what's hap-pening here tonight?"

"You don't know?"

"Ah... no, not really. Someone just. Told me to come."

"I see. Well, we're having a bit of an unveiling of sorts for a certain painting," she explains. "The ceremony's already begun, but you shouldn't have a problem sneaking in there. It's just around the corner, and to your left."

"Oh. Thank you."

"Enjoy, darling."

An unveiling... so what would Leo be hired for tonight? Like... serving food and drinks?

Toby follows Sophie's instructions, which leads him to a large set of oak doors that he squeezes through, not paying much mind to the sign out front that... well, it probably would have given him a few more details than he has. But he's already past the doors and there are a buttload of people in here, so to walk back out would be way too embarrassing. So. He's still going into this almost completely blind.

The main hall is giant, with its high ceilings and distant walls and sleek wooden floors. People in suits and ties and dresses and blazers are swarmed around a very large painting, which is currently concealed by a velvet curtain, as they listen to someone speak whom Toby can only assume is the artist. He doesn't pay much attention to their speech, considering his head is fully set on scouring the crowd and placing that lone-dimpled face. But there's way too many people here. In a moment of desperation, Toby genuinely considers pulling aside a gallery worker or caterer and asking where Leo is. Which terrifies him.

Luckily, though, something stops him from going through with that horrifying thought—a hand grasped very tightly around his arm (Jesus, what is this, the third time today?) that drags him away from the crowd and toward the wall opposite the painting.

When his arm is released and Toby can properly process what just happened/is about to happen, he turns toward Leo, an entire, improvised speech of his own on his tongue, only—

Only it's not Leo.

It's Ariel.

And now Toby is stuck in possibly the most terrifying situation he's ever been stuck in. Probably even scarier than accidentally-on-purpose coming out to Reggie.

"What are you doing here?" Ariel growls.

"I—I came to see him," Toby responds quietly. "Steph told me he was here."

Her eyes seem to bug out of her head. "You asked her? After what you did?"

"I didn't know they broke up until after, okay? You can get off my back."

"He hasn't spoken to you in a month."

"I know that. That's why I came."

"You're gonna ruin everything."

"Can you just chill out for like, ten seconds?" Toby hisses, rubbing his face. "Jesus, you exhaust me, and I don't even know you."

"Well, I know enough about you to know that you being here, uninvited, isn't a good situation," she says. "Just leave before you start something."

"I'm not a fucking stick of dynamite, Ariel. I don't go blowing shit up as if it's all I'm good for."

"Just—"

"I know you're trying to be a good friend," Toby whispers sharply, glancing around to ensure they aren't drawing attention away from the speaker. "I know you just want to protect him. But I swear to God, I am not here to cause trouble. I know I've fucked up—maybe not quite to the extent that you might think I have, but still. All I want to do is talk to him."

She sighs, and crosses her arms over her chest. "The last thing he needs right now is a distraction."

"Can you just tell me where he is?"

"What do you mean, tell you?"

"What else would I mean?"

"Are you—" Her eyebrows jump up, and she hides a scoff with her hand. "Wow, you're actually not joking right now."

Toby is so tired. Good God.

"You're telling me—you came here, and you don't know?" she snickers.

"Know what?"

"Use your eyes, genius."

She plants a hand on each of Toby's shoulders and physically turns him toward the painting and the audience. He shoots a confused glare at her, *What the fuck am I supposed to be looking at right now*, and she rolls her eyes and gives him a rough push, lurching him forwards.

Toby rolls his shoulder as he creeps up to meet the back of the crowd, eyes narrow, scanning for Leo's smallish frame among the sea of people. When he doesn't find him, he shoots more daggers back at Ariel, and she quite literally smacks her forehead with one hand and gestures to the painting with the other.

Toby's shoulders sag as he follows the invisible dotted line between her finger and the wall, and when he pushes himself up on his tippy toes just to make sure he isn't missing something, they tense right back up again.

Because the person giving the speech in front of the veiled painting, a microphone in one hand while he fumbles with cue cards in the other, dressed up in a dusty blue suit that compliment his eyes painfully well, is Leo.

Toby whips his head around to look at Ariel yet again, but she's disappeared from her spot against the back wall and relocated somewhere else, probably somewhere in the crowd, a decent distance away from Toby.

Toby is right at the cusp of six feet tall, which more often than not he is exceedingly thankful for. But even now, as he stands all the way at the back of the crowd, everyone else seems to tower over him, whether they're men, women, anyone, heels or no heels, boots or no boots. And Leo being—what, five foot seven? Yeah, that's not really helping either. They probably should have gotten him a platform or something to stand on. He looks miniature, considering that Toby can only see him from the nose up without anything impeding his vision.

So, Toby pulls the douchiest move possible and attempts to push his way through the crowd. Just a little bit. Just so he can see Leo in all his nervous, blue-eyed, shaky glory.

"I'm sorry," Toby whispers as he squeezes past a few individuals. "I'm so sorry, I just—'scuse me, I'm sorry."

Toby tries to ignore the indignant scoffs or the grumbling or that one elderly lady that stomps on his foot on purpose, and follows up with, "Damn brat."

He... kind of succeeds. So. That's what matters.

Once Toby decides he has found a satisfactory enough position, one that allows him to view Leo almost in his entirety, he both stares at him and actually listens to the words coming out of his mouth. Toby has never hated himself for being fifteen minutes late to something more than he does right now.

"Daniela meant—means—a lot to me," Leo's saying, and Toby is enthralled immediately. "There isn't a day that goes by where I—um. Where I don't think about her, and miss her, and mourn her and the chance at living a f-fulfilled life, of—of which she was robbed. So. Um. This piece... I guess you could say it..."

A chill rattles Toby's spine as Leo's eyes lock onto his, blue blue blue, seemingly more so than usual because of the suit. Dear God, the suit. Formal wear is tolerable—no, it's favorable—when Leo is the one in it.

Toby doesn't even realize that Leo has trailed off until he rips his gaze away, leaving Toby blinking—a lot—and with a weird swelling feeling in his chest. Leo clears his throat.

"S-sorry," he mumbles. "I—I spaced out for a second."

A collective, good-natured chuckle ripples through the crowd—excluding Toby. Leo clears his throat again. "So. Um. I-I guess you could say this piece is the result of my grief, guilt, and pain. It's... my catharsis. And I know that its existence doesn't make everything okay, it doesn't undo what has been done." Leo looks down and swallows. He's not reading off the cards in his hand anymore. "But the fact that it's here, about to be revealed and put on display for people to see... that means something. I'm not quite sure what, yet. I've never been good with words. But. I'm pretty sure it's a good thing." He lifts his head up, makes eye contact with Toby for a fraction of a second, and then looks out at the rest of the crowd. "So... with that, I guess... I present, Mariposa."

The curtain drops, and Toby is already attempting to process everything he just heard, but—wow. Toby can't help the small gasp that comes from his mouth, but it doesn't really matter much because his own is drowned out by those of the other guests.

The painting is... well, Toby can't even think of a proper word to describe it without coming up with something that degrades its actual beauty. The focal point—Toby thinks he's using that term correctly, but he is definitely not an artist—is a young girl with long brown hair, maybe around ten years old, if Toby had to guess, surrounded by a swarm of butterflies unlike any that Toby had ever seen before, with wings of her own attached to her back. There's a smile on her face and, even though it's a stationary image, Toby thinks that there is pure joy shining in her—her eyes. Her hydrangea-blue eyes.

Toby looks back at Leo, knowing his jaw must be touching the floor right now, but Leo doesn't see him. He's staring at his own creation, blinking a lot, as if fighting back tears. Toby has to hold himself back from fighting his way through the hoard of people and toppling him right then and there.

"So. Um." Leo's voice is shaky still, and much quieter than it had been before. He clears his throat and continues, "Dan loved butterflies. When she—when we were kids, really little, she used to tell me that she wanted to be one when she grew up." The audience chuckles again, and a sad smile of Leo's own makes it way onto his face. "Unfortunately, she never got to accomplish that dream, so. This—I know it doesn't do her justice. But I wanted to at least see that dream of hers fulfilled, and this was the best way I could think of how to do that. Thank you."

Everybody erupts into applause, and Leo takes a hesitant bow as an elderly man makes his way to the front and pats him on the back, taking the microphone in his hand and beginning to speak words that sound garbled in Toby's ear. He can't rip his gaze off of Leo, and when he begins to slip away, Toby nearly trips over his own feet trying to get to him.

God, there are so many people here. Too many. Toby really feels like he's living in a romcom now.

"Sorry. Sorry. Excuse me." It's the same game as before, only with less angry grandmas, and instead of Toby fighting his way to the front of the crowd, he's trying to fight his way out. Don't get him wrong. He would love to stand and stare at Leo's painting all day long, just like the rest of these people, but. Leo. Leo is what matters most to him right now.

When he's finally managed to escape the sea of black-tied art snobs (and some college students he's seen around campus that he thinks are probably only here for the free food), he sees Leo standing about ten feet away, having what looks like a very intense discussion with Ariel. He's swinging his hands, more so than usual, and her arms are folded tightly across her chest, as if bound there. Toby stands still for a moment, watching them, and then Leo glances up and catches his eye. So now, Toby really has only one choice, which is to simply go for it.

Leo just stares at him as he draws closer and closer, and Toby stares right back, adrenaline or something like that pumping through his veins, his heartbeat thrumming in his ears. He only blinks when he's come to a halt in front of Leo, before looking down at his feet as the routine warmth rushes to his cheeks. He opens his mouth, unsure of what might end up coming out and willing to just roll with it, but Ariel interrupts him.

"What are you doing?" she snaps.

Toby looks everywhere except directly in front of him and doesn't answer.

"Look, just do us all a favor and—"

"Go away, Ariel."

Ariel and Toby jerk their heads toward Leo simultaneously, who is still boring his gaze into Toby.

"What?" Ariel asks, looking morbidly offended. Toby folds his lips inward to keep from smiling. "Leo—"

"I need to talk to him," Leo says, finally looking in her direction. "Privately."

"But—"

Leo lets out a huff of breath, and before Toby can really process anything, seizes Toby's wrist and begins to drag him away, out of the hall. Toby is very tempted to look back at

Ariel and flip her off as they round a corner, but he's more mature than that.

Barely.

The ambient noise of the chattering guests dies down the further they walk, their own mouths clamped shut. Toby's heart is racing, and he wonders if Leo can feel it in his wrist. Probably. Honestly, he can probably hear it right now, considering Toby's pretty sure it's about as loud as a jackhammer.

They finally come to a halt in front of an abstract painting, hanging up alongside various others in a secluded area of the gallery. Toby glances at the little plaque below it. Chaos. Toby might laugh.

"I thought you wanted me to leave you alone," Leo says quietly, his eyes right back on Toby's. Piercing. Assertive.

"I know," Toby replies, his voice at an equally low volume. "I know I said that. But I was... upset. And I shouldn't have gotten so angry at you. I'm sorry."

Leo bites the inside of his cheek. "So why are you here now?"

Toby opens his mouth, closes it, then plunges his hand into his right pocket. "You—you forgot this today."

He withdraws the Rubik's Cube from where it's been hidden all night, and holds it out to Leo. Toby's honestly surprised that his hand isn't trembling. Weird.

"Oh, jeez." Leo takes the Cube and holds it as if it's his most prized possession. "Thank you. I was looking for this earlier, and nearly had a breakdown when I couldn't find it."

"Yeah, no problem."

Leo scoffs and shakes his head, beginning to fiddle with the Rubik's Cube. "I was so nervous about tonight. I couldn't focus all day. This thing was my only source of distraction."

Toby watches the Cube in his hands for a few moments before looking upward and seeing a ghost of a smile resting on Leo's lips. Toby clears his throat and it hurts to see the smile fade.

"Your painting is beautiful," he says. "I knew you were an artist, but. Really, I was... blown away."

Leo looks down at the Cube again. "Oh. Thanks."

Toby crosses his arms and shifts his weight from one foot to another. "I... got here a little late, so I didn't get to hear your entire speech," he admits. "Um. Is she—that girl in the painting—is she someone you know?"

Leo sighs, stows the Rubik's Cube away into one of the suit's inside pockets, and reaches up to mess with his hair. Toby, for some reason, really admires the fact that he didn't seem to bother putting any effort into making it look any different than normal.

"She was," Leo says. Toby watches his Adam's apple bob up and down as he swallows. "Dan was... my twin sister. She died. About ten years ago."

Toby's arms come unfolded in sync with the sinking of his heart. "Oh... I didn't..."

"It's fine."

"I'm sorry."

Leo shakes his head, then waves Toby's sympathy off, and then rubs his eyes and shakes his head again. He glances up to meet Toby's eyes, and when Toby expects him to look away again, he doesn't.

"Is the Rubik's Cube the only reason you came?" he asks softly. "Or did you track me down for something else?"

Toby blushes. "I'm... sorry," he mumbles, scratching the back of his head. "Just. For a lot of things."

"Yeah. Me too."

"You don't hate me, do you?"

"I feel like I should be the one asking you that question."

Toby chuckles awkwardly. "I'll say no if you do."

Leo cracks a small smile, actually showing teeth. "I do not hate you, Toby Wentworth," he declares, rocking on his heels.

Toby smiles too. "I don't hate you either."

"Glad that's settled, then."

"Yeah."

Toby thinks the sexual tension wafting throughout the room is just about to drive him up the wall if he doesn't do something about it soon.

"So," he begins, planting his feet and stowing his hands in his pockets to resist fidgeting. "I... heard you're single now."

Leo looks startled for a second, as if having forgotten so himself, but he regains composure rather quickly. He clears his throat.

"I am," he says. Then, after a moment's hesitation, "You gonna do something about that?"

Toby feels like he's just been slammed in the chest by a dozen anvils. But, like, a dozen anvils made out of, like, romance instead of metal. Give him a break, he can't think straight. His heart begins to bang around against his ribcage, more so than it already had been. And he also thinks maybe you could fry an egg on his cheek if you tried, because damn. He can hear the sizzling already.

"I-I'm sure they're looking for you," he says, even though that's not what he wanted to say. "Since it's. You know. Your event, and all."

Leo raises an eyebrow. "Maybe they are."

"Should we go back?"

"Maybe."

Good lord. Toby can't do this anymore.

He takes a step closer to Leo, and Leo stands his ground. So Toby takes another baby step, and then leans in until his face only a few inches from Leo's.

"Hey," he says. Leo's eyes are blue, hydrangea blue, the color of the flowers in his mom's garden back home.

"Hm."

"Are you sure you're single this time?" Toby asks through a whisper. He can't help but smile when he hears the breathy little laugh from within Leo's throat.

"Positive," Leo says, and that's it. That's Toby's word of affirmation, and all it takes for him to close his eyes and the gap between them.

This kiss is... wow. For a brief second, it's just wow, because that's all that Toby can think. Technically speaking, it really shouldn't be all that different from any other kiss, because it's just the usual. The routine press of mouth against mouth, lips against lips, eventually and inevitably the slightest amount of tongue against tongue. But this one, this kiss—the reason it's something entirely new, something un-like any of the kisses that Toby and Leo have shared before is because this kiss—this kiss is a sober kiss. A welcomed kiss. An intentional kiss. An innocent kiss. A kiss they could do all over again if they wanted to, because now they can.

When they separate, it's the hardest thing Toby thinks he's ever had to do. His hand is on Leo's face—when it got there, he doesn't know—and Leo is gripping onto the bottom of Toby's shirt as if his sanity depends on it. Toby thinks his probably depends on it, too.

"You're right. They probably are looking for me," Leo breathes, yet tightening his hold on Toby's shirt. "Are you gonna stay?"

Toby opens his mouth. I have work in half an hour.

But Toby can't go to work right now. He just can't. So.

"Yeah," he says, leaning in again, maybe involuntarily. "I'll stay as long as you want me to."

Leo accepts the second kiss without hesitation, though it's chaster, quicker, less explosive than the last one. But that's all right. That's perfectly fine. After, Leo's head falls forward against Toby's shoulder and his arms wrap around his waist. Toby returns the embrace, looping his arms around Leo's neck and pressing a kiss to the top of his head. He's happy.

I need you to take my shift at 6

You mean, 6, as in less than half an hour from now, 6?

yeah

Uhhh kind of late notice. Why can't you do it?

something came up

??

please

Ohhhhh, mayhaps is it something to do with your boy drama?

you know, you owe me one after your little escape to new york

Deflecting the question, i see. But I guess i do. Be safe. Don't do anything I wouldn't do. Use protection!!

oh my god

A bad tv drama, Toby, I'm telling you. Everyone will say it's garbage and bash on it mercilessly till the end of time, but those same exact people will kick back and eat that shit up with a bowl of popcorn for every episode you release. It's a decent thing to consider, man. I mean, you've already got me on the edge of my seat.

Chapter 25

Early June..

"What's this?" Leo takes the papers in his hands, reads the title, and looks up at Toby with one cocked eyebrow. "Something you wrote?"

Toby has to physically restrain himself from snatching the papers back and taking cover beneath Leo's blanket. He suddenly has the overwhelming urge to crawl out of his skin.

"Your birthday gift," he mutters sheepishly, looking off to the side.

Damn it, he can hear Leo smile. "You mean, the birthday I had four months ago?"

"Yeah. I didn't—I didn't get a chance to give it to you then, and then we didn't talk for, like, a month, and then I got distracted by... everything." He clears his throat. "So. There it is."

He caves and glances up at Leo, who is smiling from ear to ear.

"I'm just messing with you," he says, beginning to flip through the stapled pages. "Is this that story you wrote?'

"Yeah." Toby shoves his hands in his pockets, then takes them back out because that's an awkward thing to do sitting down and crosses his arms instead. "Except, it's not nearly as bad as it was when I turned it in," he assures Leo. "I worked my ass off editing and revising once I heard your birthday was coming up, because... I wanted you to be able to read it after pestering me about it so much. Actually, last weekend when I remembered I still hadn't given it to you, I went over it again, and emailed a copy to my creative writing professor. She said she was sorry this wasn't the paper I turned in, because it's significantly better than the last. So. Now I finally have the guts to let you read it."

Leo awwws at him as if he's a puppy learning to sit, and then ruffles the hair on top of his head as if he's finally understood how. Toby doesn't hate it.

"You're so sweet," Leo says, and presses a kiss to Toby's cheek. Toby definitely doesn't hate that either, but that doesn't stop him from blushing like an absolute fool, despite the fact that they've been going out for two months now. Already. God, maybe time still isn't.

"Cora knew her ocean to be green. Not blue, vivid and rich as a sapphire, and not turquoise either, the color of the sea glass that lined her ocean floor. But green. Venom green, dark and toxic and grotesque, as if the—"

"Okay, that's enough," Toby says, sticking his hand out over the paper to stop Leo's narration. "I know this is my gift to you and I wrote it, but please don't read it in front of me.

And, like, don't ever talk to me about it. I don't think I'll be able to handle it."

Leo tilts his head. "Why?"

"I—I don't know. It's weird, for me. I guess. Makes me feel weird."

"C'mon. What if I think it's really good?"

"Then I appreciate it, but please don't let me know."

"What if it's bad?"

"Definitely do not let me know."

"Toby."

"It's just—I don't know. Embarrassing. I guess," he mumbles. "I'm pretty sure this is the first time someone other than me or a teacher has read something I've written. I hate showing my stuff off."

Leo sighs, plops the papers down onto his nightstand, and leans forward into Toby's lips. "Fine," he agrees, his breath ghosting on Toby's skin. "But I am not making promises for when I get to the part with the handsome love interest whom I wholeheartedly consider myself the inspiration for."

Toby puts his hand over Leo's face and pushes him away, and Leo breaks into a fit of laughter as he falls onto his pillow. Toby watches him for a second, attempting and not really succeeding to bite back the smile that weasels its way onto his own face at the sight, but he eventually gives up completely and flops down next to him on the mattress. Leo, still snickering, takes Toby's face in his hands and pulls him into a kiss that Toby is more than happy to succumb to.

Making out on the bed, whether it's Leo's or his own, has very easily become one of Toby's favorite hobbies. Not only because he and Leo get to hold each other close—another one of his favorite things to do—but also because of the sheer unpredictableness of it. Sometimes, most of the time, kissing's as far as they go. Other times....

"Can you stay over tonight?" Leo asks against Toby's lips, his hand sliding up underneath the back of Toby's tank top. Toby does his best to fight the shiver that prickles his spine at Leo's touch.

"I can't," he answers glumly. "I have work till ass o'clock in the morning, so I should probably get home and nap for an hour or two so I'm not a zombie tomorrow."

Leo sighs, and begins tracing circles with his middle finger into the small of Toby's back. "I thought you said you were free tonight."

"I was, but then Blue, for whatever reason, decided to take off a week after he got engaged. So I'm filling in for him tonight."

Leo makes a hmph noise that sounds similar to how a child would react when their mother tells them they can't bring home a toy from the store. Then the image of a pudgy little toddler version of Leo pops into Toby's mind, and he sniggers to himself, not bothering to enlighten Leo when he raises his eyebrow at him.

"I should go now," Toby tells him, rolling off of him onto his back, then getting to his feet. "I'll call you tomorrow."

"Ughhhh." Leo stretches as if he were a cat, and then shuffles over to the edge of the bed to meet Toby halfway for a goodbye kiss. "Thanks for the story."

Toby shakes his head. "Happy birthday," he says, and steps out of Leo's room, gently closing the door behind him.

"Later," he says to Ariel, who's sitting on the couch with her feet propped up on the coffee table, scrolling through her phone.

"Still don't like you," she says without looking up.

"Yeah, I know."

Toby drives home with a smile on his face.

Toby staggers through his apartment door a little past 6:15 in the morning, yearning for nothing more than sleep. He doesn't hate a lot of things, but working the graveyard shift is definitely one of them.

The house is quiet and dark, as usual, because now that it's summer Reggie is absolutely refusing to wake up any time earlier than ten a.m. Which Toby supposes he can respect. He generally avoids rising and shining as often as he can, too.

The minutes during which Toby undresses, takes a quick shower, throws on a change of clothes, and brushes his teeth seem out of a delirium. He hates that weird sense of some altered form of reality that often takes over when he has to work the early mornings. It makes him itchy and, honestly, kind of freaks him out. But when everything is all crossed off the list, he eagerly makes his way toward his bed. Beloved bed.

But. One can imagine the shock in the moment when he goes to place his hand on the mattress, only to instead touch a lump of blankets that is his boyfriend.

"Hey," Leo says, his voice raspy and a little bit muffled. "Was waiting for you."

Toby pinches himself to make sure this isn't some exhaustion-induced hallucination. It's not, apparently.

"Wh—what are you doing here?" Toby asks, and Leo scoots over a little bit so he can climb in with him.

"Reggie let me in," Leo mumbles. "Been here since two."

"Why?"

"I just... I wanted to be here when you got home."

Toby's heart melts a little. An irrepressible smile slides across his face, and he reaches out to pull Leo closer to him, as close as they can possibly be, with Leo's left leg resting on top of Toby's and Toby's right arm slung around Leo's torso, holding him in place.

Leo lets out a low groan, his eyes falling shut. "I'm so tired."

"Well, you shouldn't have stayed up, dummy," Toby says softly.

"I missed you."

"It's been twelve hours."

"I wanted to fall asleep with you."

Toby sighs, his chest blooming with warmth. Leo's eyes blink back open, and he places a warm hand on Toby's cheek, his thumb sliding back and forth over his skin, a gentle wave of tenderness sweeping through Toby with each pass.

They stay like that for a while, and Leo's eyes close again, and Toby would be convinced that he fell asleep if it weren't for the fact that his thumb drifts down Toby's face and swipes across Toby's bottom lip before he leans in to press a soft kiss against Toby's mouth.

"Good night," Leo mumbles. Toby smiles again, and allows slumber to overtake them both.

Toby blinks his eyes open at some point that morning to the sound of birds chittering outside his window and the familiar citrus aroma sweeping through his nose. In his arms still lies Leo, completely out cold, his eyelashes fluttering, his hands entangled with the fabric of Toby's t-shirt, breathing in soft puffs of breath through his open mouth.

"Morning," Toby whispers into Leo's hair, not caring whether he's awake or not to hear it. But drowsiness sweeps over him again and he decides that, out of all the mornings, this one is a good one to sleep through.

Chapter 26

Mid-December of some nondescript year..

As soon as he passes through the automatic doors of the craft store, Toby books it—as discreetly as he can—toward the aisle he's looking for.

The paints he wants—well, the paints Leo wants—have been bought out every single time he's come to this place, and today he got the notification—yeah, so maybe he did sign up for their mailing list—that they're back in stock. And there's a week until Christmas, so time is seriously of the essence.

Toby has to hold himself back from sprinting across the craft store, past the displays of cheap holiday decor, past the brand new Valentine's day setup, because wow, they're already preparing for that. Toby doesn't even want to think about the panic that will undoubtedly be overwhelming him come February.

Finally, he makes it to the aisle he saw listed on the website, and he sees it. He sees the box. It's the last one on the shelf, already, but who fucking cares, because it's his. He disregards all thoughts of calmness and collectivism as he practically lunges for the paints, and he gets them, but—

He feels himself collide into another solid figure, and it's not one of those columns that tend to stand inconveniently in the middle of some aisles, as he's come to notice from his many futile expeditions to this store. It's a person. A woman. And he has just knocked her to the ground. The slap of her hands on the linoleum floors is deafening, along with the clunking and—fuck—shattering of everything that spills ot of her arms.

"Oh, shit," Toby says, vision slightly blurred from sheer humiliation. "I'm so sorry. Are you okay? Are you hurt any-where? I'm really sorry, I'll pay for everything that broke—"

"I'm fine," the young woman says, accepting Toby's out-stretched hand to pull herself up. "It's fine. Don't worry about—"

She looks up at him, the first time Toby can get a clear view of who he just sent flying, and they gasp in unison.

"Toby?"

"Lily?"

There's no mistaking it; everything about her may be dif-ferent now, from her hair length and color to her clothing to the number of piercings on her face, but Toby could never forget those two different colored eyes.

Lily's gawking mouth quickly spreads into a smile, her eyes shining the way they always used to. Toby doubts he's ever been hit by a wave of nostalgia this hard. It's like he's back in high school again, and they've just shared their first kiss, and she was ecstatic, while he was internally combusting. Except, he doesn't have to worry about that anymore.

"Wow. Wow! I can't believe it's you!" Lily exclaims. "I mean, I knew you went to school around here, but I didn't expect to see you here of all places—"

"No, yeah, I—well, what about you?" Toby says. "I thought—I thought you stayed in state for college?"

"I did, but I'm up here for the holidays. My fiancé's family lives in the area."

Toby blinks. "Fiancé?" he asks, though it comes out as more of a surprised statement. Immediately, he regrets opening his mouth, because holy fuck, talk about a whole lot of none of his business.

But Lily laughs, kind and genuine. "Yeah. We got engaged last month, actually."

"That's... wow. That's great. Congratulations."

"Thanks. Though, I guess I've kinda backed myself into a corner with the whole thing, because as far as my parents know, my breakup with you left me heartbroken and afraid to seek love ever since. They think I'm still single."

"Oh," Toby says, his eyebrows furrowing. "Why—why haven't you told them?"

Lily smiles again, though it's different from the others. Sadder. "It's complicated."

Toby nods, taking the hint to steer away from the parent thing.

"Well, anyway," he says, rubbing the back of his neck. "It's kind of surreal to see you. I mean, especially now that you're—now that you're getting married. Feels like yesterday we were going out for macarons every Friday."

And then the Lily Abraham glow is back, practically blinding Toby as her eyes glimmer with memories. "We did do that, didn't we?" She sighs. "That was fun. We had a lot of fun together."

"Yeah. We did."

Toby can only stare at her in the short silence that follows. She looks almost entirely different, but at the same time, her aura, her demeanor, is identical to the Lily he knew years ago. Her hair, once long and dirty blond, is now shoulder-length and dyed pink at the ends, falling in loose waves around her face. When she and Toby dated, she had the standard set of piercings on her earlobes, but now she's got them trailing up both ears, and even sports a septum ring, and it honestly really suits her. And it seems like she's let loose a bit with what she wears; they did go to a school with enforced uniforms, but even on weekends and breaks, she stuck to the same modest styles and soft, plain colors. Now, she's wearing a lavender turtleneck, ripped black jeans, and an oversized denim jacket with tears and neon paint splatters all over it. And Doc Martens, extremely similar—if not identical—to a pair that Leo has in his closet.

Toby blinks, realizing he probably shouldn't be examining her so closely. "Um," he says, looking away. "So. Who's the lucky guy?"

"Hm?"

"Your, uh, fiancé. Who'd you end up—"

When Toby looks back at her, a small smirk tugs at the corner of her lips. She opens her mouth to speak. "Actually—"

"Sorry to keep you waiting, turns out they didn't have it in the—whoa, what's all this?"

A woman jogs up to them and rests her arm on Lily's shoulder as she stares down at the mess of shattered ceramic on the ground. Her dark eyes immediately flick up to Toby, and a spark of fear shoots through him. Holy shit, she's intimidating.

"It's nothing, I just happened to see an old friend," Lily tells the woman, who is still eyeing Toby with a bit of a scowl twisting her face. "This is Toby."

"Hi," Toby croaks, his grip on the box of paints tightening. "Sorry about this, I promise I'm gonna pay for it all."

"I already told you, it's fine," Lily says, waving him off. She glances to her right. "And you, stop with the glaring. We're cool."

The woman looks back at Lily, one eyebrow raised, as if to ask if she's sure. When Lily shows no signs of distress, she sighs, and holds out her right hand for Toby to shake. "Nice to meet you, Toby. I'm Talia. Lily's fiancée."

Toby's entire body freezes mid-handshake and his jaw drops.

Oh.

Oh, wow.

Almost immediately, that defensive expression is back on Talia's face, and she releases Toby's hand with a slight push. "What, Blondie? Something you wanna say about that?"

"What?" Toby shakes his head frantically. "No! No, no, it's—I'm happy for you two, I just—I can't believe—"

"It's all right," Lily says, seemingly speaking to both Talia and Toby. "I know it's surprising, considering we dated for three years, but I met Talia when I went to UNC, and—I mean, long story short, she helped me come to terms with the fact that I'm gay."

Toby almost wants to laugh, but he doesn't, mostly out of fear of Talia. "Oh," he says instead, his brain too deep-fried from the shock of the situation to manage much else.

"We should head out," Talia mutters to Lily, removing her arm off her shoulder and instead reaching down to take her hand. "My mom's got feijoada cooking, and she'd never forgive herself if we had to eat it cold."

"Okay," Lily agrees. Then she looks down at the objects at her feet. "Let me just clean this up first. Why don't you get the car started so it'll be warm when I get there?"

"All right," Talia says. She kisses Lily's cheek, points two fingers at her eyes and then at Toby, and walks away.

"Let me help," Toby says, setting the box of paints on the bottom shelf and crouching down. "It's my fault, anyway."

Lily smiles, and then joins him. They pluck out the salvage-able products and place them gently in a shopping basket and organize the broken things into a pile. When they check out, Toby alerts one of the employees of the broken mer-chandise, pays for it all, and offers to sweep the mess up, but the worker insists he'll take care of it and shoos Toby away.

Lily waits for him outside the craft store, and when he steps into the bitter wind, she looks up at him with pink cheeks and a closed-mouth smile. He can't help but smile back.

"Um," he says after a moment, shoving the hand that's not holding the newly-purchased paints into his jacket pocket. "Talia seems really nice."

Lilly laughs. "No, she doesn't."

"She does!"

"Trust me, Toby, she takes it upon herself to be as uninviting as possible with every first impression she makes," Lily says. "But thank you, anyway. I love her a lot."

The genuine happiness on Lily's face creates a warm feeling in Toby's chest. "I'm really happy for you."

"Thank you."

"And, uh—I just figured it's only fair that you know." Toby takes a breath. "I'm... also seeing someone."

"Oh yeah?" Lily asks, her eyebrows jumping up a bit.

"Yeah." Toby swallows. "His name's Leo. I'm—I'm gay. Also."

Lily's mouth drops into an O.

"Surprised?" Toby asks.

"No—I mean, yes, but not because you're gay, just because—things just happened to end up like this."

Toby raises an eyebrow, and he can't help the small smile that pulls at his lips. "So I was bad at playing straight?"

"Not necessarily," Lily replies. "I just think that queer people tend to unconsciously lump together, so I've grown pretty used to people coming out."

"Yeah," Toby says. "You're right."

"Guess we were both each other's beards, then."

"Guess so."

"Well, I hope you and your boyfriend are happy together."

"We are. I—yeah. He's..." Toby's ears burn, even in the cold. "He's great."

Lily points at the shopping bag in Toby's hand containing the box of paints. "Those for him?"

"Oh, yeah," Toby says. "Can't tell you how many times I tried to get these things only to find out they were sold out pretty much everywhere."

Before Lily can say anything else, a black jeep pulls up in front of them, and the passenger window rolls down.

"Lily. Feijoada. Getting cold," Talia calls from the driver's side.

"Okay, one second," Lily replies, and then turns back to Toby. "Well, I better go. It was really nice running into you, Toby. Literally."

"Same here," Toby says.

"You know... my number hasn't changed. Um, assuming you still have it, maybe... shoot me a text?" Lily suggests. "It'd be nice to get in touch again. And I'd love to send you and Leo an invitation to the wedding. Whenever it happens."

Toby smiles. "Yeah. That sounds nice."

"Cool."

Lily dismisses herself with a two-fingered salute and climbs into the passenger seat of Talia's jeep. The two drive off, with Talia taking an illegal right turn on red out of the parking lot.

Toby's phone chimes from deep within his jacket pocket. He worms it out from the depths of the fabric and unlocks the screen.

It's a text from Leo.

Scale of 1-10 how mad woukd you be if i told you i completely ignored our no expensive christmas present rule and boyht you something anyway

Toby lets out a small laugh before replying.

8000

Toby!!!!! is Leo's instant response.

whatever happened to you being a broke art nerd?

First of all, i am not a nerd. second, money is no object when it comes to you, my little literature geek <3

you're ridiculous

Thanks <3

im on my way home, Toby types. want me to pick up dinner? burgers?

Oh my god yes.

Toby tucks his phone back away and makes his way towards his car, the box of paints weighing him down.

Christmas can't come fast enough.

Epilogue

Toby stands in front of his bathroom mirror, looking down at the enamel rainbow pin between his thumb and forefinger.

Out of the corner of his eye he notices his phone light up from where it sits face up on the counter, likely with texts from Blue. They're supposed to meet up with him and Jack in half an hour, but the rather prominent twisting in Toby's gut is making him consider canceling everything.

Toby attempts to swallow that uneasy feeling down, closes his eyes, and takes a few deep breaths. He knows, in the back of his mind, that by the end of today, everything will be fine. In fact, he'd probably regret it more if he didn't go.

But, God. It's as if he's back to his fifteen-year-old self right now; overwhelmed by shame and denial, peer pressure from everyone around him drilling into his skull and sending him spiraling.

A soft knock on the wall makes Toby jump, his eyes flying open, and the rainbow pin nearly tumbling from his grip and falling into the sink. He clutches it in his fist, turning toward the doorway.

"Hey," Leo says, a soft smile on his face. Immediately, Toby's chest fills with warmth.

"Hi," he replies, taking a moment to just look at him. "You—you look nice."

Leo's left eyebrow climbs up his forehead, his dimple digging into the left side of his face. "I'm just wearing a t-shirt and jeans."

"Well, I mean, you always look nice."

Leo releases a breathy laugh, his hand coming up to scratch the back of his neck. "Thank you."

They stand there for a moment, looking at each other. When the silence becomes just a tad too overbearing, Toby clears his throat.

"Did Reggie let you in?" he asks.

"Yeah. I, uh, texted you, but you didn't respond."

"Oh." Toby looks down at his phone. "Yeah. Sorry, I haven't—I haven't been paying attention."

Leo nods. "It's fine. Um, are you ready? We're supposed to be leaving soon, right?"

"Yeah, um. You're right. I'm almost—I mean, I just—" Toby's throat grows tight, causing him to choke on his words (not that he had any prepared to begin with), and he leans forward onto the counter, bracing his hands against the edge.

"Hey," Leo says softly, stepping closer. "You all right?"

"Yeah, no, I'm fine," Toby lies. And then he feels guilty almost immediately. "I mean, no. I'm—I'm actually freaking out a little, if I'm being completely honest."

Then Leo's hand is on his back, stable and supportive and everything Toby is the opposite of right now. "What's going on, Toby?"

"I just..." Toby curls his fingernails into his hands, the enamel pin in his right fist digging into his skin as his grip around it tightens. "I guess I'm just, like... having second thoughts. About our plans."

"Oh," Leo says. "We don't have to go, if you don't want to."

"No, I—that's the thing. I want to, I know I do. But I'm just—I just—"

"Just what?"

"I'm just scared."

There's a beat of silence; all Toby can hear is the thrumming of blood in his ears as heat rushes to his face, settling in his cheeks and below his eyes.

"Why are you scared?" Leo asks a moment later, no hint of judgment in his voice whatsoever. Toby doesn't think he deserves that.

"I don't know," Toby croaks. "I—I feel like there's a lot of reasons, but at the same time, they all seem so stupid."

"I bet they aren't stupid," Leo says, leaning his head against Toby's shoulder. "You can talk to me. I want to help you."

Toby sighs, his breath shaking. Tears burn in his eyes, and a lump is growing in his throat, and he's so embarrassed. He's acting like a child, like a pitiful, fifteen-year-old child.

"Okay," he begins, shifting his weight a bit. "Well, um—you know I'm not out to that many people. So I feel like by going to this, it—I don't know. It would just be so... public. Like I'm putting myself on blast. But it's—it's not that I don't want to be out in public with you, obviously. You—you're my boyfriend, and I really like you, and I want to go everywhere with you. I'm just not... I'm not used to it. I guess it would feel like coming out to a bunch of people all at once? I mean, coming out to Blue was something I did on a whim and I'd be lying if I said I didn't regret it for a few minutes afterwards, even though I knew he was bi, so I—I don't—"

"It's okay," Leo assures Toby, rubbing his back while Toby does his best to take deep breaths. He feels so silly getting so worked up about this. It's such a small thing, but at the same time, for God knows what reason, it's the most important thing in the world.

"I'm sorry," Toby mumbles, looking down at his clenched fists. "I'm probably making you feel like shit."

"No, Toby. I get it. It's okay."

"But you wanna go, right?"

"I mean—I think it could be fun, yeah. I've been once before. With Ariel. We had a good time. But if you really don't want to go, we don't have to. I'm sure Blue and Jack will understand."

Toby swallows.

"Okay. Let's think of it like this." Leo jumps up onto the bathroom counter, guiding Toby sideways so he can stand between his dangling legs. Leo takes Toby's fist, the one with the pin curled inside, brings it up to his mouth, and unfolds it to place a small kiss on the heel of Toby's palm, setting the little rainbow aside. "Let's say we don't go. What's the worst case scenario?"

Toby bites his cheek. "I feel terrible for canceling on Blue last minute and getting you excited over nothing."

"Okay. And if you do go?"

"I-I don't—well, absolute worst case? I guess, um, someone I know sees me, and I'm not out to them yet, and then they tell other people, and somehow it ends up spreading to my parents, and they cut me off and disown me and—"

"Okay," Leo interrupts with a light chuckle. "Don't you see how far-fetched that sounds?"

Toby frowns.

"We're going to a pride parade, Toby. The entire point is to embrace who you are, even if just for one day," Leo says, smiling gently. "How likely is it that anyone we might see there, also celebrating their identity, would go out of their way to ruin your life?"

"Not," Toby mutters after a second.

"Right. And, even if they do—which they won't—how would it ever get to your parents?"

"I-I dunno... email?"

"Toby," Leo groans dramatically, tossing his head back for effect.

"Okay. Fine. That's probably not going to happen," Toby concedes.

"It's definitely not going to happen," Leo corrects. "And even if, on the extremely off chance—I'm talking, like, less than a 0.0001 percent chance—it does, you have a whole community up here that has your back, and always will." Leo squeezes Toby's hand. "Me, Blue, Jack, Reggie, Vicki, even Ariel. And then everybody else we might see today, whether we know them or not. You're going to be okay, Toby. I promise."

Toby takes a moment, just to look at Leo, into his pretty blue eyes, glimmering with affection and—well, pride.

"Okay," Toby says softly. "I want to go."

Leo just smiles at him and reaches out to cup his face, tugging Toby in for a long, soft kiss. After, Toby leans his forehead against Leo's, and only opens them when he feels nimble fingers playing with the fabric of his shirt.

In the mirror, he watches Leo fasten the rainbow pin to a spot just above Toby's heart, and then lean forward to kiss Toby's collarbone.

"I'm proud of you," Leo says quietly, taking Toby's hands in his own and looking up at him with those beautiful blue eyes.

A blush breaks out across Toby's face. "Thanks," he replies sheepishly.

Then, the peaceful silence is pierced by the shrill, unattractive ringing of Toby's phone from the countertop, causing the both of them to jump away from one another out of shock. Leo laughs while Toby groans, snatching up the phone without bothering to check who's calling and ruining the moment. "Hello," he answers, with probably a tiny little bit too much hostility.

"Wow, what's with that tone? Wake up on the wrong side of the bed?" the familiar voice on the other end of the line says.

"Oh. Hey, Blue," Toby mumbles. "Sorry. Didn't mean to. Um, what's up? We're just about to head out—"

"Yeah. Um. About that. I don't suppose you've seen the fifteen unread texts I've left you in the past ten minutes?"

Toby's eyebrows climb up his forehead. "Uh, no, sorry. I haven't really been looking at my phone."

"Okay. Well. TL;DR, Jack and I are gonna be a little bit later than we thought. We had a bit of a, um... wardrobe malfunction, if you will."

"Wardrobe malfunction?" Toby repeats, glancing at Leo, whose brows furrow in confusion.

"Yeah. So, like, give us... I don't know. Thirty minutes? Hopefully we'll be good to go by then."

"Hold on. What kind of 'wardrobe malfunction' would warrant a half-hour delay?"

"Oh, Toby. Some things are just better left unsaid."

And with that, the line goes dead.

"So..." Leo says after a moment or two. "From what I've gathered, we have a half-hour to kill?"

"Uh, yeah," Toby says, placing his phone down. "Leave it to Blue to give the most cryptic phone call ever for what I hope is just a small issue."

Leo chuckles, wrapping his arms around Toby's middle. "Well. What do you wanna do?"

Another tsunami of heat rushes up to Toby's face. "Um. I dunno."

"I'm sure you can think of something."

Leo pulls Toby even closer to him, their hips almost flush. Toby unwillingly breaks into a miniature fit of nervous giggles, which causes Leo to echo him almost immediately.

And they just laugh together, happiness fueled by one another's smiles. And just to be here with Leo Rosales—his boyfriend, one of his best friends, his confidant—Toby couldn't be more proud.